FAMILY SQUABBLES

FAMILY SQUABBLES

CHRONICLES OF ZOEY GRIMM™ BOOK 1

THEOPHILUS MONROE

MICHAEL ANDERLE

DISRUPTIVE IMAGINATION®

LMBPN Publishing
PMB 196, 2540 South Maryland Pkwy
Las Vegas, NV 89109

Version 1.00, March 2022
ebook ISBN: 978-1-68500-636-5
Print ISBN: 978-1-68500-637-2

THE FAMILY SQUABBLES TEAM

Thanks to our Beta Team

Larry Omans, John Ashmore, Rachel Beckford, Kelly O'Donnell, Jim Caplan

Thanks to our JIT Readers

Wendy L Bonell
Dave Hicks
Christopher Gilliard
Jeff Goode
Jackey Hankard-Brodie
Zacc Pelter
Paul Westman
Angel LaVey

If We've missed anyone, please let us know!

Editor
The Skyhunter Editing Team

CHAPTER ONE

Cheers resounded throughout the coliseum as I stepped onto the ash-covered floor, holding a jewel-tipped staff that looked like a scythe from Earth.

My stomach was twisted in knots, and not just because half the underworld was here to witness my examination. No one had attempted the particular test I'd chosen to demonstrate my capabilities as a Reaper in more than a century, and as far as I knew, my father was the only one who'd ever passed it...roughly two thousand years earlier.

What choice did I have? I was Zoey Grimm. The daughter of Azrael, the Grim Reaper himself. I didn't just have to live up to my name. I was the heir-apparent; well, me or my twin brother Morty, but no one thought Morty had what it took. I was the one everyone expected to take my father's place.

You have to be the best of the best. The top of your class.

My father's words ran through my mind as the headmaster activated the crystal and three crystalline golems emerged from the floor of the coliseum. My father had said those words or some variation of them to me a thousand times. I usually rose to the occasion. I wanted to make Daddy proud.

Failure wasn't an option. Neither was being second-best.

I wondered if I'd taken on more than I could handle this time. Once the headmaster rang the bell, I'd have to dispatch all three constructs in less than a minute.

The constructs weren't large. They mimicked the appearance and behavior of disembodied human souls. They were vaguely human-shaped, though their legs were longer than what was natural, and their heads were smaller than they should have been.

I twirled my staff, preparing for my attack. Succeed, and I'd skip the first two ranks and graduate as a Level Three Reaper. Would anyone be impressed? Probably not. This was what everyone expected from me. But if I failed? Well, I could almost hear the chatter that would follow. *That Zoey Grimm...such arrogance! To think she could match her father's legend!*

I'd be the laughingstock of the underworld. I'd have to go back to the academy. I'd have to wait another year before they'd give me a second chance. My brother had already passed his exam. He'd taken down a single construct and was pronounced a Level One Reaper. If I failed, by the time my next attempt was granted, he'd probably be Level Three. If I wanted to keep up with him and remain the heir apparent, I'd have to complete this same challenge again a year from now. If I failed again, the chances that I'd ever catch up to him were slim.

Failure was not an option. Not for me, anyway.

The crystal the constructs were made of channeled red energy into their forms. It programmed them to behave like real souls that had been recently harvested by the Reapers.

Not every human resists their Reaper. Some welcomed their entry into the afterlife. They were prepared to move on and welcomed the Reaper who was sent to guide them into the beyond. Others, afraid to die, couldn't help but resist. They fought, or they'd flee.

The souls chosen to define these constructs would be less than compliant. I expected that much. What I couldn't predict was *how* these golems might resist. They'd probably be more challenging than they were when the souls were originally reaped. After all, these constructs were formed based on souls who already had experience attempting to resist their Reaper. They'd done this before. They'd learn from their previous failures.

There were more reasons why it wasn't suggested for would-be graduates to take the Level Three exam. The souls that defined the constructs had fallen to an experienced Reaper. I was a novice. I'd never reaped a real soul. They had every advantage.

"Commence the examination!" the headmaster announced, ringing a large bell and starting the timepiece mounted just below the dais.

One minute...

Two of the three constructs slowly moved toward me. They wanted to fight. The third took a few steps back, then turned and ran in the opposite direction.

I'd trained for this. There were methods for countering split strategies. I'd studied them in the academy archives.

I took off after the construct who fled my position. If I took down two at once, head-on, I'd waste most of my time on them, then I'd still have to chase down the runaway. By then, I'd probably have to traverse the full length of the coliseum before I reached him. That would take a good thirty seconds.

But if I chased the runner while the other two pursued me, I'd make better use of my time. Plus, with my back turned to the other two, they'd think they had an advantage.

My boots slammed against the ash, kicking up a cloud as I pursued the construct. Yes, the thing moved fast. Not as fast as me. In the academy, I hadn't only studied various combat arts. I'd also trained my body for strength, speed, and endurance.

As I closed in on the construct, it pivoted, realizing it couldn't get away. It swept a foot, trying to trip me. I jumped over its foot and flipped to land on the arena wall, where I used my momentum to run sideways along the wall before launching into another flip that took me over its head.

The construct collapsed in a pile of ash as I jammed the gem on my staff into its back.

"The candidate has eliminated construct number one," the headmaster announced as the crowd applauded my effort.

I landed on my knees. Not the best position for assaulting a resistant soul, but that was by design. The other two constructs would *think* I was in a vulnerable position.

It wasn't like they could kill me. But if they knocked me out or wrestled my staff from my hands, they'd buy themselves time to escape. I didn't have time to waste.

I hoped they'd try to charge me. I could pivot on one knee, swipe my staff through the air, and take both of them down with one strike. That would be the fastest way to end this.

If these were common souls, that was what they'd try to do. But these constructs were powered by souls that had likely learned a thing or two from their prior reapings.

They didn't take the bait. Instead, they split up. I glanced at the timepiece near the headmaster. I had twenty seconds left, give or take.

I leaped to my feet and charged the construct that had fled to my right. The other one—call it Construct Number Three—was running as far as he could in the opposite direction. Construct Number Two pivoted and went for my staff. With a twirl of the staff around my back, I caught it in my left hand and jammed it to the second construct's chest.

"The candidate has eliminated the second construct. A single construct remains."

I wasn't sure why the crowd needed a play-by-play from the headmaster. There wasn't any mistaking what was happening. The crowd cheered at the announcement, but not as exuberantly as they did the first. After all, they knew time was running out. They were on the edge of their seats.

Five seconds to go, if that...

I widened my stance, raised my staff overhead, and took aim. This wasn't one of the recommended strategies taught at the academy. Still, from the archives, I knew a few Reapers, including my father, who'd pulled it off. I'd practiced, but it was risky, especially in a real-world situation where a scythe wouldn't fly through the air with the same grace as a staff.

I threw my staff like a javelin, sending it arcing through the air. It pierced the last construct in the torso, and the golem exploded in a cloud of ash as the headmaster declared that time was up.

Had I made it in time?

It was up to the headmaster.

"While I cannot recommend this strategy," the headmaster began, "good Reapers know the situation on the ground. They use any skill or tactic available, given every contingency. While this method will not likely work for you again, Miss Grimm, you exercised creativity and captured all three souls before the time expired. I now declare Zoey Grimm, daughter of Azrael, a Level Three Reaper with all the rights and privileges accorded the same."

The crowd seated around the coliseum erupted in cheers. A wide grin split my face as I looked up at my father, who was on his feet. His pale complexion caught the light. There was no mistaking his smile. He was proud.

One day, I'd hold his seat. I was well on my way.

CHAPTER TWO

There are six steps to reap one's soul. I was the first in my class to memorize them all. When you're the daughter of Azrael, it's important to make a good impression. After all, one day, I wouldn't be Zoey, student, and RIT (Reaper in Training). I'd inherit my father's position and become the new Grim Reaper. I wouldn't just be one of the many Reapers responsible for harvesting the souls of the deceased. I'd be in charge of the entire operation.

The transition from life to death. It was a massive responsibility. Screw it up, and, well, millions of human souls could be left on Earth, wandering as ghosts, unable to move on. They'd be angry, and the gods, whoever and wherever they were, would probably have to intervene. If I was going to take over for Dad, I had to be the best of the best.

Of course, I had a twin brother. My dad hadn't planned it that way. When he'd hooked up with my mother to produce an heir, he never expected he'd get a two-for-one deal. I often wondered what my mother would think if she could see me now. I imagined her as a beautiful woman with long black hair like mine, a petite woman with fire in her eyes. She'd have to be a firecracker to put up with my dad. What wouldn't I give for her to be here?

This was my graduation—twenty-one years in the making, which, frankly, isn't a long time for our line of work.

Morty was graduating, too. Barely. He would receive his first assignment, just as I would. No one had high expectations for Morty, especially since I'd defied the odds and passed my examination.

When you have all the pressure in the underworld on your shoulders—and we certainly did as Azrael's children—there are two options. You can rise and meet the challenge, exceeding even the loftiest of people's expectations. Or, you can say "fuck y'all" and resign yourself to being a disappointment. I chose the former path, my brother the latter.

Did I mention that there are six steps that every Reaper must follow before harvesting a soul? I thought so. I called them the six Rs. Why? Because alliteration helps me memorize shit, and I needed a few A-plus study strategies if I ever hoped to live up to my father's expectations.

The first "R" stood for regalia. I was already wearing the proper attire: a long, black robe, made of wool, with a hood. Strictly, this step did nothing to affect the reaping. It did, however, have a few functions. First, and most importantly, it made us invisible to almost everyone except the soul we were meant to reap. Some mediums or sensitives, depending on their abilities, could detect our presence to varying degrees.

Still, that was rare. Most of the time, with our regalia in place, we'd be able to sneak in, harvest a soul, and leave. Badda bing, badda boom. Without it? Well, can you imagine the uproar it would cause every time we came for a soul? In addition, the black robe prepared the expired soul for the inevitable. Think of it like this. If you're a Catholic, and you're about to die, you expect your priest to show up wearing a white collar to administer your last rites. If the priest showed up in a leotard, you'd be all out of sorts about it, and for good reason. Dress for success. Uniforms are important.

The better a soul is prepared to accept its reaping, the easier the job will be. No one wants to deal with an insubordinate soul. My dad said he'd once spent the better part of a decade chasing a soul across Europe. It certainly wasn't the way he'd planned to spend his 1490s. While he was wearing the proper regalia, of course, he always insisted that if we weren't wearing it, the risk of such an occurrence was multiplied a hundredfold. As a Reaper, what you wore mattered.

The second R stood for "receipt." Sometimes this happened before the first R. If you were on schedule, it was better to be in the proper regalia prior to receipt. Receipt was how we got our assignments. The names and locations of the expired souls due for reaping. It was a bit of a mystery, even to my father, who chose the names or why a particular name hit the list on any given day. Some believed every soul had an expiration date programmed into it when it was made. Others imagined that the big man upstairs—you know, the fellow that some people call "God"—decides in accordance with His inscrutable will.

That's fancy-speak for saying he probably draws the names from a hat and sends them down to us in the underworld so we can do his dirty work. I'm pretty sure it's an *enormous* hat—you know, because he's God. Not saying God has a big head or anything. I mean, He probably does. If you were almighty, you'd have an enormous dome, too.

"Never let your head get too big, Zoey," my father had told me. Good advice for a semi-eternal RIT like me. God, I figured, was entitled to have as large a cranium as he wished.

I stepped up to the scroll of the day. They posted it on a bulletin board just outside the Earth portal. I'd imagined this day my whole life. Seeing *my* name on the scroll? Butterflies churned in my stomach as I traced my finger down to the Gs. Surnames were a relatively recent development in the underworld. My father didn't have one. We were born with the last name "Grimm." Why two Ms? Well, there was only one Grim Reaper. The extra M served two purposes: it made it clear that we were a part of Azrael's family, but it also maintained the distinction between the Grim Reaper and the Grimms, my brother and me, who would eventually inherit my father's domain. Well, I would, anyway. Morty gave up that dream a long time ago. I don't think he wanted to become the Grim Reaper anyway.

Grimm, Zoey.

"That's me!" I smiled from ear to ear as I looked with pride upon my first assignment.

I was about to look up my brother's name to see if he was going to get his first reaping today when the pleasant voice of Gabriel Graves interrupted me. "Congrats, Zoey."

I turned. Gabriel was the best-looking Reaper in the academy where I'd trained to prepare for this very day. Like most of us, he was the product of a union between a human and another Reaper. Over time, Reapers progress toward celestial glory. When too much of one's humanity is lost, it complicates the ability to teleport between worlds.

Humans belong on Earth. Reapers and other semi-divines belong in the underworld. Reap long enough, and you'd advance beyond the underworld into the realm of the angels. It took several millennia, of course. My father was on the cusp of his ascension. That's why I was training to replace him. It was nearly his time. He might make it another year, maybe another twenty. I couldn't imagine it would be much longer than that. Once he could no longer go to Earth, when he couldn't reap souls himself, we'd know it was time. He'd done his duty.

Gabriel was two years older than me. Now that he'd been reaping for two full years, he was excited to show me the ropes. We spent most of our evenings together. I suppose you could say he was my boyfriend, although we'd never formalized our relationship. Everyone knew we were together. We trusted each other implicitly. It wouldn't last forever.

Reaper romances come and go as quickly as the McRib. Yes, I know about that. Studying human society is one of the most important aspects of our training as Reapers. When it came to relationships, though, they didn't tend to last since we couldn't reproduce. Life can't be made in the underworld. When a Reaper *must* reproduce, before advancing to the celestial realm, he must seduce a human woman. Then, when the child is born, the Reaper parent must bring their heir to the underworld to be raised as I was.

As a female Reaper, I'd never have children. Not that my plumbing didn't work. All the parts were there. But for a male Reaper, all it took was to seduce a willing human, come back nine months later, and bring their semi-divine baby back to the underworld. If I were to go to Earth and get knocked up, well, the moment I returned to the underworld, my baby would stop developing. It wouldn't survive. Not unless I stayed on Earth.

I say all that to say this: since children Reapers couldn't have children together, marriage wasn't a thing. We didn't make lifelong commitments. We enjoyed one another until we didn't anymore. No strings attached. Eventually, we'd go our separate ways. With Gabriel, though, I hoped we'd make it at least a century or so.

Gabriel was a keeper. Half the girls in the underworld wanted him. The other half realized they didn't have a chance, so they didn't bother. He had dark hair and blue eyes, and he towered over me by at least a foot. His arms were solid, and his shoulders were broad. His skin was pale and unblemished. He was the embodiment of death. Sexy as hell.

"So, who's the lucky soul who gets to be Zoey Grimm's first?" Gabriel asked.

I smirked as I traced my finger across the page. "Soul 5-1-816-229-4417-3."

"Missouri, then." Gabriel nodded.

"Looks that way. That code corresponds with a suburb of Kansas City."

Gabriel laughed. "You seriously memorized all the codes?"

I shrugged. "Top of my class. What did you expect?"

"It's unnecessary. You can look up the codes in the directories. It doesn't take much time."

I sighed. Gabriel was right, of course. The codes defined the continent, human nation, and additional information. The final number differentiated the souls who lived in a single home. Why weren't we given names? Well, from what they taught me at the academy, it was best to keep the reaping process impersonal.

Many humans resisted it. If we hesitated, even for a moment, worrying about Joe Schmoe's life and his family, we might miss the person's designated departure time across the River Styx. If that happened, their soul would be left to wander. That was how ghosts were made. Too many hauntings on a Reaper's performance report and my old man would bench them while they underwent reconditioning—intense training to refine our skills to prevent such mishaps from recurring in the future.

"So, where are you heading today?" I asked Gabriel.

"South America," Gabriel replied. "A woman, as best I can tell, in her ninety-third year of life. Easy-peasy."

"You could discern all that from the code?" I asked.

Gabriel laughed. "You still have to look up the code in the directories, Zoey. When you do, those details will be provided."

I snorted. "Why didn't they teach us that in the academy?"

Gabriel shrugged his shoulders. "It's extraneous information. Not crucial for the reaping. But, in my experience, it's good to know what you're getting into."

"We were told to be prepared for anything. Sometimes those less than willing to go quietly into the beyond will put up a fight."

"Which is why most of our training is focused on how to subdue humans quickly," Gabriel reminded me. "There's a risk, of course, in knowing too much. We might take it for granted that, in my case, a woman who matches the description in the directory won't be a hassle at all. It's best not to make any assumptions. It's amazing how even an old, decrepit person can put up a good fight when they don't want to die."

I nodded. "I'll just stick to the code, then. It's best not to know the details."

Gabriel grinned. "To each one's own, I suppose. Good luck, Zoey. I can't wait to hear how your first reaping went."

I hugged Gabriel and kissed him softly on the lips.

"Get a room, you two," another familiar voice called, approaching from behind. It was my brother.

I smiled. "Hey, Morty. You ready for our first reaping?"

Morty shrugged, approached the scroll, and looked up his target. Despite being listed next to each other in alphabetical order on account of having the same surname, I hadn't looked at his assignment. "Well, this is weird."

"What is?" I asked.

Morty scratched his head. "They gave us the same code."

I pushed past Morty and looked at the list again. "What the hell?"

Morty sighed. "Those dumb angels, or whoever made the list, must've gotten confused. There aren't many siblings in the underworld, you know."

I shook my head. "Unbelievable. Well, I guess we're doing this together."

Morty shrugged. "Honestly, I wonder if it was a mistake. They probably don't trust me to pull it off."

"You think they *want* you to shadow me?" I asked.

Morty scratched the back of his head. "It makes sense. I mean, I barely passed the core requirements."

I took a deep breath and exhaled. Don't get me wrong; I loved my little brother. I say "little" even though we're twins. He was born a few minutes after me. He didn't appreciate being called that, so I avoided saying it in his company. Still, finding out I was supposed to chaperone him on what I'd thought was going to be my first solo reaping was mildly disenchanting.

CHAPTER THREE

The third R stood for "relocation." No, that wasn't how the textbooks defined it, but that was how I remembered it. It involved entering the code into a dial beside the Earth portal and going through it. The code calibrated the portal to spit us out in proximity to the soul we were meant to reap. According to what I'd learned, it brought us to the closest place uninhabited by humans. It rarely took a Reaper directly into the target's presence. We'd enter the portal and immediately begin the fourth R of a successful reaping: "reconnaissance."

We had to survey our surroundings. If other humans were present, well, remember the first R, regalia? Our cloaks rendered us invisible to all except the soul we were meant to claim. Before reaping a soul, we needed to examine the situation.

Was the person already on their deathbed, sick and ready to go peacefully? No problem. I'd summon my scythe—I was so excited to see what mine looked like—and catch the soul with it as it left the body. If it was a case of sudden death, or if the person was fighting it, we might have to subdue the target first.

That was why we trained in combat at the Reaper academy. I knew more than a dozen styles of what humans called martial arts. Humans are resilient creatures. They do not always go along with fate willingly. It didn't happen every time. Maybe one out of ten would put up a fight. But we had to be ready. Those cases were the ones I'd spent the bulk of my time learning to handle. A strike with the scythe and no matter how resolved the person might be to stay alive, we could remove the soul from the body and take them with us.

That's the final R—the return to the underworld, where we'd deposit the collected soul with Charon, the boatman who traversed the River Styx and took the souls to their final destination. Purgatory. Heaven. Hell. All or none of the above. The soul's destination wasn't our concern. Wherever they went, it was where they were meant to go to rest.

That R, the seventh R, was beyond our paygrade as Reapers. "Rest" was the purview of semi-divine or divine entities I'd never met. All I knew was that if we mucked up any of *our* six Rs, the soul would never reach the seventh. After twenty-one years of constant training and education, I was ready. As Azrael's daughter, I expected most of the underworld was waiting for me to return. I could only wonder what they'd think when they found out that Morty and I were tasked to tag-team our first soul.

"Just let me handle it, Morty. I'm ready for this. Watch and learn. Maybe tomorrow we'll have our own targets."

Morty wiped a bead of sweat from his brow. "I'm actually relieved, Zoey. I'm glad you'll be with me."

I shook my head. "You may not have excelled in school, Morty, but you passed all the requirements. You just need a little confidence."

Morty snorted. "I think you have enough confidence for both of us."

I shrugged. "You'll get there."

I approached the gateway to Earth and entered the code for my target into the dial. It was a series of round spheres, like globes, that had to be turned precisely to match the prescribed destination of the soul we were supposed to reap. If we didn't get the code correct, we could end up anywhere in the world. Meanwhile, we'd risk missing the window to deliver our soul to Charon.

My heart raced as Morty and I stepped into the Earth portal. That was nothing compared to the sensation of actually being on Earth. Where we came out of the portal wasn't the fanciest place in the world. The burnt-orange shag carpet on the floor and the paisley-patterned wallpaper suggested that our target hadn't bothered redecorating for some time.

Other Reapers brought back Earth relics from time to time. Collecting trophies wasn't outright forbidden, although it was discouraged. All the Reapers did it, at least occasionally. An item that once belonged to the soul they'd been tasked to reap. Usually, if they took something, they tried to make sure it wasn't anything anyone else would notice or miss. Dead people can't take their belongings with them. That didn't mean their Reaper couldn't.

From the looks of the place, there wasn't much I'd be interested in claiming. Of course, it was my first reaping. Maybe I'd find something small to take. You know, for sentimental reasons. You can only reap your first soul once, after all.

"Time to initiate reconnaissance."

Morty huffed. "Yup. Reconnaissance complete. I'd guess, based on the doilies everywhere, that we were sent to harvest the soul of an old lady. Let's do this."

"Wait." I raised my hand. "We have to check the perimeter. We must account for any other souls who might be on the property. I want to make sure I don't get taken off guard and accidentally hit the wrong soul with my scythe."

"That's not exactly a common error. It's happened...what, two or three times over the last century?"

I nodded. "Three. Still, it *can* happen. You can't be too careful, Morty."

My brother rolled his eyes. "You know, I think the way they teach it at the academy, by the book, isn't really how most Reapers handle their business."

"The best ones do," I disagreed. "That's what separates the women from the boys."

Morty raised an eyebrow. "What is that supposed to mean?"

I chuckled. "Take it however you like. It just means that while you might get away with lackadaisical reaping practices for a few centuries, the best of us, those like Dad, know that harvesting souls is both an art and a science. It takes creativity *and* precision. And that's what I intend to be. You know, when I take over for Dad."

Morty raised his eyebrow. "What if I take over?"

"You're a slacker! Do you really think he'll choose you? Plus, I'm older."

"Yeah, by, like, five minutes."

"That means I'm the first-born. I have first right of refusal."

Morty snorted. "Whatever. You know as well as I do that there aren't any clear laws about that. Mostly because most Reapers never have more than one kid."

"Look, Morty. If Dad ascended to the celestial realm tomorrow, one of us would have to take over."

"He's not leaving any time soon, Zoey," Morty argued. "Probably not for another couple of decades."

"We don't know that," I countered. "It's always possible. If it happened, which of us do you think would be better suited to take over the family business?"

"Business?" Morty asked. "This isn't exactly a business, Zoey."

I shrugged. "Call it whatever you like. You're avoiding the question. Which of us is better prepared to take over our father's affairs?"

"Well, you are right now," Morty replied. "That might not be the case whenever he ascends."

I huffed. Until now, Morty had given no sign at all that he

wanted to become the Grim Reaper. If he had, he should have studied harder at the academy. "I'm not slowing down any time soon, little brother. If you're going to stake your claim over the underworld, you have a lot of catching up to do."

"Can't we just get this over with?" Morty asked. "While we're shooting the shit, we're wasting time."

I bit my lip. "You're right. Commencing reconnaissance now."

Morty rolled his eyes as he wandered around the house, looking under tables and furniture.

I moved from room to room with precision. There was a strategy to casing a home to ensure that we examined every room, it was best to work from one end of the house to the other. I reached into my robe and grabbed a roll of tape. It wasn't the common human tape. Most humans wouldn't be able to see it at all, just as they couldn't see me. Not unless they were sensitives—like mediums or empaths. If we ever encountered one of those, the protocol was to ignore them. Act like they didn't see us. Most people thought they were loonies, anyway. No harm, no foul.

"She's in the back room," Morty offered.

"I know, but we have to finish reconnaissance first."

"Really?" Morty protested. "No one is here. We could get in there, reap the little old lady's soul in a matter of seconds, and get out."

"There are procedures to follow, Morty," I insisted.

Morty sighed. "Whatever. Sometimes you just have to trust your gut, you know? Something tells me we'd best get this done and over with fast."

I placed a piece of my tape over the front door. No sooner did I do it than I heard a honking sound from outside. I peeked through a peephole in the door. A woman, dressed in all blue, approached. A nurse, I guessed, from the photos I'd seen. They were commonly in attendance when someone was dying.

"Shit!" I exclaimed. "A nurse is coming."

"Then let's get this over with! She's less likely to hang on if she's alone when we reap her."

I nodded. Morty was right about something, for once. When people were surrounded by other humans, they often resisted the reaping. In truth, the effect of other people's presence was difficult to predict. Some souls, afraid to leave behind people they loved, would cling to them and refuse to let go. Others would do the opposite. They'd be more at peace with their loved ones surrounding them during their last earthly moment. Nurses and other medical professionals tended to prolong the process artificially, though. It would be simpler and faster to reap subject No. 5-1-816-229-4417-3 before the nurse entered the house. When she did, the tape I'd placed on the door would break. It would release a high-pitched sound, inaudible to most humans on the earthly plane. We'd hear it. We'd know the nurse was getting closer.

I rushed back with Morty to the room where our target was lying in her bed. An old lady—our suspicions were correct. She was asleep. Her breathing was shallow. It was her time. She was one of the lucky ones. She could die peacefully in her sleep. That is, so long as we got the job done before the nurse arrived.

"You ready for this?" Morty asked. "I'll have mine ready just in case."

I nodded. "Sorry. I know you were looking forward to this, too. You know, your first time."

Morty shrugged. "Honestly, I don't care nearly as much about it as you do. This is your thing, Zoey."

I smiled. "Thanks for this. I promise if they keep sending us out together, you can do it next time."

Morty nodded. "Come on, Zoey. Let's just do it and get out of here."

I extended my hand. I pressed a small marking on my wrist. It looked like a tattoo. In truth, it was more like a birthmark. All the Reapers had them. It corresponded with your lineage. As the daughter of *the* Grim Reaper, mine was fittingly in the shape of a scythe already.

I'd touched the sigil thousands of times in the underworld. There, it did nothing. Here on Earth, it would call forth my scythe from the ether. I placed the fingers of my left hand to the sigil on my right wrist. A bright, blue glow emerged in the shape of an orb in my hand. Then the orb flattened into something closer to a cylinder. A long staff grew in my palm, extending both directions. It came to a point on either end. It was warm to the touch.

Then, the good part. When the scythe formed, the blade was on the end. This was the moment I was waiting for.

Waiting… more waiting… I'd waited for twenty-one years, visualizing this very moment in my mind every day. Sort of like how human girls imagine their future weddings, I suppose. Why wasn't it happening? The magic still coursed through my weapon. It must've been building up a charge. After all, it is the blade that harnesses the power to reap souls. Nothing in the textbooks suggested it should take so long.

The magic faded, settling into the long metal scythe-less staff I was now holding. Nothing.

"What the hell?" I asked.

Morty cocked his head. "No scythe? How weird is that?"

"I don't know. It should have worked. There's no reason—"

A high-pitched ring echoed through the house. The nurse had come in through the front door and broken my tape. She must've had a key. A hospice nurse, most likely.

I touched the sigil on my wrist again. "It has to work. Maybe it was just a glitch."

Nothing about the long staff I was holding changed. My sigil did nothing. Maybe if I dispelled the staff and gave in another go, it would work. I released the staff. It disappeared. I touched the sigil again. It formed the same way. Still no scythe.

"*Damn it!*" I screamed.

"The nurse will be here any second. We have to do this now, Zoey!" Morty protested, touching the sigil on his wrist.

When he did, his staff formed in his hand, its glorious blade coursing with hellfire. It looked a lot like our father's blade. Ornate, but sleek and modern at the same time.

My forehead turned hot. I wasn't angry at Morty. This wasn't his fault. But I was jealous, and envy breeds rage. I took a deep breath. I had to hold it together. "I don't understand, I—"

Morty pushed me aside with his opposite hand. "Zoey, you don't have to do everything yourself. I know I'm not as good as you are. But I can help. Let me handle this for you. We'll figure out what the problem is later."

I sighed, nodded, and took a step back.

With a single swipe, Morty struck the woman, slicing through her chest. A white light danced on his blade as he retrieved it from her side.

"Come on, Zoey. We have to go."

I clenched my fists in frustration and released my useless staff. It disappeared. Then, I followed Morty as he carried the soul of our target, now harnessed by his scythe, back to the portal. We passed the nurse in the hallway.

"Louise, it's Anna. I'm here to check on you."

Anna wouldn't receive a response. Louise's soul was now reaped. It was our responsibility to ensure her safe transition to the beyond. We jumped into our portal and returned to the underworld.

CHAPTER FOUR

"You can't tell anyone," I told Morty as we returned to the otherworld. "I'm guessing they'll pair us together again. Maybe, you know, next time mine will work and yours won't."

Morty rolled his eyes. "I'm not going to say a word. Do you think I'd do that?"

"Don't even tell Dad," I insisted.

Morty lifted his fingers to his lips and made a twisting motion as if locking them shut. "My lips are sealed, Zoey."

I sighed. "All right. Let's get this soul to the boatman."

Morty nodded and followed me through a dark corridor and down a set of stairs that led to the deep cave where the River Styx flowed through the underworld. Charon wouldn't care or even notice that it was Morty's scythe, not mine, that delivered the soul to him. He wasn't at all plugged into Reaper politics. He probably didn't even know who I was.

Truth be told, this was only the second time I'd even seen the boatman. The first time had been about a year earlier when he was a guest lecturer in one of my classes. He'd given us the lowdown on his job, why it was important to stick to a schedule and deliver souls on time, yadda, yadda, yadda. I'd almost fallen asleep. It was as if this little speech was something he'd given a thousand times before. He probably had. He was reciting it from memory, with the same sort of cadence someone might use if giving a speech with little skill for public speaking.

In the olden days, Charon had to be paid by the dead. They'd place a coin under the deceased's tongue when he died. Reapers back then waited around to collect the coin with the person's soul to pay Charon. Nowadays, most people didn't believe in Charon, the River Styx, or even in our existence as Reapers. He still demanded payment, of course. My father saw to it that he was satisfied. What Charon did with human money was beyond my wildest guess. How my father acquired the money to pay him, though, I knew all about.

My father invested in stocks. Yes, Azrael frequented the New York Stock Exchange. When he wasn't reaping souls—which, frankly, he rarely did these days—he ensured that his accounts on Earth were secure enough to keep our agreement with Charon going. As such, my father had a New York State driver's license, a Social Security Number, and all the paperwork he needed to handle the investments. He'd secured the same for Morty and me. One day, after he ascended, we'd have to handle it. Sure, I was my father's most likely successor. But if we were co-heirs of the Grim Reaper's earthly fortune, it could only be more convenient if each of us could access all the accounts.

My father kept a stack of hundred-dollar bills in a small box that we passed on our way to meeting the boatman. I opened it, retrieved a Benjamin Franklin, and approached Charon. I handed him the money. Morty placed his hand on a crystal that Charon carried with him. He couldn't summon his scythe here, but the soul could be passed into the crystal no less.

The crystal glowed white when the soul entered it. Charon nodded at both of us. He was about to return to his rowboat when he turned and grabbed my arm.

"Your souls are not welcome here."

I cocked my head. "Excuse me?"

"I cannot take your souls where they must go."

I snorted. "Well, good thing Morty reaped this one."

Charon grunted, turned, and climbed into his boat. I narrowed my eyes as he slowly rowed across the River Styx.

"What the hell was that about?" Morty asked.

"I don't have the slightest clue."

"Do you think he knows something?" Morty asked.

I shook my head. "I think he's lost his mind. An eternity of ferrying souls from the underworld into the afterlife probably takes its toll on one's sanity."

"If you say so," Morty agreed doubtfully. "But if he knows why your scythe wouldn't work…"

"He wouldn't say anything even if he knew," I argued. "I'd wager that was the first time he'd spoken two words to a Reaper, outside of his lectures, in a thousand years."

Morty scratched the back of his head. "Well, whatever. I'm sure you'll be able to reap tomorrow. When you deliver a soul, if he accepts it, we'll know he was just speaking the nonsense of a crazed demigod."

I pressed my lips together. "Yeah. Tomorrow. We'll see."

No one thought it was odd that Morty and I were placed on the same assignment that day. I was a Level Three Reaper, after all. Morty was Level One. It was common for first-level Reapers to shadow second- or third-level Reapers until they advanced. It also wasn't strange that I'd permit Morty to do the deed. At least, it wouldn't have been if it wasn't for the fact that this was also supposed to be my first reaping.

No matter. No one aside from Charon knew that Morty had done the deed, not me. I could only hope that he was right. Whatever happened earlier must've been a fluke. In all my studies, I'd never read about a single Reaper who couldn't summon a scythe. It was supposed to be as easy and natural for us as breathing. For Morty, it had been. They say on Earth that lightning never strikes the same place twice. I was pretty sure that wasn't true. Still, the saying suggested that the odds of something so rare—like me not being able to summon my scythe—wasn't likely to occur more than once. If this was just some kind of glitch, like a misfire or something like that, then the odds were in my favor. I'd be able to reap without incident next time.

A sinking feeling in my gut suggested it might be something more. What if there was something wrong with me? What if, because I was a twin, the ability to reap could only be passed from our father to one of us? Furthermore, if I couldn't reap, what the hell was I going to do with myself? I certainly couldn't take over for my father if I couldn't reap. Even if I could keep this a secret for a while, eventually, I'd be sent out to reap alone. Morty would get promoted to Level Two. And if I returned without my appointed soul, if I left the human spirit wandering as a ghost on the Earth, *everyone* would know about it.

Word travels fast in the underworld. Secrets didn't last long in the Reaper community. I wasn't a girl known to pray much. I won't say that there weren't Reapers who prayed occasionally. We were all part human, and belief in the divine came with the territory. But if I was ever to say a prayer, this was the time.

Please God, or Goddess, or whoever the hell you are, give me my scythe. Allow me to reap.

I didn't dare speak my prayer out loud. I only spoke it in my mind. Would it work? I didn't have a clue. If it didn't, I'd rather be reaped myself, if such a thing was even possible, than go on living in the underworld as an impotent Reaper.

CHAPTER FIVE

"What is going on with you tonight?" Gabriel asked, holding my hand while we walked down Gehenna Boulevard. It was, I suppose, the Bourbon Street of the Underworld. It was where Reapers went to let loose after a day's work harvesting souls. The alcohol flowed there like water would from a tap back on Earth.

"What do you mean?" I asked.

Gabriel shrugged. "I just expected you'd be giddy with excitement after your first reaping. Ready to party."

I huffed. "I don't know. I suppose, after all that preparation…"

"Not as thrilling as you expected?" Gabriel asked.

I sighed. "You could say that."

Gabriel snorted. "You had an old person, didn't you? Someone passing from natural causes."

I nodded. "Yup. And they shackled me with Morty."

Gabriel laughed. "There's more than one reason why no graduates attempt to take out three constructs in their final examination. Yes, most of them couldn't pull it off. The whole underworld can't stop talking about how awesome you were in the coliseum. But the other reason why no one tries is exactly

27

that. Level Threes typically have more responsibility than Level Ones."

He was right. Still... "I just didn't expect they'd have someone shadow me on my first reaping. Yeah, I'm Level Three. But you'd think they'd let me get my feet wet first."

Gabriel shook his head. "No one knows why assignments are doled out the way they are. A lot of times, they don't make much sense."

"What is there to make sense of?" I asked.

Gabriel sighed. "You'd think that someone at Level Four would be given more challenging cases. Today was the fourth easy reap I've had in a row. Any Level One could have pulled it off solo without incident."

I nodded. "Maybe it's just a supply and demand sort of thing?"

"Supply and demand?"

I sighed. "Yeah. My dad teaches me all about economics on Earth. It's shit I'll have to know when I take over someday. You know, so I can keep the money flowing for the boatman. It just means that prices are impacted by how much supply there is. If there were a lot of mass casualty events or a Third World War, there'd be a lot more unwilling souls to reap. Now, though, there aren't as many challenging cases to go around. Once they're doled out to the higher-level Reapers, all that's left are the common cases."

"I suppose that makes sense," Gabriel agreed. "I get it that you'd have to be Level Twenty or higher to be dispatched to a battlefield, or maybe a genocide. But you'd think there'd at least be a car crash, a shooting, or something that I could handle. Something that would require at least a little effort on my part."

"So, that's why you check the directories with every assignment? Why do you look up the profile of each of your targets?"

Gabriel nodded. "Like you, I didn't always do that. Not for the first year or so. I followed the advice they gave at the academy.

Best not to know. But I've grown so weary of simple reapings that I'm afraid, now, that if I had the slightest challenge at all, I'd be taken off guard. I just want to be prepared, Zoey. Is there anything wrong with that?"

"I don't think so. I mean, it's not like it's illegal to check out your targets' profiles. Those files are there for a reason. It just isn't typically recommended. Usually, only the highest-level Reapers consult the directories, if for no other reason than they realize every case they're given will be complicated."

Gabriel chuckled. "Well, we won't be at that level for another century, at least. I suppose we might as well just enjoy it while it's still easy. Have you noticed, there aren't many upper-level Reapers who frequent Gehenna Boulevard?"

I smiled. "Well, if you knew you were going into battle every day, you probably wouldn't want to get drunk the night before, either."

"Fair point, but I wonder if it's more than that. I mean, we were so eager to reap when we graduated. But there's a reason why those who are nearing ascension grow weary of this life."

I pressed my lips together. "Like my father, you mean?"

"Exactly." Gabriel pulled me by the hand into one of the bars we often frequented. A fifth-level Reaper who'd been at Level Five as long as I could remember tended the bar. Every Reaper plateaued at some point. They reached their potential, and that was that.

Harley was one such Reaper. A nice enough fellow. His hair was long and black, with gray hair at his temples. Reapers don't age at the same pace as most humans. We reach our prime then stay there for a while. I suppose Harley might have been prematurely graying, but even so, I was reasonably certain he'd been reaping for at least a century.

He smiled when he saw us. Most people did. Being Azrael's daughter meant people were always eager to make an impression. It was nice, to a point. I mean, I didn't have to deal with a lot of rude people. It also meant that I doubted how genuine anyone was when they spoke to me.

"Tonight is a cause to celebrate," Harley announced.

I smiled even as I bit my tongue. "That's right."

"We'll take the usual," Gabriel told him. The "usual" was a dirty martini. I know, it's an acquired taste, but they'd grown on me over the last few months since Gabriel started taking me here. The first time he ordered me one, I'd spat my first sip back into his face. It was our second date. I was embarrassed as hell. He was a good sport about it. It was expected, he'd said, my first time. "Take smaller sips" had been his advice. I followed it. Before I knew it, I was savoring my glass. I could nurse the thing most of the night. At most, I'd order a second. Never a third. As slow as I drank it, I rarely felt more than the slightest buzz from the alcohol's effects.

Besides, alcohol only affected half a Reaper's constitution—the human half. The other part of us, the part that was semi-divine, was immune to it. So, while we could indulge in strong drinks quite liberally, it took a lot for any of us to get wasted. I won't say it never happened. It did. But it was far less frequent, I imagined, than it was for regular humans.

I took a larger sip than usual. I was still anxious about what had happened earlier. On top of that, everyone was staring at us. I was used to it. Most of the time, people at least tried to pretend they weren't looking. On this occasion, though, the people were blatantly gawking at me.

I knew why. They'd seen me at my examination. They knew today was supposed to be my first reaping. They were all curious. They wondered how it had gone. Still, deep down, it was terrifying. It felt as if every person looking at me knew what happened —that their stares were not admiration or even curiosity, but pity.

Poor girl, I imagined them telling themselves. *She had so much potential...*

I took another big sip from my martini glass, retrieved my olive from the little sword-shaped toothpick that held it in the bottom of my drink, and popped it in my mouth.

"Something's bothering you, Zoey. I think it's more than just being underwhelmed by your first reaping."

I huffed. "Whatever, Gabriel. I'll be fine."

"You can talk to me, you know."

I took a deep breath and let it out slowly. "Not this time. I'm sorry, Gabriel. I can't."

"So, there *is* something wrong." Gabriel cocked his head to his right.

I bit the inside of my cheek. "Like I said, I can't talk about it. If I could, I would. Maybe I will, eventually. Depending on how things play out."

"Your brother finished the job, didn't he?" Gabriel asked. "That's it, isn't it?"

I turned away and stared ahead as I took another sip from my glass. "Just drop it, Gabriel. I'm serious. I don't want to talk about it."

"It's not a big deal, Zoey," he assured me. "A lot of times when one Reaper shadows another, the higher-level Reaper gives the lower-level person the harvest."

I clenched my fist. "Gabriel, I'm going to say this once. After that...well, I don't know what the fuck I'll do, but our night will be over. Do you understand?"

He nodded. "Of course, Zoey."

"There's a lot more to it than that. And right now, there's nothing I can do and nothing you can say that will make me feel any better. Leave it the fuck alone."

Gabriel leaned over and kissed me on the cheek. "What do you say we get out of here?"

I nodded, gulped down the rest of my martini, and set the glass on the bar. "My place or yours?"

Gabriel raised his eyebrow. "If your dad walked in on us…"

I laughed. "He'd probably kill you. You know, if he could. All right, your place it is."

CHAPTER SIX

I wasn't in the mood to stay at Gabriel's for the night to cuddle. Screw and split. Dick and dash. Copulate and evacuate. Call it what you will. It wasn't usually my style. It did make me feel a little better. For a few moments, the ecstasy made me forget about my own impotence. My inability to "perform" earlier in the day.

Gabriel had no such issues. At least, when he was with me. He lasted five minutes, tops. I wasn't exactly satisfied, but I wasn't in the mood to lie around and wait for him to recover his stamina for a second go-round.

I think I hurt his feelings a little when I hopped up, got dressed, and kissed him one last time before I bolted out of his door. It wasn't like it was our first time, but I'd be lying if I said I didn't feel a *little* bad about it. He knew I was upset. If he knew *why*, he'd understand. Of course, if he knew, would he be interested in me at all?

If I couldn't reap, who the hell was I? That's all I'd ever wanted. It was what I'd spent my entire life preparing to do. Pull that rug out from underneath me, and I wouldn't be able to stand. Reaping was my world. Not just my goal or my dream, but my future. It wasn't just my status as the princess, as the Grim Reaper in waiting, that was in jeopardy. It was my whole identity. Everything that made me, *me*.

I knew I wouldn't be able to sleep. I went back to Gehenna Boulevard. No, I wasn't looking for another hook-up. I wouldn't cheat on Gabriel, though I'd have plenty of opportunities if I wanted to. I wouldn't do that to him. I can't say I loved Gabriel. I always suspected he was more into me than I was into him. But he treated me well. He was kind. I always enjoyed his company.

I always figured that my feelings for him would grow. Until now, time was one thing I figured we had plenty of. And he was one hell of a catch. Good looking, sensitive, and passionate. What else could a girl want? Sure, he didn't make my heart skip a beat when we were together. But really, did I need that? I had to believe that if I could love anyone at all, I'd love Gabriel eventually, so I stuck with him.

I wasn't looking for a one-night stand. I didn't need it. I didn't want it. But I could certainly use another martini. Harley was more than willing to oblige.

"Why do I get the distinct sense that this isn't a celebratory drink?" Harley asked, sliding my martini across the bar toward me.

"Mind your own business and make my drinks," I snapped. I regretted my tone the second I spoke. "Sorry, Harley."

I wasn't a bitch. Not usually. But everyone's entitled to a little bitchiness from time to time. While I had my reasons, it wasn't Harley's fault. There wasn't anyone I could blame for what happened. I couldn't even blame myself. Not really. I'd done everything right. I'd worked harder than everyone else at the academy. I'd met the high expectations placed on me and exceeded them at every turn.

No, this wasn't my fault. But that made me even angrier. If I could point to a mistake I'd made, a problem in my process that had led to this, at least I'd know what I could correct. Maybe it was just a fluke like Morty had suggested. I didn't believe for a second that was the case. Hence, the bitchiness.

"Hey, princess," a stocky, handsome fellow greeted me as he took a seat next to me. His name escaped me. I'd seen him before. He had another girl on his arm practically every time he was out. I wasn't about to be his flavor of the night.

"Hey, asshole," I shot back.

The man grinned. "I've been called worse."

I took a sip of my martini. It burned its way down my throat. "I'm sure you have."

"Nice ass, by the way."

I chuckled. "So I've been told. Is that the best pickup line you've got?"

"Not really. Usually, I just ask, 'Hey, wanna fuck?' But you're the princess. I figured I'd show you some respect."

I raised an eyebrow. "By paying homage to my royal ass?"

"I can think of less enjoyable ways to spend an evening."

I smirked. "You couldn't handle this."

"Hey, Leeroy," Harley piped up. "Show a little class. Leave Zoey alone."

I raised my hand. "Thanks, Harley. But I've got this."

I stood up from my barstool. "Leeroy, get up."

Leeroy stood up. "What do you say, princess? Wanna get out of here and blow off a little steam together?"

I laughed. Then I punched Leeroy in the face. He dropped to the floor.

A chorus of cheers erupted from the rest of the people in the bar. I imagined I wasn't the first girl at Harley's bar who wanted to feed Leeroy a fist sandwich.

I turned to leave and looked over my shoulder at Leeroy on the ground, rubbing his eyes. "Since you like my ass so much, enjoy the view on my way out."

It was the first satisfying thing I'd done all day.

CHAPTER SEVEN

I was weirdly happy that Leeroy had creeped on me the night before. If he hadn't, I probably would have drunk myself into oblivion. The way I saw it, the asshole had saved me a raging headache this morning. I couldn't be sure he wouldn't have one in my stead. At least he got what was coming to him.

I hurried to check out the daily postings, eager to see what my next assignment would be.

Morty was already there waiting for me. "Looks like we're together again today, sis."

I sighed and pressed past my brother to check the listing myself. Sure enough. Same deal as before.

I nodded. "All right. Let's hope today's reaping goes more according to plan."

"I'm sure it will be fine."

I smiled at him, then we stepped up to the portal. I dialed in the code, and we left.

This time we appeared in a hospital, just outside the room of our target. No one else would see us, of course. We were in the proper regalia.

I stared at the same damned scythe-less staff that I'd summoned the day before. "For fuck's sake!"

Morty sighed, then summoned his scythe and finished the job.

The same thing happened for the next three days. Morty and I were given the same assignments. Each time, no scythe. My frustration grew with each failure. Pointy sticks don't reap souls.

"I think we should tell Dad," Morty suggested.

I'd been hoping it wouldn't come to that. "I don't know. I'm afraid of what he'll say."

"He might have an answer, Zoey," Morty insisted. "We can't go on like this forever. Eventually, it's going to come out. It's better if Dad knows about it before it does."

I nodded. "I suppose you're right. Dammit. If just once it would work the other way around."

"We've tried everything, Zoey. I don't think this problem is going to fix itself."

I couldn't help but be skeptical. "You're just angling to become the favorite to inherit his position."

Morty looked at me blankly. "That has nothing to do with this. I know this is upsetting, but it isn't my fault, either."

I closed my eyes for a second and gathered my wits. "I know. You're right. I'm sorry. I'm just frustrated."

"Totally understandable. If it means anything, I wish it was happening to me instead. You deserve to be the heir. I really don't. You've always been the better Reaper."

I snorted. "Yeah, right. I can't be a better Reaper if I can't even reap, Morty."

"You know what I mean. You've earned this. I've skated by every step of the way. There's a reason you're Level Three and I'm just Level One."

I shook my head. "I'll be a Level Nothing once Dad learns I can't so much as summon my scythe."

Morty shook his head. "Don't jump to conclusions, sis. You

know Dad has his hopes set on you as much as anyone else does. If there's a way to fix this, he'll do it."

As much as I hated to admit it, my brother was right. If we let this go on and didn't let Dad know, it would be an embarrassment to all of us. Something had to be done, and my father was the only one who might know what was going on with me.

My father wasn't a cruel person, despite his reputation throughout the world. At his core, he was kind and decent. He was overly focused on his work, of course, but he was the Grim Reaper, and the transition of every human soul into the afterlife was his responsibility. I suppose it was understandable that he was absent a lot during our childhood. It wasn't like he could just take a week off to take us to Disneyland.

Still, I did resent one thing. He'd never so much as suggested the possibility that he would one day take us to meet our mother. As far as I knew, the last time she'd seen us was when we were born. He didn't speak about her, *ever*. I wasn't sure if that was because he didn't care about her or if talking about her was just too painful.

For him and us.

After all, she was fully human. She couldn't come to the underworld even if she'd wanted to. Still, especially when we were young and weren't fully invested in our Reaper training, one would think a weekend here or there with Mom would have been desirable. I couldn't think of a good reason why he deprived us of that.

We grew up in a castle in the heart of the underworld. For the most part, the underworld had kept up with the times. Contrary to popular belief, we didn't live in a dark and primitive world. I mean, sure, it was dark when the lights were off. We didn't have the sun shining overhead. But we had most of the amenities they had on Earth.

Over the years, the Reapers had seen to it that our world closely resembled society on Earth. It was better that way. Not just because it made life more enjoyable for us in the underworld, but because if we were accustomed to the different technologies and various intricacies of human development, we'd be better equipped to deal with whatever challenges we would have to face while reaping.

So, we had Gehenna Boulevard, our own Bourbon Street. We had bars and casinos. We even had access to most of the movies and television shows that were broadcast on Earth. Sure, we were usually a few months behind in terms of new releases, but we got most everything eventually. The upper-level Reapers took care of it. Much like my father spent considerable energy buying and selling stocks, others spent their extra time when they weren't reaping souls acquiring new technologies, new movies, new music, and the like.

The only thing we didn't have in the underworld was the Internet. Unfortunately, signals don't reach through transdimensional portals. Even if we were to create something similar to it, it wouldn't be the same Internet. It would be a shoddy imitation without nearly as much content as the real thing.

Morty and I made our way to our father's office. It was where he spent most of his time. He even had his own portal there, connected directly to Earth. He didn't use the same one the rest of us did. If he had something important to do, he wasn't about to wait in line while the Reapers set out to collect their daily harvests.

To get to his office, we had to climb a long, stone, spiral staircase to the top of one of the castle spires. It wasn't as awful as it sounds. It was about a hundred steps, give or take, which most people can climb in a matter of a few minutes. Of course, it wasn't a pleasurable climb. More than once as children, Dad left Morty and me to fend for ourselves while he slaved away doing whatever the Grim Reaper does in his office when he's not traversing between worlds. Want a snack? We'd have to get it ourselves. Couldn't reach the top shelf in the pantry? We'd have to weigh our options. Give up or make the trek to go get Dad. Most of the time, he'd dismiss us, anyway. He'd say he was busy or, more likely, just didn't want to make the climb himself.

When we made it to the top of the stairs, I knocked on his door.

A chorus of barks greeted me. The sound of claws scratching at the door signaled that our entry would not be obstacle-free. I sighed. "Cerberus."

"Damn dog!" Morty exclaimed. "Such a pain in the ass."

I snorted. Don't get me wrong. Cerberus was a playful pooch. But with three heads, that meant three times the barking, three times the chewing on random shit around the castle, and three times the mouths to feed. No matter how full he got, it took at least thirty minutes for his stomach to tell each of his brains he was full. So, he was…overweight.

"Come in," my father called, his voice barely audible over the noise of his three-headed barking dog.

No sooner did I open the door than Cerberus was jumping on my legs. His poorly trimmed claws didn't feel great on my thighs. "Down, boy!"

Morty started laughing. Then he stopped because Cerberus took his giggles as an invitation. The three-headed canine darted to Morty and jumped up at him.

"Ow! My balls!" Morty screamed. "Stop it, Cerberus."

My father looked up from his desk. He'd been reading an old book. Nothing was unusual about that. He'd collected quite the library throughout the years. He set his book aside and rose from behind his desk. "Cerberus, off."

The dog stopped jumping on Morty and sat down. My father walked over to him with a single treat broken into three pieces and gave one to each of Cerberus' heads. "You can't say 'down,' Zoey. That's a different command. He should lie down if you tell him 'Down.' You need to say 'off.'"

I nodded. "I'll try to remember that."

Cerberus curled up on his bed in the corner of the office, and each of his three heads grabbed a squeaky toy. Yes, three squeaky toys at once. It very well might have been the most annoying symphony in underworld history.

My father seemed oblivious to the ruckus.

Cerberus huffed times three. My father raised his hand. The dog lowered his three heads and resumed chewing on his toys.

Dad was wearing flannel pajamas and slippers. I know he's the Grim Reaper. You probably expected a black cloak all the time. Well, do kings and queens wear their crowns constantly? Hell no. But people tend to think of them that way. Reapers, and especially the Grim Reaper, were often stereotyped. My dad wasn't that different than anyone else in the underworld. He wore his cloak when he went to Earth for all the same reasons the rest of us did. Usually, when he was bumming around the house, it was sweatpants or pajamas. Sometimes, he'd hang out in his tighty whities and wrap himself in a velvet bathrobe if we visited. Dad worked from home most of the time. There was no reason to dress fancy,

Dad opened his arms to greet us with a hug. Thankfully, he was in the flannel pajamas rather than the skivvies. I wouldn't hug my dad in his underwear. That's just weird.

My brother and I might have been the only two creatures in the universe who welcomed a hug from the Grim Reaper. My dad might have been busier than any single father should be. He wasn't around as much as I would have enjoyed growing up. But I *never* doubted that he loved me. Morty wasn't quite as confident. To hear my brother tell it, I'd been my dad's favorite from day one. I suspected, given what we had to share, that was about to change.

"How has it been going?" my dad asked. "I see you've been reaping together. What were the chances?"

"Well, we haven't lost any souls," I replied.

My dad smiled. "I never expected you would. How about you, Morty? Have you been able to reap any of the souls yourself?"

Morty nodded. "I've harvested all of them."

My father cocked his head, then he looked at me, his brow furrowed. "You're letting your brother reap them all?"

I sighed. "I wouldn't say I'm letting him, Dad. I have a problem."

My father sat on the edge of his desk, his plaid slippers dangling from his feet. "What kind of problem?"

I took a deep breath. "I can't summon my scythe."

He frowned at me in confusion. "What do you mean, you can't summon it?"

"The handle appears," I explained. "But that's it. There's no blade. I can't harvest any souls."

My dad scratched his head. "That doesn't make any sense at all. If you couldn't summon a scythe, for whatever reason, you shouldn't be able to summon anything at all."

I shook my head. "I don't know what to say. That's what's happening."

My father pinched his chin, then he looked at Morty, narrowing his eyes. "Is this your doing, son?"

"No!" Morty exclaimed. "You seriously think I'm sabotaging Zoey? I'd never! And do you think I'd be able to pull it off even if I wanted to do that?"

My father sighed. "I suppose not. Does anyone else know about this?"

I shook my head. "We've kept it to ourselves. No one knows except for the boatman."

My father pinched his chin. "He won't say anything. He doesn't care, frankly. So long as he gets paid on time."

"So, you seriously don't know why this is happening?" I asked.

My father shook his head. "Not for certain. But perhaps, since you are twins, you can't summon your scythe together. If you were to reap alone, Zoey, the results might be different."

"But Dad," Morty protested, "that doesn't explain why my blade could be summoned every time but hers couldn't. Like, why would she be the one with the problem every time?"

"It's a fair question, son. Especially since she's two ranks your senior. This is uncharted waters. As long as I've been the Grim Reaper, there hasn't been a single heir to any of the Reapers who has been a twin. There isn't any precedent that would explain why this is happening."

"Is there a way to fix it?" I asked.

"There might be." My father slid off the edge of the desk and retrieved his cloak from the coat rack in the corner. "I have tomorrow's schedule already. You're slated to work together again. I'll make some modifications before it's posted in the morning."

"Modifications?" I asked. "You can do that?"

My father smiled. "They don't tell you in the academy where the list comes from. That's by design. Only I know. When you take my place, Zoey, I'll tell you the truth. Until then, trust me this far. I can't alter the targets, but I do have the ability to modify the assignments."

I squinted. "I was under the impression that the assignments came from above. You know, someone in the celestial realm, deciding who got to reap who."

My father laughed. "Not at all, dear. The names come from beyond the underworld. We cannot change who is targeted. But it is and always has been the Grim Reaper's responsibility to assign Reapers to souls."

"Doesn't that take a while?" Morty asked. "A lot of people die every day."

My father smiled, rested his cloak on the back of his chair, and pulled a small tablet out of his drawer. He pushed a button and powered it on.

"We don't have many of these in the underworld," my father

explained. "Without the Internet, the devices are severely limited. However, they do help me with my assignments."

I raised my eyebrows. "How does that work?"

My father smiled. "A program. The algorithm analyzes the strengths, weaknesses, and the rank of all the Reapers, along with the difficulty of the various targets and makes assignments accordingly."

"So, this algorithm put Zoey and me together every day?" Morty asked.

My father nodded. "For some reason, yes, it did. I cannot say why. The algorithm is complex. I didn't write the program."

"Who did?" I asked.

My father laughed. "A particularly gifted human programmer. The celestials hired him on my behalf. He completed the program in exchange for an extra five years of life."

"And these celestials are…what, angels?" Morty asked.

My father smiled. "To some, that's what they are. Though, they are known by many names."

"And you can contact them?" I asked.

"There are many lessons you must learn before inheriting my position, Zoey."

Morty snorted. He knew that I was the one my father intended to make his heir. That didn't mean he liked it. Especially now, I figured, since my status as the future Grim Reaper was in question. That my father didn't recognize that was at the same time encouraging, at least from my perspective, and also discouraging to Morty.

Still, we all knew the truth. If we couldn't solve this problem, then Morty would be my father's heir. If that was the case, well, it would probably take a while before he was ready. It might delay my father's hopes to ascend by several years, maybe even by decades, depending on how long it took my brother to advance in rank.

"So, what is your plan?" I asked.

My father tapped on his tablet a few times. "I'll be printing out tomorrow's list in a few hours. Zoey, I'll be accompanying you tomorrow instead of Morty."

Morty cocked his head. Then his eyes widened. "Does that mean I'll get to go solo?"

My father shook his head. "I'm sorry, son, but no. You still need to shadow someone if you go out. What do you say about a day off?"

Morty narrowed his eyes. "No! I don't want a day off, dad. I want to reap."

"What about Gabriel?" I asked. "Morty could shadow him tomorrow."

"Gabriel Graves?" My father asked. "Your boyfriend?"

I nodded. "Yes. He was just saying he was getting a little bored with his assignments."

My father scrolled through the list on his tablet. I assumed it was the next day's assignments. "Very well. Though I should say his target tomorrow may prove more challenging than those he's faced recently."

"What do you mean?" I asked.

My father shrugged his shoulders. "Never mind. Morty, just mind your manners and keep your distance. Gabriel Graves is an accomplished Reaper, nearly ready to advance to the next level. This is an opportunity for you to learn."

"What is our assignment, then?" Morty asked.

My father smiled. "You'll find out soon enough. It's best not to over-prepare, son. I'll just say that I wouldn't be surprised if this particular soul put up quite the fight."

"And what about me?" I asked.

"I'll be accompanying you, Zoey. Again, I cannot tell you much about the target. I'm confident, however, that you will be able to handle it. If this works, as I anticipate it shall, I'll ensure that you and Morty are given different assignments from here on out."

CHAPTER EIGHT

If I were any other Reaper, I'd have been nervous as hell going on an assignment with my dad. I didn't know anyone lower than Level Twenty who'd ever shadowed my dad. That he was going on a reaping with me was a move that was certain to cause a few folks to whisper. They'd think it was nepotism.

Whatever. It was a one-time deal, and since most folks believed I was one day going to take his place, it was expected that I'd be shadowing him at some point. If they didn't think it was nepotism, they might start to wonder if my father's ascension was coming sooner than anticipated. Either way, it would elicit chatter throughout the underworld.

It would be worth it if this worked. And if it didn't work, there would be bigger problems we'd have to overcome than gossip.

"You do the work. I'm just here to watch."

I nodded. "Thanks, Dad."

I approached the dial and entered the code for my assignment. We stepped into the portal and emerged on an airplane. Oxygen masks were already deployed. The high-pitched scream of the jet's engine was deafening. A loud boom nearly forced me to jump out of my cloak.

I looked at my dad. "A plane crash?"

My father nodded. "We have to reap them all."

I sighed. "No survivors."

"A few of them won't be prepared to move on. Be ready, Zoey."

I raised an eyebrow. "If you hadn't come, this would have been *my* responsibility? Mine and Morty's?"

My father nodded. "You're more than capable, Zoey. You have all the training you need."

I gripped the top of one of the seats. No one could see us. As a Reaper, the g-force of the plane torpedoing toward the surface didn't affect me. Not directly. But the optics of it was disorienting. It gave me a sense of vertigo. I glanced at my dad, who stood casually in the middle of the aisle, unfazed by the experience. This wasn't his first plane crash, I imagined. He'd been through worse.

The jet collided with the sea, and water splashed around us as the plane burst into flames. I could feel the heat. I could smell the burning jet fuel mixed with the pungent odor of cooked flesh.

"This will be easier if you can finish the job before the plane goes under," my father urged.

I nodded, extended my hand, and pressed the sigil on my arm. My staff formed in my hand. Again, no blade.

"Fuck!" I screamed.

"Wield it like a scythe nonetheless," my father instructed. "Attempt to reap a soul."

I grunted. I didn't know how he remained so calm through it all. Was it really the case that my scythe just *looked* like a staff? Maybe it still had the power to harvest souls. If that was the case, I had the lamest scythe in the history of Reapers. It was worth a shot.

I jammed the end of my staff into someone's burning chest.

Blood poured out from the wound as if I'd punctured the man's ribcage.

I shook my head. "It's not working!"

I looked up. Dozens of souls were rising from their bodies, mixed with the thick smoke that filled the plane's cabin. I charged one of them and swung my staff at the soul. It passed through the soul with no effect.

"I want you to try something," my father began.

"Yeah, anything!"

"Scratch one of the men with the tip of your staff."

"Scratch him?" I cocked my head.

"They don't teach you this in the academy. When a soul flees, if you can accumulate a bit of your target's DNA on your staff—a little skin, some hair, even some sweat—you can use it to target their soul. It will help you track them down."

I bit the inside of my cheek and stepped toward one of the men. He was in a suit and tie. He had his oxygen mask pressed to his face. I placed the sharp tip of my staff to the man's cheek and scratched him. He was already terrified and screaming. I doubted he even noticed the scratch.

"Now point your staff at the man," my father directed.

I took two steps back and aimed the sharp end of my staff back at the man I'd just scratched. A blue glow settled onto the tip.

"Good. Now pivot to your right."

I turned, pointing my staff away from the man. The glow faded. I directed it back at him, and it glowed again.

"Your staff isn't powerless," my father told me. "You can still track souls."

"That's good news!" I exclaimed. "Does that mean I can summon my blade?"

"Try to strike the man," my father told me. "Perhaps the blade will appear now that it's tuned to his soul."

I swung my staff at the man. It banged into his chest. No blade.

"Dammit!" my father shouted. "Step aside!"

I moved out of my father's way. He stepped up beside me and summoned his scythe. He widened his stance and swung his blade through the businessman's body, collecting his soul. Then, my father turned again. I ducked out of the way, taking the hint, as he spun around like a tornado, catching one soul after the next with his glorious blade. I'd never actually seen my dad reap before. If I wasn't in such turmoil over my failure, I would have been awestruck by the sight. He moved with grace like a ballerina's through the cockpit, arresting one soul after the next until the job was done.

"It's time to go," my dad insisted.

"But it didn't work!" I shouted. "My scythe, it—"

"It's time to go, Zoey."

I shook my head and followed my dad back through the portal. I dragged my feet as we approached the boatman and my father delivered the souls to him.

We stood there a moment, watching the boatman ferry the souls from the plane to their respective eternal destinations. My dad took a deep breath. "Come with me."

No words of consolation. No explanations. He was direct and to the point. My father's face was expressionless. For a man who'd always shown me so much love, I felt nothing from him. I'd worked so hard to impress him, to impress everyone. Now, I'd let him down. I'd let the entire underworld down.

We made our way back to my dad's office. He didn't say one word to me the whole way back. Not as we navigated our way through the underworld back to his castle. Not as we made our way up the stairs and entered his office.

Cerberus started to bark. All three of his heads. It sounded like an animal shelter. I swear, if that dog jumped on me, I'd probably lose my mind. My father closed the door to his office.

Then he raised his hand, and Cerberus obediently crawled onto his bed. My dad had him trained to hand signals—no squeaky toys this time. I was grateful for that.

"Please sit down, Zoey."

Tears welled up in my eyes as I lowered myself into a small, leather, four-legged chair beside my dad's desk. I was supposed to be strong. I was confident. I was the badass Grim Reaper in waiting.

"I'm sorry, Dad. I don't know what's wrong."

"This isn't your fault, Zoey."

"But I can't reap!"

"No, you can't." My father shook his head. "But that doesn't mean you can't serve our cause."

"How the hell can I be worth a thing if I can't reap?"

"Your brother needs your help," my father replied. "He is the one who will have to replace me. But he's hardly fit for the job."

I shook my head. "I can't just live the rest of my existence as his tutor, Dad."

"What else would you do?" my father asked.

"I don't know!" I yelled, slamming my fist into the arm of the chair I was seated in.

"I realize this is a hard truth to accept, Zoey. Believe me, it's every bit as hard for me as it is for you. But you did not inherit my gift."

"I'm the one who has your skill. I was the one who aced my training, who passed her examination at Level Three. Not Morty!"

He sighed. "You are not Level Three, Zoey. You are not a Reaper."

"I earned it! This isn't fair!"

My father shook his head. "You're right. It isn't fair. But this is the hand that fate has dealt. I cannot imagine how difficult this must be for you."

I snorted. "I'd be the only one in all the underworld who can't reap, dad. I can't live with that. If I can't reap, why don't you just send me back to my mom?"

My father cocked his head. "I do not know where your mother is. That's not an option, Zoey."

"Why isn't it?" I asked. "Look, I can't bear to face everyone here, especially once they learn the truth. They'll all see me as a freak."

"You're not a freak, Zoey. You just aren't a Reaper."

"Who lives in a world of fucking Reapers, Dad!"

"Watch your mouth, Zoey. I realize this is upsetting. But there's no need to curse."

I bit my tongue. It was the only way to prevent myself from responding without unleashing a torrent of F-bombs. "Send me back to Earth."

My father sighed. "You won't fit in there either, Zoey. You might as well stay here where you can still be of some use. In a world you know. And Morty..."

"Yeah, he needs me. Why is that *my* responsibility? There are other Reapers he can shadow. Leave him with Gabriel. He'll learn well enough. Maybe once I'm gone, he'll step up to the plate. Give him a chance, Dad. He's better than you realize."

"He does the bare minimum just to skate by. He's a slacker, Zoey."

"Because all of our lives, you've made it abundantly clear to him that I was your favorite."

"That's not true," my father protested. "I love you both."

"But you've always preferred me," I countered. "You nurtured my potential. Even though either of us could have been your heir, neither of us ever believed that he had a chance. That's why he didn't try. But he's smart. He can learn, and he'll do better if I'm gone. The only reason he doesn't try harder is that he figured there was no point. Like everyone else, he assumed I was your heir."

"I don't believe that's true. He looks up to you."

"No, he doesn't," I argued. "He loves me because I'm his sister. But that's it. If anything, he's jealous of me, and for good reason. You've given him every reason in the world not to try harder. It's not my job to make up for the fact that you didn't believe in him. That you still don't believe in him."

My father shook his head. "Zoey…"

I shrugged. "What, Dad? You know what I'm saying is true! If you want him to take over, let Gabriel train him. Or for God's sake, train him yourself!"

"What am I supposed to tell everyone if you leave, Zoey?" he asked. "They won't understand."

"Then make them understand. I don't care what you tell them."

"You're my daughter. I won't just send you to Earth to live as a human, Zoey. You won't make it."

I huffed. "So, I can't summon a scythe, and you lose all faith in me just like that?"

"That has nothing to do with it!" he protested.

"But it does. Tell me, until now, when haven't I risen to the occasion? When haven't I exceeded every expectation ever placed on me? I know it won't be easy, but it'll be a lot easier to live there where no one knows me. Where no one thinks I'm a princess and I can make whatever life I want. Maybe I can find Mom."

My father pressed his hands together and extended his index fingers, resting them against his lips. "If this is what you truly want, I'll let you go. But I will need to make a few preparations."

I frowned. "Preparations?"

"I'm not going to let you go to Earth empty-handed, Zoey. If you go, as a human, you'll have all the skills you've ever had. But you'll be vulnerable without your cloak. You'll be subject to all the dangers that can befall any human. One day, you may even have to be harvested. I'd prefer to see that day come later than sooner."

"So, what do I do now?" I asked. "Just hang out and wait?"

"There may be people you'd like to visit before you go. Of course, you can return at any time. That is one of many things I must arrange before I allow you to leave. You'll always have a home here, Zoey."

I shook my head. "This place can never be my home again. I don't belong here, Dad."

I could swear that tears were forming in my father's eyes. I'd never seen him cry. The Grim Reaper *doesn't* cry.

"Zoey, this isn't the first time I've had to say goodbye to someone I love. This isn't easy for me to accept."

I snorted and cocked my head. "Are you talking about Mom? I thought she was just, you know, like an incubator. Some chick you knocked up to make an heir."

My father took a deep breath and exhaled. "Your mother was much more to me than that. But like you, I suppose, she didn't belong here. She couldn't live here, and I couldn't stay on Earth. Not if I ever was going to fulfill my duty as the Grim Reaper. Fate demanded something different for us both."

"But she's still alive?" I asked.

My father nodded. "I've checked the records every day since you were born, Zoey. Her soul has never been reaped. She's alive. Somewhere."

"I'm going to find her, Dad."

My dad stepped toward me. I stood, and he hugged me. "I hope you do, Zoey. I really hope you do. Come back tomorrow. If you still intend to leave, I will send you to Earth. Think about where you'd like to live. I can open a portal to any place in the world."

I shook my head. "I don't have to think about it. You might not know where Mom is, but you can send me back to the last place you knew she was."

"That was more than twenty years ago, Zoey. She could be anywhere in the world by now."

I nodded. "Maybe I can use the Internet to locate her."

"Perhaps. However, I've tried it myself many times. When I refused to give up my place here and took you and your brother with me, I broke her heart. I believe she's moved on. She must've changed her name. If she could be found, if she wanted to be found, I would have a long time ago."

"That doesn't mean I can't try. I'll see you tomorrow, Dad."

My father nodded. "I love you, Zoey."

I sighed. "Yeah. I love you too, Dad."

CHAPTER NINE

There was only one person I wanted to see before I left. No, not Morty. He was the last person I wanted to see. I left him a note to say goodbye. I couldn't bear to face him. Call it childish, if you must. Perhaps I was being petty. But he was taking my place. He was taking over the family business if you could call it that.

Reaping was, after all, an enterprise. I'd been the heir in waiting. Now I was the outcast. My brother, who hadn't done a damn thing to earn it, was taking over what I'd busted my ass for my entire life.

If I was honest, jealousy was only half the reason I didn't want to see him. If anyone could convince me to stay, it would be Morty. I didn't want to risk that. I couldn't allow it. If I let him give me those puppy-dog eyes and beg me to stay in the underworld, I'd probably give in. And if I did, I'd be miserable for the rest of my eternal existence.

I didn't write much in my letter to Morty. I told him I loved him. I explained my choice. I told him not to come looking for me. I wished him luck. I wanted him to succeed, don't get me wrong. But dammit, there was a part of me that sort of hoped he'd fail. Not because I wished him ill. I wanted to give fate itself the middle finger. Whatever power in the universe had decided to give him my father's abilities instead of me deserved to eat a little crow after making what could be the dumbest choice in supernatural history.

That was saying something, considering the long history, full of demigods and even full-blown gods making stupid decisions. I'd never met any of the Olympian deities. Dad insisted they were real and that most of the stories were true. Take Chronos, for example. He was the father of Zeus. As the story goes, after he learned that one of his children would overthrow him, he *ate* all of his children. If Zeus' mother hadn't disguised him as a rock, wrapped in swaddling clothes, he would have been eaten, too.

How Chronos mistook the taste of granite for the flavor of a baby was beyond me. But it takes a special kind of asshole to do that. Especially since, supposedly, Chronos had overthrown *and castrated* his father. The dickwad got what was coming to him when the real Zeus delivered Daddy Dearest his comeuppance. The point is this. Just because things happen with supposed divine fate in view doesn't mean they aren't colossally stupid and downright wrong. Whatever so-called god had chosen to make Morty the next Grim Reaper over me was just another in a long line of dumb jerks who probably didn't know his divine ass from his pretentious face. That the gods had screwed me over was probably par for the course. I should have seen it coming.

The way I saw it, the gods were far more interested in the affairs of the underworld than they were with Earth. They hadn't done shit on Earth in thousands of years. Not that they might not someday decide to get involved in human affairs. So far as I knew, the only thing they were concerned about when it came to humanity was ensuring that every person died when they were supposed to. That we reaped their souls and didn't leave too many behind as ghosts. Yeah, they cared about human death. They didn't give two shits about human lives.

If I went to Earth, I could make a life for myself and create my own fate. At least until they decided it was my time to get reaped. I knew the deal. When that happened, well, I'd put up one hell of a fight.

I met up with Gabriel at our usual spot on Gehenna Boulevard. Everyone in the place went silent when I stepped through the doors. Leeroy wasn't there. He was probably too ashamed to show his face.

"What are you all staring at?" I asked as I stepped up to the bar where Gabriel was waiting for me, two dirty martinis already prepared for us.

People started chatting again, returning to the conversations they were engaged in before I walked in. Yeah, I wasn't going to miss that kind of attention. I could only imagine how quiet it would get when I stepped into the bar if everyone knew the truth about me.

"So, I heard about what happened the other night," Gabriel began.

I chuckled. "You know that Leeroy asshole?"

Gabriel shrugged. "I don't generally spend a lot of time befriending assholes."

"I don't blame you." I took a sip from my martini. "You know what they say about assholes, right?"

"What's that?" Gabriel asked.

"Get too close to them, and they'll inevitably shit all over you."

Gabriel laughed. "In that case, I suppose it's a good thing I don't befriend a lot of dicks either."

"I don't either," I agreed. "Doesn't change the fact that I keep getting fucked."

Gabriel turned and stared at me. "What is that supposed to mean?"

I sighed. "Nothing. But I wanted to tell you I'll be going away for a while."

"Going away? I heard your dad took you on an assignment today. Does that have something to do with it?"

I nodded. "It does. But probably not in the way you're thinking."

"Would you care to explain?"

I bit my lip. I might not have been in love with Gabriel. But I did care about him, and I knew he was in love with me. I owed him the truth. "I'm going to Earth."

He grinned. "I assumed as much. Doing some major harvests with your dad?"

I shook my head. "Not like that, Gabriel. I'm leaving the underworld. I'm going there to live."

"Why would you do that?" he asked.

"I can't reap, Gabriel."

Gabriel scratched his head. "What do you mean? You're one of the best Reapers to graduate from the academy in decades."

"I can't summon a scythe. I literally *can't* reap."

Gabriel grabbed his glass and took a drink—a bigger gulp than he usually did. "That's not possible."

"Trust me, it is." I shrugged. "I've tried everything. My dad has tried everything. There's nothing we can do to change it."

"When will you be coming back?" Gabriel asked.

"I don't know. I might not ever come back, Gabriel."

Gabriel clenched his fist. "No. I can't accept that, Zoey. You have to come back."

I shook my head. "I don't belong here, Gabriel. I can't live here anymore."

"I don't care, Zoey. Don't you understand? It doesn't matter to me that you can't reap. I don't care if you're the next Grim Reaper or just some girl in the crowd. I love you, Zoey."

"I know you do."

"Don't you love me, too?"

I cringed. "I—"

"You don't, do you?"

"I didn't say that!"

"If you love me, then stay!"

"Gabriel, if you loved *me*, you wouldn't ask me to stay in a world where I don't fit in. Where I'll always be looked at as the girl who used to have potential but became...*nothing*."

"I don't care what people think. You shouldn't either, Zoey."

"You're not listening, Gabriel. Say I stay here, and we stay together, I'd be nothing here but your...whatever. I need to make something of myself."

"I'm not enough for you?" he asked. "Is that what you're telling me?'

"Yes, that's exactly what I'm saying. You shouldn't want that for me. To live my entire existence with no goals, no aspirations, other than being your girl? You know me, Gabriel. Do you think I'd be happy if that was all I could ever be?"

Gabriel shook his head as he took another drink. "No, you wouldn't be happy. You're right."

"That's why I have to leave," I insisted.

"Then go to Earth," Gabriel suggested. "I can visit. Not for long. But it's possible. Other Reapers do it."

"When they have to reproduce, Gabriel. You're not old enough for that."

"But your dad will allow it if you ask him to. And you can still come back here to visit, right?"

"I can," I agreed. "My dad wants me to."

Gabriel gave in. "Then go have your life. Find whatever it is on Earth that you think will make you happy. I'll still be here for you. We can still make this work."

"Gabriel, do you really want a long-distance relationship?"

He nodded. "If that's what it takes to be together, then yes."

"I don't know..." Dammit. I'd come here expecting to break up with him. But he was determined.

"What's the harm in trying, Zoey? If it doesn't work, if we aren't happy, we can break up. I don't want to give up on us."

I closed my eyes. He was committed to figuring this out, even though it was bound to fail. I might be tough, but I wasn't cold-hearted. I couldn't bring myself to break his heart.

"Fine." I regretted it almost the moment the word escaped my lips.

"So, will we stay together?" Gabriel asked.

I sighed. "I suppose."

Gabriel smiled and kissed me on the cheek. "This is going to be hard, Zoey. But think about it. How romantic would it be, two Reapers in love, separated by worlds, overcoming it all to be together forever."

I snorted. Yeah, it *sounded* romantic. It also sounded like an impossibility. It was a sweet sentiment. I wanted to believe him, even as I wanted to love him as much as he loved me. That forever bullshit might have worked out for Bella and Edward. I highly doubted it would for Zoey and Gabriel.

"When I come back, I don't want to meet here. I don't want other people to see me. When people find out why I left, or even worse, if they think I just abandoned my place here, I'm not sure I could deal with that."

"I understand," Gabriel replied. "This is just a bar. The under-world is a large place. There are other places we can go."

I nodded. "Well, I'll leave it up to you to plan something."

"When will you come back, then?" Gabriel asked.

"I don't know, Gabriel."

"Once a month, at least."

"Gabriel, I—"

"Don't make me wait longer than that, Zoey."

I sighed. "Fine, I'll come back the first of the month. But I'm serious, Gabriel. I don't want anyone else to know I'm here."

"Not even your family?"

"*Especially* not them. I mean, my dad can know. He probably will. But not Morty."

Gabriel cocked his head. "Why not?"

"He needs to move on without me," I replied. "He shadowed you today, didn't he?"

Gabriel nodded. "He did. I can't say I was too impressed."

"That's my point. He's not incapable of rising to the occasion. But if I keep showing up and he knows it, it'll only hold him back."

"I don't think that's true, Zoey."

"Trust me, Gabriel. I know my brother. He needs to know that I'm gone. He needs to believe I'm not coming back. Ever. That's the only way he'll ever become what he needs to be."

Gabriel shook his head. "I don't think you're giving him enough credit."

"You're the one who just said he wasn't impressive. Who isn't giving him credit, now?"

"That's not the point," Gabriel countered. "I just don't see how seeing his sister from time to time would be such a hindrance. He's shadowed you for several days, and he finished all your assignments. I assume if what you're telling me is accurate, that he was making progress."

"Only by necessity. When I'm gone, it will still be by necessity that he has to improve. He needs to be able to do this without me. I won't be here forever."

"But you can come back here forever. If you're coming back because of us, he won't ever have to do it alone, without you."

"But he needs to." I tucked my hair behind my ears. "If he's going to become the Grim Reaper someday, he can't look up to me. He has to surpass me. That's the only way."

"Look, I don't agree. But if that's what you want, I won't let him know you're here when you come back."

"Those are my terms. That's the only way I'll agree to this."

"I can live with that," Gabriel agreed. "Are you sure you'll be okay?"

"On Earth?" I asked.

Gabriel nodded.

I took my martini glass from the bar and raised it to my lips. "When have I ever not been okay?"

"It's a different world, you know. The skills you have, they don't exactly translate to success on Earth."

I shrugged. "Then I'll learn new skills."

Gabriel laughed. "Well, you're nothing if not determined, Zoey. That's one thing I love about you. That's one reason why I know we can make this relationship work. When you want to do something, there's not a power in even the celestial realm, not even on Olympus itself, that could stop you."

I smiled. "That's what I'm counting on."

CHAPTER TEN

I spent the night with Gabriel. He made love to me. I tried to make love to him back. My heart wasn't in it. In truth, I was thinking about all the possibilities that lay ahead. I allowed him to cuddle up next to me as he fell asleep. I was wide awake. Too much was churning through my mind. The more I thought about it, the more my anxiety started to give way to excitement.

I was still in pain from the loss of my dreams. The hopes I'd had all these years for what I would become were dead. New hopes were about to be born. Gabriel represented my old life.

Was I making a mistake by not cutting the cord? Maybe. But it's hard to let go of everything familiar. Gabriel was, if nothing else, the one thing I'd promised to keep in my life that connected me to the underworld. I was excited about my future, but I was also afraid. I didn't know what was coming. The only thing I knew was what I'd always known. Strangely, agreeing to try to make things work with Gabriel made my decision to leave the underworld easier. It was like I was diving into an abyss, and he was the tether that could pull me out of it if I started to drown.

I kissed him as I rolled out of bed and got dressed. I'd

intended to sneak out of his bed and leave. He got up and met me at the door and kissed me again—passionately, on the lips.

"I love you, Zoey."

"I love you, too," I told him, knowing that it might have been a lie. Then again, I didn't know it wasn't true, either. Love is complicated. In my case, it was more complex than it was for most. Maybe that was why something felt wrong about telling Gabriel I loved him as I left. Shouldn't love be simple? If I did love him, why was I questioning it? I'd seen my share of romcoms. We'd imported a bunch of them. One night, Gabriel and I had binged a few. We'd watched Adam Sandler and Drew Barrymore fall in love in at least four different ways. In none of those instances had it been anything like what I'd experienced with Gabriel.

I realize that romcoms are mostly sappy, overly sentimental, and unrealistic. But it wasn't like I had two parents whose relationship I could use as a baseline for what my understanding of love should be. Isn't love something you should recognize, no matter what? If I loved Gabriel, why would I consider breaking up with him? If I loved him, dammit, why would I allow him to talk me into trying to make this long-distance, transdimensional relationship work? Was it because I didn't love him? If I loved him, wouldn't it be better to cut him loose, let him find someone who could love him the way he deserved?

I dismissed those questions from my mind as I left and returned to my father's office. He was waiting for me with a large footlocker waiting on top of his desk.

"What's all this?" I asked.

"Some things that I hope will help you get started in your new life, and a few items that may or may not help you track down your mother. I couldn't figure out where she'd gone, but perhaps you'll have more success than I did since you'll have more time to dedicate to finding her. Don't open the chest until you arrive."

I nodded. "I should probably pack a few things, as well."

My father shook his head. "You can only take so much with you through the portal, Zoey. This is all you will require."

"What about clothes?"

"There's a prepaid credit card in the box in your name," he explained. "There's plenty on it to provide for you until you get situated."

I cocked my head. "So how much is on this card, anyway? I'm not taking too much of the money required for the boatman, am I?"

My father laughed. "I've already arranged for temporary lodgings in an apartment. I've paid for your first three months in advance, and I've seen that you have sufficient transportation."

"A bus ticket or something?"

Dad smiled. "Or something. I think you'll be quite pleased when you discover your graduation present."

"What is it?"

My father smirked. "You'll see, Zoey. It's a surprise. You'll find out when you open the footlocker."

"Well, that's a big footlocker. I'm guessing there's a lot more there than a debit card and a set of car keys."

My father nodded. "There is. Everything will be clear when you arrive. The portal will take you to your new lodgings."

"Where is this apartment? New York? That's where you got us IDs."

My father shook his head. "No, not New York."

"Paris?" I guessed. "Los Angeles? Somewhere in the Caribbean? Oh! What about Vegas?"

My father smiled. "Kansas City."

"Kansas City?" I asked, raising my eyebrows. "Isn't Missouri like America's butthole?"

My father cocked his head. "Excuse me?"

I sighed. "Of all the places in the world, why would you send me there? I reaped a soul there the other day. Well, Morty did. Trust me, I saw nothing there that was remotely impressive."

"I've spent quite a bit of time there myself. It's quite the town if you give it a chance. It's also where I met your mother."

"So that's why you're setting me up there."

"It's the best place to start. So far as I know, all her family is in the region. There's no reason she'd move too far. Unless she met someone."

When he said, "Unless she met someone," I saw pain on my dad's face. He didn't talk about Mom often, and maybe that was why. It was too painful. Did he still love her after all these years? I suppose, for a semi-divine being who'd existed for so many centuries, a heartbreak from two decades ago was still tender and fresh.

"Thanks, Dad. I'll make the best of it."

"If that's not where you'd like to go, well, I can make other arrangements. It may take some time..."

"No. That's perfect."

My father nodded. "There's a crystal in the box. You can use it to cast a portal directly into my office at any time."

I snorted. "At any time? Is there some way I can warn you before I show up?"

"Not really. You'll appear here instantly. I won't have much warning at all."

"Please don't hang out in here in your underwear, then."

My dad raised an eyebrow. "Why not? It's my office. I'll do what I want."

"Then I'm not coming through that portal without covering my eyes." I was only half-joking.

My father laughed. "I'll try to remain decent."

I took a deep breath as my father formed the portal that, presumably, would drop me square in my new Kansas City apartment.

My father looked at me and brushed a stray strand of my hair away from my eyes. "Be careful, Zoey. I'm always here if you need me."

"I know, Dad. Thank you for this. I promise I'll be fine."

"Come back and say hello soon."

I nodded. "Yup. Definitely. Love you, Dad."

"Love you too, baby girl."

CHAPTER ELEVEN

Six Months Later

My sports bike nearly skidded out beneath me as I turned the corner sharply. The last thing I wanted to do was lay it down. Sure, Daddy's money had paid for my motorcycle, but it would take more of Daddy's money to fix it—and I didn't know how I'd even begin to explain how it happened.

More than that, though, I couldn't let the asshole get away.

He reminded me of that Leeroy dickwad who'd harassed me that time at the bar on Gehenna Boulevard, back in the other-world. Only this guy wasn't so forward and direct. He was more of a silent stalker. His tactic was different from Leeroy's. His goal was the same.

I'd watched the creeper eye Sienna, my eighteen-year-old coworker, during my shift at Cup-O-Joe's as I made lattes and cappuccinos and poured plain-Jane cups of coffee for the customers. Sienna was short but spunky. She had one of those round faces that made her look younger than her actual age. She had wavy, dishwater-blonde hair, a petite frame, and a button nose. She had a cute smile. This was her first job.

Hell, it was my first job, too. Sienna had trained me despite the fact she'd only worked there a couple of months longer than me. She'd also covered for me more than once. I wasn't a great barista, but she always had my back. When I screwed up customer orders, she was quick to fix my mistakes. I was grateful for that. Joe, my boss and the owner of the shop (hence Cup-O-Joe's, get it?) probably would have fired me already if it wasn't for her. Our shifts usually ran concurrently.

The first red flag had been the way the creep followed Sienna with his eyes over the top of his newspaper. I suspected he was a no-good POS. He was young, maybe nineteen or twenty. Since coming here, I had seen no one under fifty reading an actual newspaper. Most everyone in the younger generations got their news from their phones. The second was when he got up and left only seconds after Sienna took off. Thankfully, our shifts ended at the same time.

I suspected the guy had unsavory intentions. I was only a half-minute behind Sienna as I made my way to my motorcycle in the parking garage across the street.

Mister Creepo was waiting for Sienna at her car. Another sign that this dude was a stalker. He hadn't only been leering at her during her shift, but he knew what she drove. He'd apparently had his eye on her for a while.

He was getting a little handsy when I entered the parking garage. Sienna had tried to push the guy away, but he was aggressive and insentient. Aw, hell no, dude.

I yelled at him as I ran toward Sienna's car. He took off. Most people would say that a young woman should just let a guy like that flee. Report it to the police. Whatever. They trained me to handle worse back at the Reaper academy. The police wouldn't do squat to the guy even if they caught him.

I didn't even have to think about it. Sienna had my back at work. I'd have her back now. There *was* something I could do about it. I'd make sure this jerk never bothered my girl again.

I had my bike parked two spots down from where Sienna had parked. I ensured she got in her car safely and took off through the parking garage. The guy leaped over a divider meant to separate one row of traffic from the next. It was a shortcut to the parking garage exit. I had to go around and speed down another row of parked vehicles before I could turn the corner and pursue Sienna's assailant.

It was my turn out of the parking lot at speeds in excess of what is generally recommended when making a ninety-degree turn that almost left my bike lying in the middle of 14th Street. I also had to be careful. The Power and Light District was one of Kansas City's busier areas. Traffic was heavy. But I could see the guy weaving through the crowd that was assembling outside the T-Mobile Center for a concert.

I weaved around a few cars and blasted down Grand Boulevard.

I had a keen eye. I hadn't lost sight of the guy, although his black jacket and jeans didn't exactly stand out in the crowd. Call it a gift, a focus that I'd gained over years of training to fight against souls that didn't want to get reaped.

The crowd was too dense. I had to leave my bike on the side of the street. I didn't know what I was going to do when I caught up to the creep. But I had to make sure he knew he couldn't get away with that stalker crap.

He was slick. He was fast. I was faster. He ducked down an alley between a restaurant and a bar further down Grand. I was right behind him.

Then he turned and pointed a gun at me.

"Leave me alone!" the guy shouted.

"You shouldn't have messed with her," I replied.

"Yeah, well, you'll do well enough to take her place. Take off your shirt."

I raised an eyebrow. "Excuse me?"

"You heard me. I've got the gun. That means you do what I say."

I shook my head. Pressed the sigil on my wrist and, summoning my staff, I spun, and with a swipe, I knocked the gun out of the guy's hand. Then I kicked him in the chest. He flew into the wall.

I stood over him, the pointed end of my staff aimed at his neck. "You were saying? Oh yeah. You thought you were in charge. That I should do what you say because you have the gun."

"Wha…" the creep stammered. "What the hell is that thing? You pulled it out of nowhere!"

I smiled. "I admit, it's not as deadly as I'd like it to be. But I imagine it would do the job. If I just applied a little pressure…"

"No, please!" the guy begged. "I'm sorry! I just thought she was hot You are too, but that other girl…"

I rolled my eyes. Sienna was pretty, but she was also shy, and from the way she carried herself, she probably didn't realize her beauty. I didn't know why Sienna might be insecure. There are a lot of things that can happen to someone to make them that way. But I knew what this guy meant. She was his type if only because she looked vulnerable, maybe a little desperate for attention. He was a predator, and he was looking for wounded prey—someone who wouldn't fight too hard.

I detected a sharp odor. The wet patch on the front of the guy's pants likely explained it. I pressed the sharp end of my staff into his neck a little harder. With a quick jab, I could end the guy's life and ensure he wouldn't hurt anyone else. But if I did that, someone who knew me would show up to reap him. Knowing my luck, it would probably be Morty. Since the Grim Reaper's blood was in my veins, I could see Reapers even if they weren't there for me.

I didn't want any of them to see me. They'd recognize me, every one of them. I'd have to settle for scaring the piss out of the guy—literally. "Here's what's going to happen...*if* I let you go, that is."

"Please, just let me go," he begged. "I'm sorry I won't bother your friend ever again."

I snorted. "What's your name?"

"I don't..."

"Tell me your name, or I'll take your wallet and find out."

He hung his head. "My name is Chad. Like I said, I'm sorry. I'm so sorry!"

I huffed. "You're only sorry because someone stood up to you and because the tip of my staff is pressing against your carotid artery. I don't think you're sorry about what you hoped to do to my friend. You're just sorry you got caught."

"Please! I swear, never again."

"I never want to see you in my coffee shop again. If you ever so much as talk to my friend again, if you come in for even a drink, I'll finish this. Trust me, Chad. I'll find you. And you won't get away from me."

"I-I-I understand," Chad stuttered.

I released my staff. It disappeared in a flash. Chad struggled to his feet and took off down the alley.

I smiled as I watched him run.

For the first time in six months, my skills came in handy. I wasn't a great barista. I was pretty bad at it. I didn't need the money, but it was something to do. I'd learned in short order after arriving on Earth that coffee shops were great social spaces. I could meet people there. I'd ask Sienna how she was doing the next day when we were scheduled for the same shift again.

75

CHAPTER TWELVE

I laughed as I returned to my motorcycle, thankful that the authorities hadn't yet ticketed or towed it, and headed back to my studio apartment. I dismounted my bike and checked my phone. I had a text from Sienna. She was worried about me.

Zoey, u ok?

She didn't know about my...skills.
That guy won't be bothering you again, I texted back before realizing I hadn't answered her question. I texted again. **I'm fine. He isn't. I'll just say he needs a change of pants**.
Sienna's reply came a few seconds later.

LOL! Thanks, Zoey!

I chuckled at the kitty-cat smiley face she ended her message with. I was still working on my emoji game. The whole smartphone thing was pretty new to me, relatively speaking. I couldn't figure out why anyone would use the little pile of smiling poop emoji that was pre-programmed into my phone. Like, really? If turds had any emotions, I doubted they'd be smiling. Think about it. The only relationship it ever had before was with a real asshole. Then, it got dumped. Angry poop emojis might make sense. Jaded ones with attitude? Sure. Happy ones? Not likely. Hard to be happy if you have a shit life.

My first reply was a simple thumbs-up. That was weird, too. It wasn't like I went around thumbs-upping people, mostly because I didn't want to be a douchebag. Thumbs-up via text message seemed more natural. Less dorky or dickwad-ish than a real-world thumbs-up.

I like made-up words. "Dickwad-ish." "Douchebaggery." "Kickassery." Just to name a few of my favorites. I'm from the underworld. I'm not beholden to the Queen's English.

I decided to follow up my text with another one. **Any clue who that guy was? Like, have you ever seen him before tonight?**

I stared at my phone blankly, waiting for Sienna's reply

He looked familiar. Like, I'm sure I've seen him before, but I can't place him.

She probably *had* seen him before. The way he'd eyed her from the moment he walked into Cup-O-Joe's, it was like he'd come there just for her. Either way, I'd scared the crap out of the guy. Well, not literally. I did scare the piss out of him, and that was enough. Maybe it was a close enough call that he'd rethink a few things about his life. Not likely. Guys like that don't change their ways easily.

I'm not going to lie. It felt good to kick a little ass. And it was nice that my scythe-less staff could be good for something. I might not be able to reap with it, but the tip was sharp, and it could do some damage.

More than that, it felt good to help out Sienna. I didn't have a lot of friends. I suppose since she was a few years younger than me and we didn't hang out outside of work, she probably didn't think of me as a friend at all. Still, she was a lot of fun. We had a blast when we worked together. She was one of only a handful of people I'd connected with since I came to Earth. Sure, I hit the clubs and bars. I talked to a lot of guys, but it was clear from the start that they all had their own agendas. They spent a lot of time talking about themselves.

Like I was supposed to be impressed about their jobs, or that they used to play quarterback in high school or belonged to an unknown rock band. Usually, my yawns signaled my lack of interest before most guys ever got around to asking me any questions about myself.

I had mixed feelings about that. I wanted people to ask me about myself, to show me they were interested in me as a person. On the other hand, if they did, I'd have to feed them a load of bullshit since I didn't have any earthbound history, and my real past wasn't exactly something I could reveal to most people.

I kicked off my shoes and changed into sweats. My apartment was a studio loft halfway between the Power and Light District, where I worked, and Country Club Plaza. It was a five-minute drive between my job and home, depending on traffic. I had to hand it to my dad. The place was quite a find. I was close to the happening spots in the city but far enough from any of them that I didn't have to deal with all the noise.

I enjoyed being halfway between these two destination spots in the city. They satisfied different sides of my personality, the refined and the rambunctious. The Plaza had expensive restaurants, fancy fountains, upscale shopping, horse-drawn carriages, musicians on the corners. It was a calm, though enjoyable, experience. The Power and Light District was home to sports bars, clubs, and concert venues. It didn't get too crazy there usually, but the crowds were younger overall and partied harder than the folks who frequented the Plaza.

I was finally getting my apartment the way I liked it. I'd found a large furniture store just across the state line that could deliver and set up most everything I needed that wasn't already included in my apartment. After I got the big stuff—a bed, a table and chairs, a bedroom set, and the biggest television I could find—it was a matter of fine-tuning the look of the place. Most of the modern art, while cool, wasn't what I was used to from the underworld. Most of the paintings I'd seen there were lifelike pieces, dark portraits of famous Reapers who'd long ago ascended. Some of them depicted the Olympian gods. Far be it from me to hang a portrait of Zeus on my wall. I was starting over. I wasn't about to bring the style of the underworld with me into my new life.

So, I'd been taking my time to get acclimated to the culture. I'd toured museums and spent way too much time watching HGTV. I was slowly forming taste, I suppose. More importantly, I was starting to figure out how to blend into this world.

Part of that was getting my job. I didn't want to rely on Dad's money forever. I appreciated his generosity, but I wanted to build a life I controlled. If I paid my own bills, if I earned my own money, then no one could pull the rug out from under me. No unnamed, divine consciousness could decide that the fates didn't favor my choice to make a life here. I wasn't beholden to the promise of a scythe or any other magical item that may or may not appear. Whatever life I made for myself in this world was going to be *mine* completely.

So, I treated Dad's money like a get-started loan. I intended to pay it all back. Not because he demanded it, but because I wanted to be able to say that I'd earned everything I got.

I realize it was a bit artificial. Dad's money was still there. Since I didn't have to ask permission to spend it, it was tempting if I was running short to just tap into his bank account. Technically, I suppose, since my name was on the account, it was also mine. But I didn't put the money in there. Who did, really? Not my dad. He'd invested it in stocks and collected it over centuries to pay the boatman.

Unless Charon had intentions to upgrade his rowboat to a cruise liner sometime soon, there was more than enough money to keep him satiated for several centuries. That is, given population growth rates, corresponding death rates, and the likely number of souls he'd have to ferry across the River Styx over the next few hundred years. It wasn't my department. The actuary Reapers handle all of that data. If you think field reaping is a grim affair, it was nothing compared to the work the actuaries did. I'd rather get reaped myself than become an actuary. They had different skills than the rest of us who were sent to reap souls on Earth. They were responsible for the administrative side of reaping, the calculations and number-crunching that bolstered the enterprise. They weren't suited to doing the dirty work I'd trained to do my whole life.

Of course, the actuaries could summon scythes. If push came to shove, they *could* reap souls, which was more than I could say for myself.

So far, I'd paid all my bills for three months straight. Just barely. The way I saw it, I didn't have much excuse. My first three months' rent had been paid. My sports bike had been paid for in cash. The keys had been waiting for me when I arrived—a graduation gift, along with stacks upon stacks of letters and several volumes of my father's journals.

The letters mostly consisted of correspondence between my parents. Some of those written by my dad were stamped Return to Sender in red letters. Presumably, most of those were sent after my dad took Morty and me back with him to the underworld. It was an attempt on my dad's part to reach out and communicate with my mom. All the letters he'd saved from her, the ones she wrote when they first met and he was off managing the life and death enterprises of the universe, were written before we were born.

I assumed if there was anything my dad could tell me about the letters that wasn't in them, he'd have said so. Perhaps he sent them with me so I could use them to try to piece together some clues to locate my mom. He'd lost track of her. She'd stopped writing him back. There wasn't anything in the letters about how he'd have to take us away, how we'd leave her and never see her again.

If my mother was pissed at him for that and wanted nothing to do with him, could I blame her? It wasn't like I could blame my dad, either. From what I'd read in the letters, he really did love her.

My dearest Josephine...

That's always how he addressed his letters. He wrote her poems and songs. I could tell from his letters that he'd paid careful attention to every word he chose. I grabbed one of them from the table. I'd read them all a dozen times. Still, I could have missed something. My dad's words, while certainly romantic, were so sappy I almost wanted to puke.

Your golden hair is more radiant than the sun. Neptune himself envies the ocean of blue that fills your eyes. Your touch warms my heart like a cold coal when set ablaze.

Apparently, my father thought similes and metaphors were romantic. I could go on reading, but it was more of the same. Nothing that helped. These descriptors didn't even give me an accurate description of what my mom looked like. I didn't need that. One of the envelopes included a photograph of my father and mother shortly after they met. They were leaning on my dad's motorcycle—his was a touring bike, nothing like mine. I had that particular photo attached to my refrigerator with a magnet.

I also read several of my mother's letters. Comparatively, they were less formal. Almost casual, but equally nauseating in tone.

Hi, Azrael! I miss you soooooooo much!

That was an example introduction from one of her letters. Most of them began similarly. She varied the number of Os, and sometimes it wasn't that she missed him but that she loved him or couldn't stop thinking about him, or that her whole world was turning on account of his love, but all of it was pukeworthy. Worse were the parts where they said things about each other... Things they wanted to do. Things I wished I could delete from my mind the moment I read them.

Ugh.

I mean, everyone knows that their parents did it at least once. *No one* wants the details. I didn't even know my mom, and the thought of it was gross.

I assumed the reason my dad bought me a motorcycle was because that's what he had when he'd come to Earth. Of course, at the time, he was trying to woo a potential mate. He probably thought that his motorcycle was an aphrodisiac. It's not an uncommon mistake for men to lead with what's between their legs rather than what's between their ears.

Not that what's between the legs doesn't matter. Size is somewhere on my list of desirable attributes, but it's way down there. Yes, I know it's always "down there," but bear with me and get your mind out of the gutter for just a second. I'd say there are at least ten or fifteen attributes I'd rank higher than that. Things like a sense of humor, compassion, a balance of confidence and humility, and ripped abs.

He hadn't factored in the fact that I had to buy insurance for my bike. That was on me. As were my utilities, and now my rent since the initial three months had passed. The smartphone bill was non-negotiable. An essential if I wanted to get by as a part of this world, which I'd come to realize existed as much in "cyber-space" as it did physically.

My phone reminded me via the alarm I'd set that I was due to go back to see Gabriel. It was always awkward when I returned. He wanted to hear about what I'd done, what Earth was like, the things I found most surprising, blah, blah, blah.

I didn't have much to ask him. I knew what he was up to. Morty was shadowing him. Learning to be what I was supposed to become. I didn't want to hear about it. If anything bad happened, he'd tell me. I didn't need to hear about how well he was progressing, how many souls he'd successfully harvested, or even if he advanced beyond Level One.

I wanted the best for Morty. I couldn't do the job. But dammit. It just wasn't fair. For my whole life, I'd busted my ass. While I was training, refining my skills to ensure that I'd become the best Reaper I could be, he was sitting around playing with himself. Yet now he was training to take my dad's place while I was a fledgling barista at a local coffee shop that only got business when the line at Starbucks was too long.

Yes, it was petty. It wasn't Morty's fault. It wasn't my dad's fault, even. It certainly wasn't Gabriel's fault. Still, at the end of the day, Morty had gotten everything I wanted and earned.

I didn't hate this new life. I was struggling with trying to fit in and finding real friends, and more than that, finding myself in this crazy world. But all of that was a part of the charm of living as a human. The pain made the pleasure all the sweeter. The uncertainty about the future and what I might become was intimidating, but it also came with a sense of adventure.

Before, I had one path. Become a Reaper, and eventually the Grim Reaper, and that was that. I didn't have a chance to consider other vocations or nurture other talents or hobbies. It wasn't just because I was one of the thousands of Reapers in training. A lot of Reapers do other things in their downtime. But that wasn't an option for me. I had to devote all my energy to preparing for what I thought was my destiny.

Still, it was hard to turn off that lingering sense of envy, that fury I felt in my gut that I couldn't be what I'd always wanted to be. And while I did enjoy my new life, I still didn't have a clue what I was supposed to do with it. I didn't know who I was. I knew a few things I enjoyed, of course. I appreciated a lot about my city and the people I'd met. But I didn't have a clue who Zoey Grimm truly was without reaping.

I wasn't sure if I was looking forward to seeing Gabriel or dreading it.

I had a day or so before I'd have to go back. A good night's rest and another shift at work. The first time I went back to see Gabriel, I was excited about it. I'd missed him. The second time, I still missed him, but I wasn't as thrilled about going back as I was the first time. For the last few months, I had begun to dread it. Sure, I had a good time with Gabriel when I arrived back in the underworld, but I didn't shed a single tear when it was time to leave again. I didn't have the heart to love him.

I didn't have the heart to break up with him, either.

CHAPTER THIRTEEN

I took time for another read of the old letters my mother had written before bed. I learned, while studying at the academy in the underworld, that if I studied something before sleep I remembered it better the next day—one of my many ninja study tips. I combined it with the use of flash cards.

At the time, most of what I learned was to prepare me for difficult reapings. From time to time, resistant souls would fight or flee. We had to be prepared to subdue both embodied and disembodied souls. Those who fled, no matter if they remained corporeal, would go somewhere. As would-be Reapers, we studied not only human culture and geography but human sociology and psychology. We were supposed to be experts in human behavior.

This was useful for at least two reasons. First, it helped to track fleeing souls. We could examine a target's behaviors, review their profiles, and even remove our cloaks and ask known associates of said targets about his or her patterns. Second, it also provided an alternative means of subduing a resistant soul—no matter if it resisted through fight or flight—by engaging the subject on a psychological level.

In other words, our studies provided the knowledge and skills necessary for tracking down the rare soul that escaped our initial reaping attempt.

So, my flashcards covered a wide array of subjects. It was a simple process. I'd go through them, returning any I missed to the back of my stack while setting aside those I knew. Once I made it through the whole stack, I set the cards beside my bed and went to sleep. First thing in the morning I went through them again. Most of that time, that was all it took to ace my exams.

This was different but similar. If I read the old letters my mother sent to my dad just before bed, my hope wasn't merely to commit them to memory but to allow the subtle details to percolate in my subconsciousness. Perhaps there'd be something I'd missed before that my mind would consider while I was sleeping. I may or may not remember it in the form of a dream. Either way, my hope was that when I reviewed the letters again in the morning, whatever insight my subconscious mind had extracted would jump out at me. I could then process them more consciously and intentionally.

Tonight, I took a different tactic. Rather than reviewing the love letters my parents exchanged, I decided to review my father's journal. I doubted my mom had one. If she did, my father didn't have it. Still, journaling isn't especially common for humans. For Reapers, it was considered an important discipline. It worked similarly to my flash card technique. The idea was that by writing about our experiences in the field, we would commit them to memory, consciously or subconsciously. It helps us process our experiences so we could learn from them in the future. So we could become better Reapers.

It wasn't mandatory, by any means. It was a suggestion. Though, from my dad's perspective, journaling was a suggestion akin to the recommendation that it's a good idea to pull the ripcord when you're jumping out of a plane. You don't have to do it, strictly speaking, but the suggestion will greatly improve your chances of survival if you follow through. After all, while it wasn't unheard of to reap skydivers, it was a rarity. Most people followed through with that suggestion.

The first journal entry I read before bed was full of mostly drivel. I figured I'd give my dad's retelling of the first time he met my mom another read before hitting the sack.

February 12, 2009

I may have met the one. She was dancing alone when I first saw her. Her long blonde hair caught my eye. I had to wonder why a creature so alluring was all alone. Surely any number of single men lurking around the perimeter of the room would have gladly joined her. But this wasn't the sort of woman you just ask to dance. She moved gracefully, which set her apart from the other bodies that gyrated haphazardly to the beat. She was a doe amidst apes. Or, better, a dragon among common lizards. There was fire in her eyes. Something I couldn't quite define. Was she even human at all? I'd seen goddesses before. I'd met more than my share of the Olympian deities. None of them compared to this woman.

This Josephine...

What a name! The way it fell from my tongue was like nectar, drawn from the flowers of Olympus itself. I approached her, extending my arm. She correctly discerned my intentions. I wanted to dance. Together, we moved on the dance floor as if we were in another world. It wasn't the bass-heavy dance number that guided our movements. There was another song in the air. An inaudible symphony, enveloping our frames, as if played by the strings of our hearts, and forged into a haunting melody. I told her my name first. There aren't many mortals who know it. But I could hardly ask this remarkable creature to dance with death. It was not this woman's soul I came to collect. I was here for her heart. Her heart and her womb.

There could have been a thousand beautiful women in the club that night, and I still would have found Josephine. She wasn't the most striking woman, perhaps, by human standards. But there was something about her, something different than any human I'd ever encountered. There was a depth to her soul that was lacking in all the thousands of those I'd harvested before.

The crowd around us disappeared. The music faded. The lights on the dance floor went out. We continued to dance. I didn't want it to end. She didn't either. Our dance could have gone on forever if it wasn't for the bouncer who insisted we leave.

I bid her come with me. To join me on a stroll through the streets. Josephine kissed me on the cheek. She invited me to her place instead. There, our bodies engaged in another dance. We were enthralled by passion and desire. We said few words. Our bodies told us all we needed to know.

She is not yet with child. Had her womb accepted my seed, I would have known it. I'd have sensed it. I must see her again. I will visit her again soon. I can only hope she longs for me as much as I do, her. I must learn more about my Josephine. I came to Earth looking for a mate. Someone who would provide me with an heir. I fear I found something more. Can it even be? How could it be? She is a mortal. She could never join me in the underworld. I could never leave my post to be with her. Still, there must be a way. I won't settle for anything less than what my heart now craves.

I'd read this account before. I should have been moved, inspired, by his account of how he met my mother. Instead, every time I read it, I felt nothing but envy. Could I ever find love like that? That wasn't at all what I felt for Gabriel. Gabriel was kind. He was sweet. He was safe. But there was something about this forbidden love, the passion infused in my father's words, that I couldn't shake. Reading his words only made me feel dissatisfied with my relationship with Gabriel. But there was at least one similarity. The tragedy that eventually tore my parents apart, that they could not live together in the same world, was one I now knew.

Still, it didn't feel the same. My heart was torn, but not

because I couldn't be with Gabriel. It was because he still chained me to a world that could never be my home. For my father, his love for my mom was what could never be. In my case, it was Gabriel's love for me and my unwillingness to break his heart that prevented me from finding the love I desired and deserved.

I had to tell him the truth. But how could I? It wasn't like I'd found another love or even that I had any guarantee that I might. But so long as I was with Gabriel, if I refused to let him go, I'd never be free to find out. I knew what I had to do. I just wasn't sure I could find the words to say it.

I flipped through a few more pages of my father's journal. About a half dozen more entries detailed various encounters between my parents. Long conversations, none of which were particularly helpful in terms of information that might help me locate my mother. There was only one that might have clues. The time my mother introduced my father to her mother. I placed the journal in my lap as I curled up in my bed and started to read.

April 2, 2009

It isn't every day that a girl invites Death to dinner. Even rarer, I suppose, is bringing the Grim Reaper home to meet her parents. I'd intended to tell Josephine the truth many times before. How could I possibly tell her that I was the Grim Reaper? I was afraid if I did, and if I revealed my true intentions, I might never see my love again. I thought, eventually, our love would grow enough that I could tell her without risk. The longer I waited, though, the harder it became. Would she resent me for not telling her sooner? Would she even believe me if I told her, or would she dismiss it as a delusion?

Either way, I was terrified that the truth might end it all. Many Reapers took mates before me. Their stories were not like mine. They were forthright. They told their prospective mate the truth from the start and, with a celestial blessing, offered their prospective mate an additional ten years of life if they'd agree to bear their heir. To give up a child for but ten years of life? For some women, it wasn't worth it. But I had more to offer. I could give upon her both life and riches. Not merely one decade, but two. Would she accept it? The longer we were together, the more we fell in love, the more I feared she'd reject any such proposal. The truth meant that she'd not only have to give up our child, but she'd lose me.

I don't think I was so terrified that she'd refuse the offer. I was more afraid she'd accept it. If she did, I'd lose her.

I hoped that meeting Josephine's mother might offer some clarity. After tonight's meal, I'm even more perplexed than before. What can I do?

Josephine's mother, Rose, is an endearing woman. She was older than I expected. She'd had Josephine later in life. Now, she was a widow. Josephine is her world. She still lives in the same home where Josephine was raised. One side of a duplex in a suburb of Kansas City called Grandview. The house is painted olive green and is situated across from a small park.

Conversation was awkward, as I suppose it must be whenever a human introduces someone they've been seeing to their parents. She asked me what I did for a living. For a living? I wasn't sure how to answer that since what I did had nothing to do with living at all. Josephine told her I was a hospice worker. I worked with the dead and the dying. That's what I'd told her. I suppose it was the closest vocational equivalent to what I truly did that a human might have. Yes, I helped people move on when it was their time. It was a noble profession, Josephine's mother said. One that requires someone with a big heart. I took it as a compliment.

I shouldn't have checked. Josephine's mother is scheduled to expire a year from tomorrow. I couldn't bear to do it myself. I'd have to assign it to another Reaper. I don't know how I'll even begin to tell Josephine. Should I tell her at all? Perhaps, at the very least, if I accelerated my plans, Rose could see her grandchild born before she died. But what would become of us after that? How could I tell Josephine the truth now? I'd not only be the one she loved, who took her child with him back to the underworld, but the Reaper who was in some sense responsible for *ending her mother's earthbound life. She'll never forgive me. How could she? Perhaps this is why Reapers are not meant to fall in love with their chosen mates...*

I closed my father's journal and set it on my nightstand. Several pages were missing after that. I could ask him about it, I suppose. I'd have to. Did he tell Josephine the truth? Did he wait to reveal it to her until after my brother and I were born? I'd have to ask my dad about it later. I was going back for my obligatory date with Gabriel the next day, anyway. Surely my father had more answers than his journal revealed.

CHAPTER FOURTEEN

I woke up more resolved than the night before. Perhaps my dad could tell me more about the location of Josephine's home. Presumably, Rose was no longer alive. She was meant to die a year from the time my father penned his journal entry. Finding the old house was probably a dead end—no pun intended. However, my dad might be able to tell me how he went about telling Josephine the truth. That might explain why she stopped communicating with him after Morty and I were born. Again, that knowledge wouldn't give me much of a lead to follow, but it was more than I had to work with based on the love letters and journals my father left me. Perhaps, if I could get inside my mother's mind, I might be able to find a trail of breadcrumbs to follow.

I got dressed for work. Cup-O-Joe wasn't a fancy coffee house, but its owner Joe roasted some of the tastiest coffee beans around. He hired me on the spot. It was the first and only job I applied for. I didn't have much of a résumé, but for a barista job, all I needed was an application.

My father had told Josephine he worked in hospice. I had told Joe that I'd trained to prepare the dead for the beyond. He took it to mean I'd studied embalming. I didn't confirm or deny his assumption. I simply told him I'd discovered after my studies that I didn't have the constitution for the work.

Understandable, given what he thought I was studying for. It was also true. That was all he needed to hear. Many baristas, it seemed, were between careers or waiting for some kind of spark of inspiration. They knew whatever they were doing before wasn't satisfying. They were looking for a new career path. Very few wanted to make lattes and cappuccinos forever. So long as I was willing to learn the job, showed up on time, and didn't do anything dumb, he said I'd be a great addition to the team.

I was willing to learn. That was covered. I wasn't learning the job particularly well. That wasn't Sienna's fault. She was doing her best to train me, and she'd only been working there a little while longer than me. It just didn't come to me quickly. There were so many drinks. I needed to make myself flash cards. I was so obsessed with examining my father's love letters and journals, though, not to mention binging random shows on Netflix, that I hadn't gotten around to it.

While we had access to some human shows in the under-world, without the Internet, there was a whole world of streaming that I'd never had access to. And there was no waiting between episodes! I watched the whole first season of *Stranger Things* in one night! Then, I'd stayed up to watch the first two episodes of the next season because I couldn't wait to find out what was going to happen next. After that, I'd watched *The Chilling Adventures of Sabrina,* which was oddly more comforting than chilling. Strangely, the odd evocation of devils and demons and the passage between this world and Hell reminded me of home.

It wasn't at all accurate. It didn't represent the underworld very well at all. But I did relate to the show's witch-heroine, who was torn between two worlds. In my case, though, my journey was the opposite. Sabrina struggled to maintain her human life and her friendships at her human high school while she embraced her role as a half-witch. I was a half-Reaper who couldn't reap at all, who was trying to sever my connections to my old life and find something new entirely. She was journeying into a world of the fantastic and extraordinary. I was trying to forge a normal, ordinary life. But like Sabrina, who'd lost her parents as a baby, I was trying to find my mother. It disappointed me that the show was over. Revealing no spoilers, I also feared that I'd be as disappointed with my true mother once I found her as the show's protagonist was with her true father.

I slipped into my leather pants and top. I checked myself in the mirror before I left. I loved the way I looked in this outfit. It accentuated my assets. Plus, since I rode a motorcycle, leather was a necessity. I loved wearing tight dresses, but for obvious reasons, I couldn't wear one on my bike. Not unless I wanted to show the world my hoo-hah.

People also recommended leather pants in case of an accident. They were supposed to save my skin if I crashed. I'd never taken the risk all that seriously. Until a white van peeled out of the parking garage as I turned into it, nearly cutting me off.

"What the hell!" I shouted, skidding to a halt and extending my middle finger at the van as it accelerated down the street. The driver probably wouldn't see my single-fingered salute, but it made me feel better.

I was almost late for my shift. I had a good mind to chase down the asshole and give him a piece of my mind, but showing up on time was probably the only qualification I had for my job. It wasn't worth the risk. Besides, it wasn't the first crazy driver I'd encountered downtown. It probably wouldn't be the last.

I pulled my bike into a vacant parking space next to Sienna's car. She was always early for her shifts. I dismounted my bike and noticed something under the front tire of Sienna's car. I bent down and picked it up—a phone case. I'd seen it before. The floral pattern confirmed it was Sienna's. Shards of shattered glass were lodged in the case's rubber.

I figured she must've dropped it and broken her phone when she got out of the car. She was probably frustrated and left the case behind.

I bit my lip. It was still strange. Those cases were supposed to protect a phone from damage. Sure, they weren't a hundred percent effective. But why would she pick up her broken phone and leave the case behind? Also, phones didn't usually come out of their cases when they dropped. I'd dropped mine a dozen times without any problem.

Something didn't feel right.

I wasn't sure if my fears were logical or amplified on account of the incident involving that Chad dickweed the night before. I didn't have a lot of experience dealing with real threats. I'd knocked out a few handsy Reapers back in the underworld, but humans were capable of a whole other level of evil. I'd trained to subdue flighty souls. But I'd never encountered the kind of villainy that dominated the nine o'clock news.

I hoofed it to the coffee shop. If Sienna was there, ready to start her shift, I could set aside my worries. When I stepped through the door and only Joe stood behind the counter, my stomach sank.

"Joe, is Sienna here?" I asked.

Joe shook his head. "Not yet. I assume she'll be here shortly."

I grunted. "I think something happened. Last night, someone tried to assault her, and I intervened. Her car is parked in the garage. I found her phone case and some shattered glass by it. I'm worried that something might have happened."

Joe shrugged. "She probably broke her phone and made a quick stop to replace it before her shift."

I sighed. "I don't think that's it. I mean, I hope you're right."

Joe's expression turned from stoic to concerned. "Should we call the police?"

I scratched my head. "Maybe. I'm not sure. If she's replacing her phone, maybe she has a new one activated already."

I reached into my back pocket and grabbed my phone. If Sienna had a new phone already, I could call her and settle the mystery once and for all. I didn't get that far. I saw I'd missed a text from Sienna. She'd sent it fifteen minutes ago. That meant her phone was broken just minutes before I found her case.

There was a video attachment.

I clicked it.

I gasped. There were three men, their faces shrouded in ski masks, getting out of a white van. It was the same white van that cut me off as I was pulling into the parking garage.

"Zoey," Sienna called from the background. "These guys are coming after me. This is all I could think to do. I think they're connected to that guy from last night. If you get this, please help!"

Then, the image on the phone shifted as she attempted to get a shot at the plates on the van. It was a blur. Maybe if I froze it, I could make it out. Then, I heard a scream. She must've managed to hit send before one of the men ripped the phone out of her hand.

I could connect the dots. They took her phone, smashed it, and retrieved it. In a hurry, they'd left the case behind and kicked it under her car.

"Joe. I have to go. Someone took her."

"Zoey, we should call the police," my boss countered.

I nodded. "Do that, Joe. I'm sorry. I saw the van that took her just as I was pulling into the garage. If there's any chance I can catch up to them, I have to try."

"Zoey, it isn't safe."

"I'll be fine," I assured him. "If I find the van, I'll call the cops, all right? Or I'll text you my location. You can tell the police. I'm going to forward you the video she sent me so you can get it to the cops."

Joe nodded. He was about to speak, probably to dissuade me

from leaving, but I was out of the door before he could get another word out. I ran back to the garage, forwarding Sienna's text to Joe as I sprinted to my motorcycle.

Sienna had sent the text fifteen minutes ago. It was maybe a five-minute walk from the garage to Cup-O-Joe's. Based on the time frame, I guessed that she probably struggled with the men for a few minutes before they took her.

If I'd arrived just a minute sooner, I would have been there. I could have stopped them. Handling three goons at once couldn't be any harder than besting three soul-infused constructs as I'd done in my examination.

That Chad guy the night before, he wasn't just trying to assault Sienna. He was trying to abduct her. He'd been studying her habits, her behaviors, the whole time. Then when I screwed up his plan, he'd showed up with extra manpower to get the job done. How long had Chad been watching her? He probably knew she showed up early for her shifts. Since Joe had a fairly steady schedule, he also knew when she'd start working.

I knew what I was facing. It wasn't the first time something like this had happened in Kansas City. The I-70 corridor was a hotbed for human trafficking. Very few of the cases made the news, but there was a story shortly after I arrived here that highlighted the problem. No individual cases were mentioned. All I knew was that very few of those abducted were ever found. These men might not be trained fighters. I'd bested Chad fairly easily the night before. But they were professional kidnappers. They knew how to hide and how to get away.

This time, though, they'd been sloppy. They came after the same girl two days in a row. All I could figure is that they had a buyer lined up, someone who was looking for a young woman fitting Sienna's description.

I jumped on my bike and fumbled my key into the ignition. Revving up my engine, I sped out of the parking garage like a bullet.

Several interstates intersected with downtown Kansas City. While the trafficking issue was associated with I-70, there was no guarantee that was the highway they'd take.

What the hell was I even doing? My chances of finding Sienna were slim to none. I could catch up to the van fairly easily if I knew which direction it had gone.

In my training, we were taught to try to put ourselves in the mind of our target if a soul fled its reaping. If I was one of the kidnappers, what would I do? What was my biggest risk? The Power and Light District was on the Missouri side of the city. If they crossed state lines, it meant that the police would have to communicate with Kansas. They wouldn't know any better than I did which direction the van went. Not until they examined traffic cameras. That would take time. Too much time. More than that, the police would take time to assess the situation. Crossing state lines wouldn't buy the abductors much time—maybe an hour or more—but given what they were attempting, that might be all it took for them to disappear.

I couldn't make out the plates on the van in the video. Maybe the cops could make some sense out of it. I assumed the van was a rental. The kidnappers surely used fake identification to secure it. They'd leave it somewhere, move Sienna to another vehicle, and take her wherever they were going.

Still, if I was one of the kidnappers, I'd cross state lines if only to complicate the search. I didn't know much about how law enforcement processes worked. That wasn't a part of what we were trained to engage in as Reapers. If they crossed state lines, wouldn't that get the feds involved? I didn't know. But I imagined whatever the case, they'd take time to act.

My staff wasn't a scythe. It couldn't reap. That didn't mean it was useless. My father had taught me that little trick when he took me on that plane crash. It was the only thing my staff could do. Still, it was worth a shot. If I could somehow impose my will on it, if I could define the target, maybe it would show me where I needed to go.

I pulled over and touched my sigil on my right wrist with my left hand. My staff formed in my hand. I tucked my staff under my arm and directed the pointy end forward.

Focus, Zoey. Direct the staff. Identify the target....

I pictured Sienna in my mind. I shouted her name. Nothing happened.

When I was on that reaping with my father, he had told me to scratch the man's cheek when the plane was going down. That was how I could target his soul. It was how I could use my staff like a homing beacon to track a fleeing soul. It wouldn't take much. A single strand of hair. Even a bit of sweat.

I needed to find another way to target Sienna. I didn't have any of her DNA. Or did I? I still had her phone case. She usually carried it in her back pocket. Maybe a little sweat was on it. Perhaps some saliva from a conversation or even a few dead skin cells lingered on the surface. It didn't matter. If there was any DNA on the case at all, my staff could use it to target Sienna's soul.

I reached into my pocket and retrieved Sienna's phone case. A blue glow settled on the tip of my staff. It worked! I pointed the staff to my left. The glow faded. I moved it straight ahead. The glow returned. All I had to do was follow its lead.

I pulled onto I-70, darting around the cars that were accelerating down the entrance ramp. I accelerated my crotch rocket up to full speed.

"I'm coming, Sienna. Hang in there, girl."

CHAPTER FIFTEEN

I followed the lead on my staff, but I was beholden to highways and roads. It was more like a compass. It gave me a direct path as the crow flies to Sienna's location. As the glow started trending to the right side of the highway, I figured my best shot was to take the next exit.

From there, I followed probably five or six more turns, hitting a few dead ends along the way. I was somewhere on the Kansas side of the Missouri River. My staff directed me to a freight yard. There were probably three or four hundred shipping containers, many of them stacked upon others. I parked my bike. Chances were the fuckers who had taken Sienna heard me approach. Even so, it was better to move silently between the containers. She had to be here somewhere. My staff took me over the river into Kansas. Now it directed me in the direction of the river. My best guess was the trafficking operation they were running used the barges to move their victims.

I ducked between two containers and checked my phone. I quickly shot a GPS link of my location to Joe. I didn't want to deal with law enforcement here, but I wasn't a fool. There was a chance I wouldn't get out of this alive. A slim chance, granted, but I hadn't done anything like this before. If something happened to me, I sure as hell wasn't going to let them get away with abducting Sienna on account of my prideful insistence to go at it alone like a real-world Batwoman.

I followed my staff, covering the tip with my hand so the glow wouldn't give my location away. I only saw three men on Sienna's video, but there may have been more in the van. There were probably others here since this was the avenue the traffickers used to transport their victims elsewhere. It might have been possible for just a few men to pull something like this off. More likely was that there were dozens of men involved in the operation.

I'm not a pessimist by nature, but it was wise to prepare for the worst-case scenario. I couldn't bank on the assumption that there were only three men here to deal with. There could have been more. A lot more. I imagined, considering the nature of what they were doing, most if not all of them would be armed.

A woman with a big stick versus a bunch of men with guns. Normally, that wouldn't sound like great odds. But I wasn't your run-of-the-mill lass.

I uncovered the tip of my staff just long enough to check my bearings. It was easy to get lost between all the crates. Still, I was moving in the right direction. Unless these traffickers had gunmen on top of the stacked containers, which was admittedly a possibility, I was most vulnerable when I ran from behind one crate to the next. Unfortunately, the containers were stacked in fairly neat rows. That meant long corridors, almost like hallways, between the stacks. It also meant a greater chance someone would see me.

I pressed my lips together. If these were traffickers, hell, I was pretty enough. I might not have been who they were targeting, but they'd think a single woman going after Sienna alone was less a threat than another potential sale.

The way I saw it, I had two options. I could go in looking to fight my way to Sienna and get shot at. Or I could come out into the open and use myself as bait to lure them out. Then, when they weren't expecting it, I could summon my staff and beat the shit out of them.

There was only one problem with that option, which otherwise might have made it the best bet. Chad had seen me summon my staff the night before. He knew I could fight. The wet spot in his pants the night before testified to that fact. He wouldn't underestimate me, and if he was in cahoots with these traffickers, they probably wouldn't either.

I might have the appearance of a desirable asset, a trafficable target for their illicit venture, but if they thought I'd be more trouble than I was worth, they might just opt to shoot me rather than risk it. Sienna was their ideal target. A shy, pretty young woman. Someone timid, who would cower rather than put up a fight. I didn't know how long they'd been watching her. Since we worked together, they'd probably been watching me, too. Maybe they targeted her because she fit the profile one of their buyers desired. Or maybe they just judged her an easier mark than me.

Of course, I was walking right into their operation. No matter how risky it might be to take me, I was at the very least presenting them with an alluring two-for-one deal.

The question was whether their greed exceeded their common sense. Because they were engaged in such a risky criminal enterprise, I presumed that money was their motivator. They'd already sacrificed common morals on the altar of a healthy pay day. But these weren't dumb men. Idiots can't pull something like this off without getting caught.

I had two options. But so did they. Once they realized I was there, they'd either try to capture or kill me. Which would they choose? I had to be prepared for either possibility.

I tucked my head as I ran from one crate to the next.

Bang! Bang! Bang!

The gunshots confirmed they were opting for the kill over my capture.

At least they quickly resolved the dilemma for me. I now had one option. I had to fight, and since they had deadly weapons, I couldn't let my fear of encountering a Reaper dissuade me from using lethal force.

They had guns. Ranged weapons. I had a staff better suited for close combat. Or was it? It wasn't unlike the staff I'd used in my examination.

I was close to Sienna. She was a few crates down the corridor from which the gunshots had come.

I heard footsteps running in my direction. I had to act fast. I rolled out into the corridor, and from one knee, I tossed my staff like a javelin. It caught one of the two armed men in the chest.

I somersaulted behind another crate and touched the sigil on my wrist. My staff reformed in my hand.

"Brilliant," I muttered under my breath. I could reload and take out the second man.

Then I heard footsteps behind me. They were trying to corner me.

I pivoted and tossed my staff, spearing the man who'd come at me from behind. I touched my sigil again as I pivoted, then tossed it at another man who was running full steam toward my position. He fired even as my staff flew toward him.

I didn't hit him, but I'd forced him to dodge my attack, which set his shot off-target, too.

I re-summoned my staff before it hit the ground and threw it again, catching the asshole right in his shoulder. His gun fell to the ground.

I ran to his position, still checking my surroundings for other possible attackers. I knew there were at least three, and he was the third.

I approached the man. Blood was spurting from the wound in

his shoulder. Some of it struck my boot. I reached down ripped off the kidnapper's ski mask.

It was Chad. Some fuckers never learn.

I kicked him in the chest, forcing him onto his back. I re-summoned my staff and was about to jam it into his heart when a flash of light to my side caught my eye.

"Zoey, what the hell?"

I turned. It was Morty. Gabriel stood just behind him. Their scythes were ready. Based on the glow that had settled on their blades, they'd already reaped the first two souls of the men I'd killed.

"It's not his time," Gabriel argued. "Let him go."

I pressed the tip of my spear to Chad's throat. "His time or not, he deserves it."

"That's not your decision," Gabriel countered.

"It sure as hell is," I insisted. "I can't let him hurt anyone else!"

Chad looked at me, his brow furrowed in confusion. "Who the hell are you talking to, you crazy bitch?"

He couldn't see them. They weren't here for him. It wasn't his time. That's what Gabriel said. Only the targeted souls, those set to expire, could see their Reapers.

I gripped my staff tightly. I wanted to take his head clean off his shoulders. It was a paradox, I suppose. If I could kill him, well, it *would* be his time. Whatever divine entity set the expiration date of souls must've known, somehow, that I wouldn't kill the bastard.

So, I kicked him hard in the face, knocking him out cold. I turned to Morty and Gabriel. "It might not be his time, but at least he can spend the rest of his life in jail."

"It's for the best," Gabriel offered. "These guys are a part of something bigger. He might be the only lead the human authorities have to whoever is issuing the orders."

I sighed. "Yeah, you're probably right. Either way, I have to save my friend."

"Zoey," Morty began. "You can't do shit like this. It isn't safe."

I glared at my brother. "Isn't safe? No one is safe so long as monsters like this are roaming free."

"Is this really the life you want to make for yourself here, Zoey?" Gabriel asked, gazing at me in concern.

I clenched my fists. "First, it's none of your business. Second, my friend was in trouble. I had to do something."

"The humans have authorities to handle this sort of thing," Gabriel replied. "I've done my reconnaissance. You know that's one of the six Rs. Law enforcement is on the way."

"They'd never have known to come here if I hadn't come," I shot back, turning around and running to one of the crates.

Sirens sounded in the distance as I swung the doors open.

Sienna was there, her hands and feet bound and her mouth gagged. There were also two other young women. From the looks of them, they had been there a while.

I removed the piece of cloth that was tied around Sienna's mouth.

"My God, Zoey!" Sienna cried as I evoked my staff again and used the sharp end to sever the ropes that bound her hands and feet. She wrapped her arms around me. "You got my message!"

"I did!" I exclaimed. "You're safe now."

"I don't understand. How did you…" Her eyes drifted to my staff. "What is that?"

I smiled as I released the staff. It dissipated in the air. "Maybe we can keep this ability of mine a secret?"

Sienna nodded. "Yeah. I mean, of course. Oh, my God, Zoey! I was so scared."

"You're safe now," I assured her.

Sienna shuddered. "But those men…"

"They're dead. Well, two of them are. The guy who attacked you last night is out cold."

"Hands in the air, where I can see them!" a man shouted from the door of the container.

I stood up and turned around, holding my hands high.

"She's the one who saved us!" Sienna shouted.

The officer still held his gun at me as two others ran to the other two women and freed them.

"Ma'am, please step outside," the first officer requested.

I nodded. "Certainly, Officer."

As I stepped out of the crate, I noticed another officer already had Chad in cuffs. Chad sneered at me when I glanced at him.

"You don't know what you've gotten yourself into, bitch!" Chad screamed.

I glared at him. "Correction. You don't understand who you were fucking with when you went after my friend."

Chad laughed, even as the officer led him away. "Just wait, Zoey! Yeah, I know your name. You'll be dead by tomorrow! He won't show you any mercy! You're dead, Zoey!"

I shook my head and glanced at the officer, who lowered his weapon. "What happened here, ma'am?"

"You can call me Zoey," I offered.

"I know your name," the officer replied. "Your boss sent us the tip."

"And you are?" I asked.

The officer smiled at me. "I'm Detective Schroeder. Kevin Schroeder. I don't know how you managed this, Miss Grimm."

I shrugged my shoulders. "Honestly, Kevin, it all happened so fast."

"But those other two men, they're dead. Did you do that?"

"Dead?" I asked, feigning ignorance. "Are you sure?"

Detective Schroeder nodded. In the distance, I saw Gabriel and Morty disappear into a portal back to the underworld. They had a couple of souls to deliver to the boatman.

Courtesy of yours truly.

CHAPTER SIXTEEN

The whole freight yard was swarming with police. I assumed they had to secure the area. It was a crime scene. Chad had confirmed, as I already suspected, that there was someone higher up in the chain of command who was ultimately responsible for their trafficking operation. Whoever it was, Chad seemed to think he wouldn't take kindly to my interference.

I wasn't as worried about it as I should have been. Whoever was in charge of this operation wasn't likely to show up anytime soon. With the cops on his trail, it would be too hot for him to risk exposing himself or any of his operatives for a vendetta. If the mastermind behind the operation had any smarts at all, he'd steer clear of me and anyone else connected to the incident.

Detective Schroeder led me to his squad car. He was a remarkably handsome man. He was tall, an inch or two over six feet. The bulletproof vest he was wearing gave him the impression of being more muscular than he probably was. Still, he wasn't one of those out-of-shape, doughnut-eating cops that I usually saw patrolling around the city. He had dark hair and brown eyes.

The way he looked at me, his eyes wandering below my chin periodically before he caught himself and looking into the distance again, suggested he found me at least as attractive as I did him. He was trying to hide it, of course. But men are notoriously bad at hiding it when they're checking a woman out. The fact he was trying his best to remain professional was kind of cute.

"So, what's the deal? Are you going to arrest me?"

Kevin chuckled. "No, Miss Grimm. The way I see it, you're a hero. But I still can't figure out how you pulled this off. Could you be so kind as to enlighten me?"

I smirked. "I suppose you want the complete story. Everything that happened the moment I arrived here?"

Kevin nodded. "Yes, but before that. How did you track them here?"

I shrugged my shoulders. "Got lucky, I suppose. I assume you saw the video that Sienna sent me."

"I did."

"I imagined they were likely going to cross state lines. You know, to slow you down."

Kevin laughed. "We operate in a city on state lines. We are accustomed to working that way. Still, these wouldn't be the first criminals who thought they could escape us by crossing the border."

"Like I said, I must've gotten lucky. I took off down the highway and saw the van. I followed it here, and that's when I sent my location to Joe."

"And rather than wait for us to arrive, you tried to save your friend yourself?" Kevin asked, raising one eyebrow.

I nodded. "I know. It wasn't smart."

"It wasn't." Kevin laughed. "What gave you the idea that you could face these men yourself?"

"I had little choice. They saw me. I ran. After that, well, everything was a blur. They shot at me. I ducked behind the crates. The next thing I knew, someone showed up and took two of them out."

Kevin narrowed his eyes. "Some hero just showed up out of the blue, dropped three men, and disappeared?"

"I guess. How am I supposed to know? But the guy you arrested, Chad, was wounded but still breathing. So I kicked him as hard as I could right in the kisser."

"Then what happened?"

"I went in and freed Sienna. Then, you showed up. That's it. Not much more to tell."

Kevin bit his lip. "Well, that Chad fellow certainly seems to think you're responsible. He directed his anger at you, Miss Grimm."

I smiled. "I was the one who called you. I outed them."

"But you weren't the one who killed the other two and took him down?" Kevin asked. "At first, I mean. Before you kicked him."

"All I know is that there was someone else here, maybe two others, who ushered the other two into the afterlife."

Kevin chuckled. "That's certainly a colorful way to put it."

I grinned. "I'm a colorful person. What can I say?"

"You realize, Miss Grimm, that we will question the suspect, along with the three victims. If there's anything else you'd like to tell us, it would be a good idea to come clean now."

"Look, Kevin, is anyone going to believe that I could take out three armed men alone and without a weapon?"

"I believe you had help, Miss Grimm," Kevin countered. "I'm not so sure that you don't know who it was. How would anyone other than you just happen to show up at precisely the same time you did if you didn't contact them?"

I scratched the back of my head. "You can look through my phone if you want, Kevin."

"Detective Schroeder," Kevin corrected.

I grinned, then unlocked my phone via facial recognition and handed it to the detective. "Like I said, check out my call history and messages. I texted Joe the location. That's the only person I contacted."

Kevin scrolled through my phone, then handed it back to me. "Well, that checks out. I'm still not sure what to make of this, Miss Grimm."

"You and me both." I nodded. "But if you figure it out who it was, would you be so kind as to let me know? I mean, whoever fought those guys is my hero, too."

"I can't make any promises," Kevin replied. "Anything we discover will be classified as evidence. But if it all checks out, and there isn't any reason to keep your hero's identity under wraps, I'll let you know who to send the thank you card to."

"Aren't you going to ask for my number?" I asked, winking at Kevin.

"Excuse me?"

I smiled. "For a follow-up, Detective Schroeder. I'm a witness, right?"

Kevin turned his face to the side, trying but failing to hide his red cheeks. "Yes. Obviously. I mean, I'll need your number, Miss Grimm."

"Have a pen?" I asked.

Kevin nodded and retrieved one from his pocket.

"Give me your hand," I ordered.

"Excuse me?" Kevin asked, raising an eyebrow.

I smiled. "I have to write it on *something*."

Kevin rolled his eyes. Then he reached into his pocket and retrieved two business cards. "Write your number on the back of one of them. Keep the other. If you remember anything else that might help, call me."

I took my pen, jotted my phone number on one of the cards,

and handed it to Kevin, then stuck the second card in my bra. "Don't be a stranger. Call me anytime."

Kevin narrowed his eyes. "Likewise. I'll be in touch, Miss Grimm."

CHAPTER SEVENTEEN

I texted Joe before I mounted my bike to head home. He gave me a pass on coming into work for the day. I was grateful for that. Killing human traffickers can be exhausting, and given all that had happened, my mind wasn't in the game. Plus, Sienna was in no shape to come into work, and I was afraid that I'd screw something up. Since Joe would be the only one there to look over my shoulder, it wouldn't do much for my ongoing employment status.

Thankfully, both Sienna and I had the next day off. I didn't know if she'd be up for coming in to work in two days. The last two times she'd come to work, she had been attacked. Who could blame her if she needed some time or if she never wanted to come back to work at Cup-O-Joe's?

It was a relaxing ride home. My sports bike was built for speed rather than comfort. Still, there was something calming about riding it. Provided, of course, I wasn't chasing down creepy kidnapper vans. The wind in my face, fluttering through my hair, cleared my mind. There was a sense of freedom that came from riding out in the open, and an undeniable power, represented by the rumble between my thighs.

No, not that. Stop it. I know what you're thinking. It wasn't like that. But riding a motorcycle is different from driving a car. If you've ever ridden a bike, you know what I'm saying is true. It feels almost like my bike is an extension of my body. As if the bike's power was my own.

That mixture of clarity of mind and empowerment gave me some perspective on all I was facing. I was worried about Sienna, but I also had other issues. I knew Chad was probably full of shit when he said that his boss, whoever he might be, would be coming for me. But somewhere in the recesses of my mind, I was afraid that his threat had legs. Then again, maybe that would be a good thing. Law enforcement has to deal with a lot of red tape when they go after an organization like the group behind the trafficking. If Chad's boss was dumb enough to come for me, I could sever the head from the beast. It would make the world a better place.

See, clarity of mind and empowerment—a deadly combination, especially in the hands of a former would-be Reaper.

There were other issues I wasn't sure how to navigate. Detective Schroeder was suspicious that I was hiding something. At least he didn't think I was involved with the traffickers. Still, if they were going to prosecute Chad and go after the organization he worked for, they'd be digging deeper into the events of the day. If they did, would they be able to find out what I'd done? Were there cameras in the freight yard? I hadn't seen any, but in the twenty-first century, there's almost always something watching and recording you. What would they think if they saw me summon my staff from the ether and wield it like an Olympic javelin thrower turned ninja assassin?

Riding my bike gave me the calm and confidence to set aside any worries about whether the traffickers would come after me. It didn't do much to settle my nerves about what Detective Schroeder might find out.

Maybe I should just call him Kevin. Look, I resent men who

objectify me or other women. But I also know that men are remarkably susceptible to the allure of a woman they find attractive. If it worked to my advantage to encourage the detective to turn a blind eye to my involvement, I could keep up our flirtations.

Yeah, that was a good excuse to keep flirting with him without feeling guilty about it....

I sighed as I dismounted my bike. Gabriel and I never said we were exclusive. Not officially. But I'd be kidding myself if I didn't admit that it wasn't understood. He expected that I'd be loyal to him. The truth is, I'd been hoping that he'd lose interest, eventually after a few months of separation. In some ways, I was bold, badass, and courageous. With nothing but a staff—albeit an ethereal one—I'd taken down three armed criminals. I was fearsome. Why the hell was I so chickenshit when it came to matters of the heart?

I wanted to break up with Gabriel, but I didn't want to break up with Gabriel. I was attracted to other men and wanted the kind of romance my parents had, but so long as I was stringing Gabriel along, that wasn't a real possibility.

Then again, after the way Gabriel had lectured me about what I was doing with my life when he and Morty showed up to reap those traffickers, I was annoyed with him. If I was ever going to muster up the courage to break up with him, this was the time to do it. And since I was supposed to meet up with him back in the underworld later that night, the timing was right.

I still had three or four hours before I was due to leave. Hopefully, I could maintain my resolve in the interim.

I inserted my key into my apartment door, and dogs started barking.

I didn't have a dog.

And yes, that was the plural...*dogs.*

There was only one person in all of Earth and the underworld who had access to my apartment and might come with multiple dogs... Well, one dog, with three heads. If my dad had let Cerberus pee on my new furniture or claw up the leather of my couch, there'd be hell to pay. I might be the only person in history to threaten the Grim Reaper with hell, but I was his daughter. I could get away with it, especially since the threat remained confined to my mind.

I swung open the door as Cerberus charged at me.

"Off!" I shouted.

"Good!" my father exclaimed. "That's the right command!"

I stared at my dad blankly. "You can't be serious. You brought your dog to my apartment?"

"I didn't just bring him here to visit, Zoey. Cerberus is staying here. Your brother told me what you were up to earlier today. I can't stop you from doing what you need to do, but at least I can leave him here to ensure you don't get in over your head."

I cocked my head. "He's a dog, Dad."

My father smiled. "He's not just a dog, Zoey. He's a hound of Hell. A guardian of all worlds. He's quite powerful, and he'll make sure you stay in line."

I snorted. "Excuse me? Stay in line?"

"Poor choice of words." Dad smiled. "He's mostly going along to protect you."

I shook my head. "A three-headed dog isn't going to go over well on Earth."

"He only needs one of his heads here," my father countered.

"You're going to perform a double decapitation on your dog, Dad?"

My father laughed. "No, not at all. The underworld is a nexus between worlds. Cerberus has a head for each domain, one that corresponds to Hades, the second to Olympus, and the third to Earth. Strictly speaking, only his Earth head is necessary here, though he can invoke all three heads at any moment. I suppose you might say he's a three-dog pack unto himself. The head that corresponds with each realm claims alpha status depending on where he's at."

"So, if you sent your dog to Hades or Olympus, he'd only have use of those respective heads?"

"That's not how it works!" Cerberus piped up. "Weren't you listening at all? Those heads would become alpha. That doesn't mean my other heads would be useless!"

"Holy crap! You can talk?"

"Yep. Yep. Yep!" Cerberus' center head agreed with me and the other two yipped in concert.

Cerberus wasn't a small dog. Average size, I suppose. Probably a good fifty or sixty pounds. His hair was short and black. Each of his heads was identical aside from the color of their eyes. It never occurred to me that they corresponded with the three realms. One had red eyes, likely giving him sight in Hades. One had white eyes with golden flecks, likely corresponding to Olympus. And his middle head had common, brown eyes. That, I guessed, was his Earth head.

"So, tell me how it works with your three heads?" I asked, holding onto my words as I spoke since, admittedly, it felt a little strange talking to a dog. Not that it would be weird to talk to a dog if it was just a dog, but now that I realized he could communicate back, it felt weird as hell.

Cerberus stretched. His middle head turned and barked at the other two. The heads on his left and right whimpered and retreated into his body. "I'm the only one of us who can speak on Earth because I'm the head that becomes alpha when on Earth."

"His other two heads would become alphas in their respective realms," my father added.

"And you couldn't talk in the underworld because you weren't in any of the three realms that correspond with your various heads?"

"B-I-N-G-O!" Cerberus yipped back.

I cocked my head. "That's not your name-o."

Cerberus just stood there, wagging his tail.

"As you might have gathered, Cerberus isn't a common canine," my father explained.

I huffed. "Ya think? As if the whole three-headed thing didn't give that away."

My father ignored my snide response. "While he has all the energy of a puppy, in truth, he's thousands of years old."

I rolled my eyes. "Here I thought you just took him in to deal with empty nest syndrome after Morty and I graduated."

My father laughed. "Well, that might have been a part of it. Before everything happened, I'd intended him to accompany you as you began your training with me. For extra protection as your reapings got more challenging."

I bit my cheek. "If that was the case, why not send him with Morty? He's your new heir, after all."

My father shook his head. "It will be a while before Morty has advanced enough for that. Right now, you're the one who needs him the most."

I sighed. "Well, I wish I knew all his commands."

Cerberus laughed. Coming from a dog, it was a bit unsettling. "You can't command me! I respond to Azrael because I respect him."

"And what about me?" I asked.

"You'll have to earn my respect," Cerberus replied.

I scratched my head. "I seriously have to earn a dog's respect?"

"I'm not just a dog!" Cerberus protested. "Haven't you been listening to your father at all?"

I smiled. "Obviously not! You talk."

My father reached down and scratched Cerberus behind the ears. "Look, Zoey. I'd be foolish to tell you to stop trying to fight injustice."

I placed my hands on my hips. "That's not what I was doing. My friend was in danger. I have skills. I chose to do something about it."

My father chuckled. "Zoey, I know you better than that. Now that your friend is safe, do you intend to stop going after the people who kidnapped her?"

I hate it when he's right. In truth, I'd spent half my ride home thinking about how I might be able to use Chad's threat to take down the whole human trafficking organization. At least, the thought had crossed my mind. My father might have been a workaholic, but he loved me, and he probably knew me better than I knew myself.

I shrugged. "I suppose you're right."

"Cerberus can be a great sidekick if you let him. Like I said, he may look like a dog, but he's really a demigod."

I chuckled. "A dog is a demigod? I mean, if he was a cat, it would fit..."

"Excuse me?" Cerberus huffed. "Don't compare me to one of those vile creatures!"

"Not a fan of cats?" I asked.

Cerberus narrowed his eyes but didn't respond. I suppose I didn't require a genuine answer.

I chuckled. "Well, 'god' is 'dog' spelled backwards. Maybe he's just a dyslexic demi-dog."

My father laughed. Cerberus barked. He didn't find my joke as funny as my father and I did. My dad raised his hand, and Cerberus obediently stopped barking.

"You realize that I live in an apartment in the city. There aren't a lot of great places for a dog to go outside to run around."

"What kind of dog do you think I am?" Cerberus asked. "I can use a toilet just like you."

I raised one eyebrow. "You use the toilet?"

"I talk," Cerberus stared at me blankly, "and you find it hard to believe that I could pee in a bowl?"

I smiled. "All right, fair point."

"I should leave you two to it." My father started to get up. "I have business to attend to. But before I go, have you had a chance to review the letters and journals I gave you?"

I nodded. "I have. I do have a few questions, if you don't mind me asking."

"I suppose I can take a few minutes to answer them." My father sat on my couch. Cerberus jumped into his lap.

I sat down on the opposite end of the couch, tucking one leg under my butt. "What pissed Mom off the most? That you took her babies away, or that you had to reap her mother?"

My father narrowed his eyes. "I didn't reap her mother."

"Someone did," I argued. "You wrote about it. You said her time had expired."

My father sighed. "There are some pages missing in my journals. I'm sure you noticed."

I nodded. "I did."

"I knew it would upset Josephine when she learned the truth," my father explained. "I went to Olympus. I petitioned the gods to extend Rose's life. I knew it wouldn't be enough to assuage your mother's anger when I took you and Morty back with me to the underworld, but it was the least I could do."

"And the gods granted the petition?" I asked.

My father nodded. "With certain conditions. One of them was that I could not visit Josephine's mother until her time came. Another was that I would have to be the one to reap her."

I shrugged my shoulders. "You removed those pages to protect her? So I wouldn't go look for her?"

My father scratched his chin. "Not exactly. I removed those pages long ago. Before we knew you couldn't reap. The truth is, what I did hadn't been done before. Reapers rarely intercede on behalf of human lives. The gods didn't want my heir to take what I did as precedent. I wrote those pages because I used my journal to process my decisions. When I write things down, it gives me clarity. After I wrote it, I realized the whole thing was a mistake."

"Why is that?" I asked.

"Not all the gods agreed to my petition. Zeus denied my petition straight away. But one of his daughters, Athena, came to visit me in the underworld. It's a long story, but she has long hoped to overthrow her father. Something to do with how Zeus turned her mother into a fly and ate her, then conceived Athena from within his mind. She emerged with a desire to avenge her mother. It's a strange tale, and I'm not sure how much of it is true. But I knew that Athena had her sights on dethroning Zeus in Olympus."

"And for some reason, she saw your petition as an opportunity to advance her agenda?" I asked.

My father nodded. "I cannot say why, or how she intended to manipulate the situation to her advantage. I suspect one of the reasons she demanded that I never visit Rose again had something to do with it. Be that as it may, if Zeus were ever to learn of what happened, I shudder to think how he might react. I may be powerful, Zoey, but I wouldn't stand a chance if Zeus left Olympus and came after me. If he unsettled the underworld and souls could no longer be reaped, the balance of life and death for all of humanity would be disrupted."

"Zeus has no idea that you and Athena managed to extend Rose's life?" I asked.

My father shook his head. "I suspect that whatever Athena had planned, she presumed that he'd never discover the truth since Rose was but a single human life and the Olympians no longer concern themselves much with human affairs."

"So, you ripped the pages out of the journal just in case because they were evidence of what you and Athena agreed to?"

My father nodded. "I never should have written those pages to begin with. Even telling you the truth now is a risk, Zoey. You mustn't speak of this to anyone."

"I'm guessing Athena demanded that you be the one to reap Rose was another way of covering her tracks?"

"I suspect that's the case. Be that as it may, Rose's time draws near. When I believed you were to take my place, I intended her reaping to be my final act as the Grim Reaper before I ascended."

"How soon before Rose's life expires?" I asked.

My father sighed. "One week from today."

I stared at my father blankly. "Your journal said she lived in a house in Grandview. Can you give me her address? I need to speak to her. If anyone knows where my mother is, it's her."

He shook his head. "That may not be the best idea, Zoey."

I shrugged. "Why the hell not?"

"If her long-lost granddaughter arrives just before her time comes, she may resist her reaping," my father offered.

"So what? You're the Grim Reaper, Dad. You can track her down and make sure she doesn't become a ghost."

"That's the thing," my father countered. "I'm not sure I can. My abilities have started to wane. The closer I get to ascending, the more difficult it is to reap."

"You didn't have any problem doing it the other day on that plane. You were pretty damn impressive."

My father smiled. "The reason I assigned that particular harvest to you and joined you on it was that I knew there was little chance of anyone escaping. It was a plane crash, after all. If Rose tries to escape and she evades me, I might not be able to track her down."

"What happens if she becomes a ghost?" I asked.

My father shrugged. "I don't know, but it will violate the terms of my agreement with Athena. If that happens, I may lose my chance to ascend."

"Then you'd remain a Reaper?" I asked.

My father shook his head. "I'd remain in the underworld. But my powers would continue to wane."

I took a deep breath. "Fine. I guess I'll have to find another way to track down Mom."

My father shook his head. "I did not tell you this to dissuade you, Zoey. I only told you the truth so that you'd know what was at stake and act with prudence. It's your choice. If you want to seek out Rose, I won't stop you."

"Dad, I couldn't live with myself if I somehow screwed up your chance to ascend!"

"And I couldn't ascend in good conscience if I stopped you from finding your mother, Zoey. You already have the address."

"I do?" I asked.

My father smiled. "One of the letters I attempted to send to your mother was addressed to her mother's house. All the rest were sent to the apartment where Josephine used to live. I didn't expect that the letter I sent to her mother's home would also be rejected."

I snorted. "The ones returned to sender went to a post office box. I saw that on the letters."

My father nodded. "It was what she used back then to reach me."

"It wasn't that long ago. They had e-mail twenty years ago, Dad."

My father laughed. "I'm an old Reaper, Zoey. Managing the algorithms on my computer is a more recent development. Back then, I knew nothing about how such technologies worked."

I nodded. "Thanks, Dad. I'll be careful, I promise. I don't even need to tell Rose who I am. I might be able to learn Mom's location without telling her the truth."

"Possibly," my father agreed. "Now, dear, I really must be going."

I sighed. "I might as well go with you. I'm supposed to meet up with Gabriel tonight."

My father cocked his head. "You won't find him in the underworld, Zoey. Not tonight."

I furrowed my brow. "What are you talking about?"

"There was another soul today that required reaping. He was originally designated for another Reaper, but given the sensitivity of the situation, I reassigned the harvest to Gabriel and Morty."

I furrowed my brow. "Are you talking about Chad? The other kidnapper I fought today?"

My father nodded. "That is correct."

I huffed. "They said it wasn't his time!"

"It wasn't," my father agreed. "But it is now."

I shook my head. "But we need him alive. He has a boss, someone higher up, that he said would be coming after me. I need to question him before he dies. I need to find out who it is. It's the only way I can stop the traffickers."

"His wound was infected, Zoey. Your staff might appear a common weapon, and perhaps it cannot reap souls, but a wound from it will kill. The magic within it is not compatible with the human body. The doctors will call it sepsis."

"How much time do I have?" I asked. "I need to get to him before it's too late."

"I'm sorry, Zoey. I sent Gabriel and Morty just before I left to meet you here. The soul will be harvested within the hour."

I grunted. "I have to go. I'll probably be too late. But I have to try."

My father nodded. "I understand."

I leaned over and kissed him on the cheek. He kissed me back, then formed a portal to the underworld and left.

Cerberus jumped up on my thighs. After everything my dad had told me, I'd almost forgotten that I was going to have to figure out how to deal with a dog now.

"Down, boy," I snapped.

"I need food! Bring me back some food!"

I sighed. "I will. What's your preference? Purina? Science Diet?"

"Are you kidding?" Cerberus asked. "We're in Kansas City. Get me some barbecue."

CHAPTER EIGHTEEN

There were two ways I figured I could track down Chad. The first involved calling Detective Schroeder. I doubted he'd give me any information. Why would he? That was a long shot. But a bit of Chad's blood had struck my boot. I summoned my staff and scraped at the stain. My best bet was to use his DNA to track him down.

I assumed he'd be at a hospital somewhere. Since he was under arrest, he'd probably be guarded. Getting to him would not be easy. I had less than an hour. Just to find him, even with my staff and the speed of my motorcycle, would take the bulk of the time. Then, getting into whatever room he was in would be the second challenge.

Gabriel and Morty would be there, too. I wasn't exactly looking forward to that encounter. I could only hope that I could convince them to delay their reaping until I got the information that I needed out of Chad.

That was going to be a third difficulty to overcome. The guy was dying. If he realized it, I wouldn't have a lot of leverage to force him to talk.

What the hell was I doing?

If I forced my way past the officers probably guarding Chad, that might get me into some trouble. Kevin was already more than a little curious about my involvement in this. Confronting Chad would only confirm his suspicion that I had more to do with it than I'd admitted.

The only thing that emboldened me and allowed me to set my qualms aside was my father's blessing. Sure, he'd pressed me to excel more than a parent probably should. He had his reasons, and I couldn't blame him for that. But he also believed in me. He hadn't questioned my intentions when I told him I needed to get to Chad.

Somewhat to my chagrin, he'd left Cerberus with me. He could have told me to back off, to be more careful, to live a normal, peaceful life. Instead, he'd tasked Cerberus to protect me. To help me encounter whatever forces of nasty I would end up confronting on Earth.

I rode fast, using my staff as a homing beacon. It led me to the doors of St. Luke's Hospital, near the Plaza.

I dispelled my staff. Walking into a hospital with a weapon probably wasn't wise. I'd have to resort to more conventional methods of investigation to locate Chad. Could I ask the front desk? Well, I wasn't his family, and I didn't know Chad's last name. Since he was also in police custody, there wasn't much of a chance they'd give me his room number.

From the perspective of the detectives, Chad wasn't just a criminal. He was also a witness. A connection they could leverage, probably by offering a more lenient sentence in exchange for giving up his superiors.

I saw a police officer strolling through the hospital foyer and approaching an elevator. I stood back and watched as he entered. Then, I watched the numbered lights above the elevator as it ascended, then stopped. The third floor.

Unless the police had any other subjects in custody, chances were better than not that Chad was on the third floor.

I pressed the elevator button and waited. I watched the three elevator doors in anticipation of whichever one might open first. The middle one dinged, and the doors parted.

I was about to step inside when I saw Detective Schroeder waiting inside.

His eyes met mine as he cocked his head. "Miss Grimm? What are you doing here?"

I grunted. "I've come to visit someone."

Kevin chuckled and placed his hand on the elevator door to hold it in place. "You can't visit the suspect, Miss Grimm. Why would you want to?"

I grunted. "He threatened me. I don't know. I was just anxious. I wanted to try to get him to talk. If I knew who might be coming after me, I might feel better."

Kevin sighed. "First, Miss Grimm, you should leave that to us. If you think you're in danger, we can offer you some protection. But second, it won't do you much good."

"Why?" I asked.

"The suspect died moments ago." Kevin shook his head.

I clenched my fist. I wanted to punch something. I was too late. "Did he tell you anything that would help? With the investigation, I mean."

Kevin shook his head. "He didn't, Miss Grimm. But I should say, I'm not as surprised to see you here as you might think."

I cocked my head. "Why is that?"

"You don't know?" Kevin asked, raising one eyebrow. "Surely you knew that your accomplices were here ahead of you?"

"What are you talking about?" I asked.

Kevin laughed. "You could have told me the truth before, Miss Grimm. Though, I suspect you had your reasons to want to protect your boyfriend and brother."

I sighed. Gabriel and Morty were there to reap Chad. Of course they were. But how the hell had they appeared to Detective Schroeder? There was only one way that might have been possible. They must've taken the portal in my father's office. They weren't here on a reaping. Then, they must've removed their cloaks. They'd *intended* to be seen. "What did they tell you?"

"Only that they were there with you in the freight yard. They were the ones who handled the kidnappers."

I rolled my eyes. They were trying to cover for me. Trying to protect me. I wasn't sure if I was grateful for that or pissed that they came, like a pair of white knights, to protect the poor earth-bound damsel in distress. "Where are they now?"

"I questioned them. They were quite cooperative, which, I should say, was nice for a change."

I rolled my eyes, annoyed by the tone of Kevin's voice. "You realize why I couldn't tell you about them, right?"

"Of course," Kevin replied. "You were trying to protect them. But rest assured, I have no intention of prosecuting them for killing those men. Technically, I could. Vigilantism isn't legal. But in this case, there are bigger fish to fry. I'm willing to overlook their involvement and yours and dismiss it as a matter of self-defense. Provided, of course, you back off and let me do my job."

I cocked my head. Now that Kevin knew I had a boyfriend, I suppose flirting with him wasn't going to get me anywhere. "Was that a threat, detective?"

Kevin shook his head. "More like a warning, Miss Grimm. Don't force my hand. I'd much rather we maintain a cooperative relationship. We may need your testimony and theirs when we figure out who these men were working for."

Kevin stepped out of the elevator and let it close as we both walked back through the foyer and out of the front doors of the hospital. "I'll tell you what, Kevin."

"Detective Schroeder," Kevin interrupted.

"Detective Schroeder," I continued, "I won't get in your way. But Chad threatened me. I need to see this through. I need to find out who might be coming after me."

Kevin shook his head. "I doubt you have much to worry

about, Miss Grimm. His threat was made in a moment of desperation. I can assure you he hasn't had contact with anyone since his arrest. Consider it a blessing in disguise that he's deceased. He won't be able to give your name to anyone else who would do you harm."

"I'm not sure I can trust that. This wasn't my first encounter with Chad."

Kevin nodded. "I spoke to Sienna. She told me what happened the night before."

"Then you know he might have already given my name to someone in his organization. I can't trust that I'm safe just because he's dead."

Kevin smiled. "We'll keep a watch on your apartment for the next few days if that makes you feel any better."

I grunted. "I'm not sure it does. You can't watch me forever. Even though I'm sure you'd like to."

Kevin smirked. "Can we please try to keep this professional, Miss Grimm?"

I rolled my eyes. "Yeah, sure. Whatever."

CHAPTER NINETEEN

Since I was near the Plaza anyway, I picked up a slab of ribs from Fiorella's Jack Stack Barbecue. I wasn't a huge barbecue fan myself, which would make me a pariah in Kansas City if anyone knew. From what I'd been able to tell, there were two things that Kansas Citians were proud of—their sports teams and their barbecue. I wasn't a huge sports fan, either.

Of course, the ribs weren't for me. They were for Cerberus.

I grabbed a bottle of spicy barbecue sauce to go with it. It was a spur-of-the-moment decision. While I was waiting for the ribs, I'd googled "how to dissuade your dog from eating human food."

One result that came up was an article on how to train your dog to stop eating its poop. Good Lord! I didn't realize how common a problem it was. Man's best friend is a poop eater? Seriously? You'd think that was something you kept under wraps. You know, like if your best friend was the kid in school who picked his nose. You might still be friends in private. There's no shame in that. I mean, pretty much everyone goes mining for the green gold when no one else is around, anyway. What does it matter? But when you're around the cool kids in school or even any other civilized human beings, you might be tempted to under-emphasize the "best" part of being "best friends" with the kid who frequents the all-you-can-eat booger buffet. All right, I thought my metaphor was good at first, but now I realize it's snot.

Most people pick their noses when no one is looking. I don't think too many people privately sample their poo. But the point is that when someone or something has a disgusting habit, having an intimate association with the said social misfit is a bit of an embarrassment. If dogs so frequently eat their shit, why are humans so inclined to choose them as their preferred species for companionship? Monkeys and apes are much closer to humans, evolutionarily speaking, but there's one major reason people don't befriend them on the regular. They play with poop! I've been to the zoo. I've seen the vile things they do.

Then again, maybe that's why humans like dogs so much. It reminds them of what they used to be back in the day. They embrace their poop-eating pooches for nostalgia's sake.

I digress. The article said that one way to break your dog from its poop-eating habit was to season it with hot sauce. Dogs don't like spicy things. They'll associate their poop with it and stop the habit. My hope was a little spicy barbecue sauce might dissuade Cerberus from his inconvenient and *expensive* food choices.

I doused the slab sufficiently with the sauce before I opened the box and placed a few ribs on a plate for Cerberus.

He sniffed at it. Then he swapped heads. The one with red eyes, the Hades head, emerged and devoured the whole plate. Bones and all.

Cerberus belched, and a blast of flames emerged from his hellish jaws. Then he switched back to his Earth head.

He wagged his tail. "Delicious! Thanks, Zoey!"

"I'm not sure what's stranger, that you just showed me you can breathe fire like a dragon or that you ate the bones."

Cerberus snorted. "You're not supposed to eat bones?"

"Dogs *chew* on bones. They don't eat them."

Cerberus licked his chops. "Well, if you haven't noticed, I'm not like other dogs."

I snorted. "Yeah, the three heads thing sort of gave that away."

"I won't hump your leg either," he assured me.

I smirked. "Well, that's good to know."

"My anatomical interests are north of the legs."

"Cerberus!"

The hellhound laughed. "Relax, honey. I'm just messing with you. You aren't my type."

I cocked my head. "Not furry enough for you?"

Cerberus snorted. "Not exactly what I meant."

I scratched my cheek. "Well, I'm mostly human, so that makes sense."

"I'm not talking about your species, Zoey. I only hump dudes."

I furrowed my brow. "Wait, you're gay?"

"Ding! Ding! Ding! We have a winner! But if you had a wiener, I'd be even happier!"

I laughed. "You could have just said something. It's not a big deal. To each one's own."

Cerberus nodded. "Good. Because I get a lot of head."

"Too much information!" I protested.

He popped out his other two heads. "Hellhound joke. Get it?"

I laughed. "Hilarious. Want more of the ribs? I'm not a fan. They'll go to waste if you don't eat them."

"There's more?" Cerberus asked. "Why are you holding out on me?"

"Because I can't afford to buy you barbecue for every meal," I explained. "I was hoping to stretch this slab out for a couple of days."

Cerberus snorted. "Bitch, please. You've got Daddy's money."

I narrowed my eyes. "I'm trying not to use his money."

Cerberus stared at me blankly. "Why the hell not? Have you seen the boatman?"

"Of course."

"He looks like death warmed over! What do you think he needs so much money for, anyway?"

I shrugged. "I don't know. Mani-pedis?"

"Honey, Charon doesn't put on a pleasure cruise," Cerberus replied. "He's ferried souls across the River Styx in that rickety old gondola for centuries, and I've never seen him wear anything more than rags. You'd think with all the money he's collected through the years, he could at least get a nice pair of pants, but no. He does nothing with that money."

"He must have a use for it," I pressed. "If we don't pay him, souls don't move on."

"It's a power play if you ask me. He knows nothing else than that dumb boat and the river. He'd do it for free, probably, if push came to shove because he has no other purpose. But if he did it for free, well, then he'd be a slave. And Charon ain't gonna be no one's bitch. He makes you pay so you realize he's in control."

I shrugged my shoulders. "I don't care what his motives are. The fact is we have to make sure there's plenty of money to ensure all the souls on Earth can cross over. And with the pace of population growth and the interest rate on my father's current investments, I have to be careful about how much of his money I take."

Cerberus narrowed his eyes. "That's the stupidest thing I've ever heard."

I furrowed my brow. "Excuse me?"

"Tell me, Zoey. How many people die every day all around the world?"

I knew the answer to that. I'd learned it in the academy. "On average, approximately one hundred fifty thousand."

"The boatman collects a hundred bucks for each one. I don't have to do the math for you, Zoey, but that's a lot of money."

"Exactly! Which is why I have to be careful about how much I'm spending!"

Cerberus growled. "I'm talking about fifty or sixty bucks a day for barbecue. It's a drop in the bucket."

"It all adds up!" I protested.

"Oh, stop it. What's the real reason you won't use his money?"

I took a deep breath. "I'm here on my own. I want to make it on my own. To stand on my own two feet."

"If you want to live poor on principle, that's up to you. But your daddy made me come here. I don't share your principles. I demand luxury!"

I rolled my eyes. "What do you think you are? A cat or something?"

Cerberus narrowed his eyes. "I'm going to pretend you didn't just say that. I'm no pussy."

"Well, just so you know, I didn't ask my dad to send you here, either. We have that much in common. Neither of us is thrilled that you're here. Since my dad is the one behind all this, I suppose it's just desserts that he be the one to pay for your lifestyle."

"Desserts?" Cerberus asked.

"Sweet justice," I returned.

The hellhound cocked his head. "And you were saying you have dessert?"

I sighed. "Not what I was saying. Whatever. We can stop for something later. I have an errand to run."

Cerberus nodded. "I'll be right behind you."

"Right behind me? I'm not sure you could hold on behind me on my bike."

Cerberus grinned, flashing his canines. "I told you before; I'm not a normal dog. I can run fast. Besides, I'm not supposed to leave your side."

I scratched my head. "You didn't go with me to the hospital earlier."

"I didn't?" Cerberus titled his head to the right.

I frowned. "You followed me?"

"Of course!"

"What would people think if they saw a dog running at eighty miles an hour down the highway?"

"They won't see me. No one sees me unless I want them to. My Earth head might be alpha here, but it's not like I can't use the other two. The domains of heaven and hell are invisible, but they are all around us all the time. It's not like you go down to Hades or up to Olympus, Zoey. They are different planes of reality, all overlapping one another. All I have to do is use my other heads, run alongside you through Hades or Olympus depending on my mood at the time, and reemerge with my Earth head when I want to show back up here."

I furrowed my brow. "You're saying you can run *between* the realms?"

Cerberus huffed. "Yes, and now I can't go to the underworld, the in-between. I need your father's help, or maybe your crystal portal, to do that. But I can run through Olympus and Hades as easily as I can on Earth."

"But you can see me on Earth when you're doing that?" I asked.

Cerberus nodded. "Of course. I can see all three realms at any given moment. You know, on account of my heads."

As Cerberus said it, his Hades and Olympian heads belched. Again, his Hades head expelled flames. His other head burped out a cloud of something that resembled glitter.

"You going to clean that stuff up?" I wondered.

Cerberus laughed. "Honey, there's no cleaning up glitter. It's the herpes of craft supplies. There's no getting rid of it."

I narrowed my eyes. "Then at least try not to burp it all over my apartment."

CHAPTER TWENTY

It was only one week before my grandmother (it felt weird to say that since I'd never met the woman) was due to expire. My father was slated to do the job. If he didn't, or if he somehow violated his bargain with Athena, he could lose his chance to ascend. I knew little about what a Reaper's ascent was like. I suppose it's as mysterious to us—well, to Reaper-kind—as it is for humans who are preparing to move on to heaven.

It's supposed to be better, a new existence. Something closer to the gods. Perhaps my father would become an angel. Might he end up an Olympian himself? I doubted that. Those gods weren't likely to welcome one of our ilk to their pretentious country club in the celestial mountains. At least that's how I imagined it. Zeus, Aphrodite, Dionysus, and the rest, and sipping on tea and munching on crumpets (what the hell are crumpets, anyway?) talking about how much better they are than mere mortals or semi-divines like us.

"Aren't we wonderful!" I can imagine Zeus exclaiming, sitting out on the greens of Olympus beneath an umbrella as a servant whose name he never bothered to learn poured him a fifty-thousand-year aged glass of pinot noir.

"Yes, darling," Hera would respond, probably sipping on a daiquiri. "We are quite splendid! Breathtakingly fabulous!"

Meanwhile, Dionysus, who is the god of winemaking (what a thing to be the god of!), would go streaking across the greens while Zeus playfully shot lightning bolts at his bouncing bare butt.

Now, I know Olympus is probably nothing like that. It's probably far more snooty and highfalutin' than I could ever imagine. You know what they say about the gods, right? Their beauty, their glory, their majesty is so far beyond that of lesser, limited beings that to even behold it would overcome a mere mortal to the point of death. Pssshh. You know who that idea came from, right? The gods themselves, that's who.

No one knew what it was like on Olympus, nor what it was like for a Reaper after ascending. It was supposed to be better, in some way. No one ascends into shit. They wouldn't call it "ascending" if that was the case. It had to be desirable on some level, but how could we know if it was? Maybe "ascending" was just a euphemism for "Welcome to Olympus. No, you're not a god. Ha! Did you think? You're here to be Zeus' everlasting bitch."

Yeah, that's a lot to pack into a single euphemism. But you get my point. No one knew what was next. Humans didn't. Even those who supposedly had faith couldn't tell you more than their platitudes and speculation about what they thought heaven was like. It was no different for Reapers contemplating their ascension. Still, it was what my dad wanted. He was ready, or at least close to it. Once he had Morty ready, which knowing my brother would take a lot longer than my dad would like.

Is it possible to be grateful and also resentful at the same time? Certainly, gratitude can defang the bite of resentment. That doesn't mean it goes away.

That's how I was feeling about Gabriel at the moment. I felt the same way about Morty, truth be told, albeit for totally different reasons.

Regarding Gabriel, taking credit for downing the bad guys at the freight yard had helped keep the police off my back. But I hated that he had treated me like his damsel in distress. He didn't take down those traffickers. I did that. With two badass javelin-like throws of my staff.

It wasn't that I wanted credit. If anything, it was better if Kevin—sorry, *Detective Schroeder*—didn't know what I could do. Practically speaking, Gabriel and Morty solved a big problem for me. But they didn't talk to me about it before they acted. They hadn't asked me if I wanted or needed their help. They'd just showed up and Gabriel had taken it upon himself to play the role of my knight in shining armor.

I imagined Morty just went along with it. After all, Gabriel outranked Morty for now. Eventually, once Morty took over for my dad, the roles would be reversed. That brings me to how I felt about my brother. I was happy that he was growing up and growing into his given role. I still wasn't over the fact that it was supposed to be me who assumed that place. I didn't blame Morty for it. It wasn't his fault. I could let Morty slide because he wasn't the center of my resentment. With Gabriel, well, it was different. It was more personal.

Thankfully, I'd missed my monthly date with him. Maybe after a month to cool off, to see how the situation with the police and the traffickers developed, I'd see it differently. After a month, what was now a giant wall between us might become something like a chain-link fence. Still a barrier, but not too hard to overcome. So much for resolve.

I needed to find my grandmother, Josephine's mother. It felt weird thinking of a woman I'd never met as "Grandma." I had the address. All I had to do was program it into my maps app and drive there. But that was a path that would forever tie me to this

143

world. Connecting my mother's side of the family and, eventually my mother, meant I was selling out for Earth. I had to cut the rope that tied me to the underworld.

It was time to break up with Gabriel.

CHAPTER TWENTY-ONE

I set up the crystal that formed the portal to take me back to the underworld. Cerberus, full of barbecue, was curled up on my couch. He didn't need to come with me. Not this time. He was supposed to be my guard dog on Earth, after all. I didn't need his…companionship in the underworld.

It was a simple process. For the crystal to work, I had to set it atop a small pedestal and shine a little light into it. Before, during the day, I'd just set it up in front of my window. The sunlight passed through the crystal and the portal formed in a small, golden circle on the opposite side.

It was too late for that. The sun had already set. So, instead, I set up my phone on my kitchen table. I wedged it between two glasses full of water. They were short glasses, the weight held my phone in place, and the phone light shone over the glasses into the crystal which I had sitting on its pedestal just in front of it.

Thankfully, the crystal didn't discriminate between light sources. The way it refracted light, conditioned by the molecular structure of the unique crystal itself, was the same. The portal formed, and I jumped through it.

I landed in my father's office.

I was grateful that he wasn't there. Not that I didn't want to see my dad, but I'd have to at least engage him in a brief conversation if he was there. I wanted to get this over with.

I grabbed one of my dad's Reaper cloaks from his closet. He had about twenty of them in there, all of them identical. Would he miss one? It wouldn't make me invisible in the underworld. Wearing it, though, I'd look like any other Reaper fresh off a reaping. With my hood up, no one would recognize me.

If I could get away with it, I'd take it back with me. My dad *probably* wouldn't mind. It would give me invisibility if I used it, and that could come in handy, especially if I had any more encounters with the traffickers.

I made my way down the stairs from my dad's office, out of the castle, and through the streets that led to Gabriel's apartment. I knocked three times. I don't know why three knocks. Two seemed too few. Four felt excessive.

Gabriel answered the door. I didn't need to drop my hood for him to recognize me. I just had to look up. He smiled as his eyes met mine. Damn. The way he looked at me. This was going to be hard.

"Zoey!" Gabriel sounded exuberant. "I wasn't sure you'd be coming after everything that went on today."

I nodded. "We need to talk, Gabriel."

Gabriel sighed. "You're right, Zoey. We do."

He stepped aside, and I walked into his apartment. I pushed back the hood from my borrowed cloak and sat on his couch. Gabriel came over and sat beside me.

"This isn't working, is it?" Gabriel asked.

I cocked my head. "It isn't. I didn't expect you'd feel that way, too."

"It's obvious, Zoey," Gabriel replied. "The last couple of times you visited, it was like you weren't really here. Your mind was somewhere else, back on Earth. And now, after all that happened…"

I bit my lip. "Are you breaking up with me?"

Gabriel nodded.

I laughed.

"That's not how I expected you to react." Gabriel shot me a disbelieving look.

"I came back to break up with you." I put my hand on his.

Gabriel pulled his hand away and wiped a tear from his cheek. "Well, I'm glad I said it first. That way, you're the one who is getting dumped, not me."

I laughed. "If that makes it easier."

Gabriel shook his head. "It's not easy, Zoey. I'm in love with you, but it's pretty clear to me you don't feel the same way. It would be selfish of me to ask you to stay with me even though your heart isn't in it. It wouldn't be fair to me, either."

"You're right," I agreed. "You deserve to have someone who loves you the way you do them."

"And you deserve to love someone the way I still feel about you, Zoey."

I smiled. "I thought this was going to be a lot harder. I was prepared for you to beg me to stay with you again, to try to make this work."

Gabriel took a deep breath. "I'm sorry, Zoey. I knew you didn't feel the same way when you left. It shouldn't have taken me so long to accept that, to understand that if I loved you, I had no choice but to let you go."

I shook my head. "You know, this would be so much easier if you weren't such a good guy. Like if you were an asshole, and I had a good reason not to love you."

"The heart wants what the heart wants, Zoey. It doesn't always make sense. If it did, well, I wouldn't still love you when I know you don't feel the same way, when you're trying to forge a new life for yourself and I'm holding you back."

"You didn't need to cover for me with the detective," I told him.

Gabriel nodded. "I know. It wasn't my place. I couldn't help myself. Every instinct I have was telling me I needed to protect you."

"I don't need your protection, Gabriel."

Gabriel laughed. "You've never needed my protection or anyone else's. You're a force of nature, Zoey. Honestly, I don't think there is anything you couldn't do well if you set your mind to it."

I chuckled. "You should see me try to make a latte."

Gabriel smiled. "Still struggling with your job?"

I nodded. "But maybe you just told me why that's the case. I haven't set my mind to it. If I had, well, I'd make flashcards. I'd put in the work to be successful."

"You should find something you're passionate about, Zoey," Gabriel urged. "Living in the human world, there are endless possibilities. You could be almost anything you want."

I shook my head. "I can't be a Reaper."

"But you still have your skills," Gabriel replied. "Your training. Maybe you could become a cop."

I laughed. "I'm not sure I'm cut out for that, either. There's too much red tape. Too many rules to follow. I'd have to do it their way."

"No magical javelins to take down the baddies?" Gabriel asked, raising one eyebrow.

I smiled. "You saw that?"

Gabriel nodded. "Morty and I watched you take those men down. I think it might have been even more impressive than your examination at the coliseum."

I laughed. "You know, I realize I shouldn't feel this way, but it felt *good* to down those bad guys."

Gabriel nodded. "The world is a better place with you in it, Zoey."

I blushed as tears welled up in my eyes. "Thank you for saying that, Gabriel."

Gabriel leaned over and kissed my cheek. "Take care, Zoey. I'll miss you."

"I'll miss you, too." I meant it. "Take care of Morty, will you?"

Gabriel laughed. "Honestly, he's doing better than I expected. Did you know he's already Level Two?"

I shook my head. "I had no idea."

"Almost Level Three. He'll be going solo soon if your dad allows it. Morty's under a lot of pressure, but he's risen to the occasion."

I sighed. "He's not in my shadow anymore. I imagine that's good for him."

Gabriel nodded. "I know this isn't the life you wanted, Zoey. But it might just work out for the better in the end."

I sighed. "I have a long way to go before I'm ready to accept that. But I appreciate you saying it."

Gabriel walked me back to the door, kissed me on the cheek again, and I left.

I didn't linger. I had things to do back home. Back home? I realized, for the first time, I'd referred to Earth as "home." It was true, though. Now that Gabriel and I weren't together, I was free. I could call the Earth my home. There was nothing left for me in the underworld. My dad was still there. So was my brother. I might come back to visit them from time to time. But when I did, it wouldn't be going "back home." I was still trying to find myself. I didn't know what my role was going to be on Earth.

But I knew I'd find my place in the world. Somehow, someway, I'd discover my path, I'd forge my destiny, and scythe or not, I'd find a way to be happy.

CHAPTER TWENTY-TWO

Cerberus jumped on my thighs the moment I appeared back in my apartment, almost knocking me right back into the portal.

"Down, boy!"

I kneed the dog lightly. No, not hard. Just enough to communicate to him the fact that jumping up on me was unacceptable behavior.

Cerberus took two steps back, turned toward the door, and started barking.

"What is it, Cerberus?"

"Someone knocked," Cerberus told me between barks. "Just before you came back."

I cocked my head. I didn't get many visitors. Sienna was the closest thing I had to a friend, and she didn't know where my apartment was. I sighed. There was only one person who had my address.

Detective Kevin Schroeder.

I reached down and scratched Cerberus behind the ears. "I think I know who it was. The detective said he'd send someone to check on me. I'll see if I can catch up with him."

Cerberus nodded, huffed, and disappeared. He was going to

follow me. I removed my dad's Reaper cloak and tossed it over the couch. There might be times when I needed it, but so long as I was wearing it, the officer assigned to my "protection detail" wouldn't be able to see me.

No one was in the hallway near my apartment door. I figured the cop might still be nearby. I ran down the stairs as fast as I could without falling and stepped outside.

Sure enough, a police car was parked outside. It didn't have all the markings of a squad car. The antennas and unusual license plates gave it away.

I stepped up to the door and knocked on the window.

The officer inside lowered the window. I knelt to look inside.

"Kevin? I thought you'd send a lackey to look after me."

Kevin laughed. "I'd tell you again to call me Detective Schroeder, but I'm beginning to think it's a lost cause."

I shrugged. "I'm not much for formalities."

Kevin snorted. "Yeah, I've gotten that impression. Want to get in so we can chat a moment?"

I grinned. "Is that appropriate, Detective Schroeder? Inviting a woman to get in your car? What will people think?"

Kevin raised an eyebrow. "Now you decide to use my official title, Zoey?"

I smiled, picking up on the fact that he didn't call me Miss Grimm for once. "Just keeping you on your toes, Kevin. Just when you think you've figured me out."

Kevin chuckled. "Just get in the car."

I stepped around the car, flashing Kevin a wink as I slid my fingers across his hood and opened his passenger-side door.

Kevin reached over and grabbed a file folder that was sitting on the passenger seat and tossed it onto his dashboard. I got in and closed the door.

"I went up to your apartment," Kevin began. "Your dog wasn't too happy to hear you had a visitor."

I smiled. "Yeah, he's an excellent guard dog. When you're single and live alone in the city, you can't be too careful."

"I thought you had a boyfriend?" Kevin asked.

"I did. We just broke up."

Kevin raised his eyebrows. "Oh, really?"

I nodded. "Yeah, he didn't like how this dude in a uniform kept following me around."

Kevin rolled his eyes. "I'm sure that's not the reason."

I smirked. "Sorry I didn't answer. I was taking a dump."

Kevin laughed. "You know, you throw me for a loop sometimes, Zoey. One moment, I could swear you're flirting with me. The next, you're telling me about your bowel movements."

I cocked my head. "You thought I was flirting with you? Don't flatter yourself, Detective!"

"Right…" Kevin shifted in his chair, realizing that he was opening up a can of worms he shouldn't. After all, I was a witness in his case. If he got too close to me, it might compromise his objectivity.

I laughed, noticing Kevin's nervousness. "I'm just giving you a hard time, Kevin. Don't worry about it. If you think I'm flirting with you, well, you are a detective. I'm sure you can figure it out."

Kevin nodded. "I'm here to make sure you're safe."

"I'm fine," I assured him. "But you could have sent anyone. A low-ranking officer could do the job. You're a big shot detective, aren't you? Shouldn't you be researching the case? Sifting through evidence? Tracking down the bad guys?"

Kevin glanced at me briefly, then looked back straight through his windshield. "On such short notice, I figured I'd handle your protective detail for tonight. I can't promise I'll be the one here tomorrow. Besides, I have all my files here in the car. It was either sit in an empty office and try to make sense of everything or come here and kill two birds with one stone."

"I'm not a birdie and killing me wouldn't do much for your career."

Kevin smirked. "Yeah, sorry. Bad metaphor. But you know what I meant. I figured I could get as much done here as I would back at the office."

"Have you found anything yet?" I asked.

"I'm not at liberty to discuss the case with you, Zoey."

I looked at Kevin and cocked my head. "Seriously? You can tell me!"

Kevin chuckled. "Given your track record of trying to go after the bad guys yourself, even if I knew something and I *could* tell you about it, I wouldn't."

"So, you're here just to watch my apartment?" I asked.

Kevin shook his head. "I wondered if you could give me your schedule. It will help with our detail. We'll make random patrols past the coffee shop where you work when you're on shift."

"And you'll stalk my apartment randomly, too?"

Kevin cocked his head. "This is protection detail, not stalking, Zoey."

"Uh-huh." I glanced at the files on Kevin's back seat. "Which is why you're poring over your files while you sit here."

"I assumed you weren't home. I was waiting to see if you showed up so I could make sure you were safe."

I narrowed my eyes. "One of two things is true. You either *wanted* to come just so you could see me, or you have reason to believe I'm in real danger. You have evidence that suggests Chad's threat wasn't as hollow as it seems. Either way, I'm fine with it. But if you had reason to believe that someone was coming after me, you'd say something to me about it. You'd give me more direction as to the things I should or shouldn't be doing, or at least you'd tell me what I should be looking for."

Kevin pressed his lips together and nodded. He said nothing in response.

"Based on your silence, I'm guessing you don't have any evidence about the threat yet. That means you just wanted to come to see me."

"Think what you want, Zoey," Kevin replied. "I take my job seriously. Just because we don't have any evidence that you're in any danger, that doesn't mean you *aren't* in danger. All it means is that I haven't found the evidence yet. Until I'm convinced that you aren't in danger, the best course of action is to proceed as if Chad's threats were credible."

As Kevin was talking, three men walked past us on the sidewalk. One of them moved toward the door that led up to my apartment. The other two men said something, and the third guy scurried back over to his group. If they were a part of the trafficking organization, and they had come for me, I guessed that they'd seen Kevin's car and decided to move on. Kevin picked up on it too.

"Stay here," Kevin told me. "It's probably nothing, but I'm going to check on it."

I nodded as Kevin stepped out of the car and locked the doors.

I watched for a moment as Kevin walked toward the three men. They turned around and acknowledged him. I couldn't hear what they were saying. I glanced at the file sitting on the dashboard in front of me. I quickly grabbed it and flipped through the pages. There was a lot there about the supposed trafficking organization that the police suspected might be involved. I couldn't steal the files. Kevin would realize they were missing.

I retrieved my phone from my pocket and quickly took shots of each of the pages. I could review them later. If there was any evidence that could help track down the traffickers, well, I'd have it.

Yes, I was flirting with Kevin. I was attracted to the man. He was sexy, especially in his tight navy-blue pants. I wasn't seriously interested in the detective. He was right. It was a conflict of interest. Besides, Gabriel and I had just broken up. I didn't want a relationship with anyone. Certainly not with a cop. Still, if flirting with him presented me with opportunities to get information like this, it was more than worth it.

I tossed the file back onto Kevin's dashboard just in time. Kevin dismissed the three men and returned to the car.

"Everything check out?" I asked.

Kevin shrugged. "I'm not sure. They said they were on their way to a get-together at a coworker's apartment but that they weren't sure which door to take."

I nodded. "Not unusual. These studio apartments have entrances that aren't obvious to people who don't know where to look."

Kevin nodded. "They were probably telling the truth. I think I'll hang out a while, just to be sure."

I smiled. "Well, as much as I'd love to stay here with you and chat, I have somewhere to go."

"I can follow you if you'd like," Kevin offered.

I shook my head. "Just keep watching the apartment. If anyone is looking for me, this is where they'll come first."

"Where are you going, if you don't mind me asking?"

I sighed. "I haven't seen my mother since I was a baby. I recently acquired my grandmother's address. I'm heading over there to see if I can track her down."

"What's your mother's name?" Kevin asked. "I might be able to help you out. You know, under the table. Just don't tell anyone."

I smirked. My flirtation was paying off if the detective was willing to offer under-the-table favors. "Josephine Collins. But I think she's going under a different name now."

"So, Collins is her maiden name?" Kevin asked.

I nodded. "Yeah, but I mean I think she's using a different first name, also. After my brother and I were born, we went to live with my father, and she disappeared. I think she was running away. She probably changed her name so my dad couldn't track her down."

"Why do you think she wants to meet you, now?" Kevin asked.

I shrugged. "I don't know. But the way I see it, if she was overwhelmed by raising twins, or whatever, I'm all grown up now. If she wants to meet me, I'm hoping to take the first step to let her know I'd like to meet her, too."

Kevin nodded. "Well, good luck with that, Zoey. It's hard to know how situations like that will pan out. I wish you the best."

CHAPTER TWENTY-THREE

I had ten or twelve pages from Kevin's file to review. Trying to make the little reverse-pinch motion of my phone screen zoom in to make it big enough to read, then navigate the screen by dragging it around, was going to be a major pain in the ass. I'd have to look at it in more detail later. It was already after dark, and given that my grandmother was within a week of dying, whatever the cause might be, I imagined she was probably pretty tired.

One page looked like Chad's bank statement. Yellow highlights marked some of the transactions. Exchanges with his superiors in the organization he'd been working with? Most likely. This wasn't a statement from a well-known bank. I didn't even see the name of whatever financial institution the files came from at the top of the page. Nonetheless, these were electronic financial transactions.

I'd have to dig into it later. More than likely, I'd need help. For all my skills, navigating digital media wasn't one of them. If your phone and computer were in perpetual "airplane mode," you'd have an experience comparable to the most I ever had with those technologies before leaving the underworld.

Sure, I'd gotten better with it over the last six months. I was pretty good with the Facebook and the Twitter. Sorry, Facebook and Twitter. Sienna almost gagged on her tongue the first time I told her I was looking at something on *the* YouTube. She said I sounded like a Boomer, whatever that meant.

I waved at Kevin as I mounted my bike, which was parked about twenty feet in front of his car. I could almost feel him undressing me with his eyes as I climbed aboard. I turned back and winked at him. He pointed to his head. I sighed. Yeah. he was a cop—helmet laws.

I pulled my hair back into a ponytail. He flashed his lights at me. I looked back. He was shaking his head while making a two-handed gesture as if he was placing an imaginary helmet over his head.

Charades!

I placed an imaginary helmet on my head. Then I turned my key in my ignition and took off down the road. Was he going to ticket me? He was on assignment, watching my apartment. Since I didn't see any flashing lights in my mirrors, I ascertained he was going to let it slide.

I had the address programmed into my phone already. I slid my phone into the holder on the left side of my handlebars as I took off down the road.

Based on the estimated arrival time from my GPS app, it was only a fifteen-minute ride from my apartment to my grandmother's house. I didn't even have to go over the river or through the woods to get there.

The house it took me to matched the one described in my dad's journals. It looked like the place hadn't been repainted in over twenty years. It still had olive green paint, although now it was peeling from the windowsills. There was a white four-door Ford Taurus in the driveway. I parked my bike next to it and went to the door.

I pressed the doorbell. A woman with dark hair wearing scrubs answered the door.

"Can I help you?" she asked.

"I'd like to see Rose," I requested.

"Are you family?" the lady, who I assumed was a nurse, asked.

I nodded. "My name's Zoey."

The lady smiled and gestured inside. I stepped inside. "I'm Helen, from the hospice."

I nodded. "How's she doing?"

"She's in good spirits, all things considered. Right this way."

I followed Helen down a narrow hallway to a bedroom on the right side. I walked in. An old woman, who I guessed must be my grandmother, was sitting in bed with several cords and hoses hooked up to her body. She had a smile on her face, which widened when she saw me. She placed a hand to her mouth.

"I can't believe it!" Rose exclaimed.

I cocked my head. "I'm Zoey. I don't think we've met."

"Oh, we've met," she replied. "You were a lot smaller the last I saw you. Just a baby."

"You know who I am?" I asked, wincing. I was sort of hoping she wouldn't know who I was. My father had said that it might risk his deal with the goddess Athena if she did. There was no going back now.

"You are the spitting image of your mother," Rose continued. "My, how you've grown. How did you find me? Did your mother send you?"

I shook my head. "I'm sorry, ma'am. I was hoping maybe you'd be able to tell me where I could find her."

Rose sighed. "I see. Why don't you take a seat, dear?"

I pulled over what looked like a kitchen chair that had been set next to Rose's bed. I sat down. "I'm sorry to barge in on you like this."

"Are you kidding?" Rose asked. "I've been praying that my Josephine would come to see me before I go. But for my lost

161

granddaughter to show up, I'll say the Lord sure works in mysterious ways."

I cocked my head. "My mom hasn't been here?"

Rose shook her head. "I haven't seen her since the last time I saw you, dear."

I furrowed my brow. "Seriously? You don't know where my mom is?"

Rose shook her head. "I'm sorry, child. I wish I did."

I braced myself for the worst. "Is she…"

"Oh, she's alive. She's out there somewhere. She's sent me letters." Rose gestured at one that rested on her end table beside her bed. "She writes often. But she's never given me an address so that I can write her back."

"May I?" I asked.

Rose nodded. "Of course, dear."

I picked up the letter and examined the envelope—no return address. There was a postmark with a zip code. "Do you know where 64015 is located?"

Rose nodded. "Blue Springs."

"Is that local?" I asked.

Rose cocked her head. "Where have you been all these years, dear?"

I sighed. "Nowhere near here. I just moved to the city six months ago. I've been trying to find my mom."

Rose smiled. "The postmarks are not always the same. I have more letters in my dresser. You can take them if you'd like."

"Are you sure?" I asked. "I mean, these were sent to you."

Rose laughed. "Dear, I might not make it through the night. I've read them all a hundred times. I dare say I've even memorized most of them. Perhaps you can make use of them now."

"Are all the postmarks local?" I asked.

Rose nodded. "I believe my Josephine is living somewhere nearby, but she sends her letters from a variety of places. I don't believe she wants to be found, dear. Though, in truth, I haven't looked too hard for the last several years. If my Josephine wanted to be found, she'd come to me herself."

I sighed, then stood up and opened Rose's dresser drawer. There were probably thirty letters or more, all stacked together and tied together with twine. "Thank you for these."

Rose nodded. "I wish I could tell you more, dear. But I'll call it a dying wish realized that you've come."

I smiled and tried my best to choke back a tear as I took my grandmother's hand. "I'm sorry, ma'am. If I could have come sooner…"

"I know, dear. It's not your fault. I'm only happy you're here now."

"And you don't know why my mom disappeared?" I asked.

"She only said it was necessary. It's all in her letters, but she's revealed little else about her activities or why it was necessary, other than that it might kill me if she were to return."

I bit my lip. Was my mom bound to the same agreement my father had made? Did she have to agree to remain absent in exchange for Athena granting her mother a longer life? It was the only explanation I could think of that made sense.

If I could tell my grandma what I suspected, I would. But how do you tell a dying woman that her daughter and her daughter's former lover made an agreement with a Greek goddess to save her life? She wouldn't believe it if I told her. Even if she did, would it help her to know? It would probably only cause her more trouble and anxiety.

Still, it was something for me to go on. Why would Athena demand that both my parents never see Rose again? The gods could be cruel. I knew little about them, but I knew that their decisions rarely took the emotional well-being of mortals or even Reapers into account.

I sat back down in my chair. "I hope she comes back to see you soon. If I find her, I'll be sure she does."

Rose smiled at me. She had a twinkle in her eye and a glow in her face that was comforting despite everything. "Would you just sit with me a while?"

I nodded. "Of course, ma'am."

"Call me Grandma. Or Grandmother. Something else. I wish I'd known you as a child. I can imagine, if you were anything like your mother, you were quite the firecracker."

I chuckled. "You could say that. My father's often said as much."

"Ah, your father. How is he?"

I shrugged. "As well as he could be. He's preparing to retire. I think he'd like to find Mom, too."

Rose pressed her lips together. "When your mother left, she broke a lot of hearts. But I have my theories, as well. She's written about you many times. I think she loves you and your brother, both."

I took a deep breath. "I'll have to read about it later."

"How is your brother?" Rose asked.

I smiled. "He's doing well. A bit of an underachiever growing up. But he's a capable young man. I trained my whole life to take over the family business, but I recently learned I wasn't suited for it. Morty is preparing to take over when Dad retires."

"Well, tell me about yourself, dear. What do you like? What are you doing with your life? I have so many questions!"

"Well, I guess I'm an athlete," I told her. "I'm still trying to find my path."

"What sort of athlete?" Rose asked.

I smiled. "Martial arts."

Rose raised an eyebrow. "That's something. Perhaps could start your own dojo?"

I chuckled. "You know, that's not a bad idea. I'll have to think about that. Thank you, Grandma."

"And your father's business?" she asked.

I pressed my lips together. "He operates something similar to a funeral home. It's a much larger enterprise than most, though."

Rose chuckled. "Well, that's not a bad line of work. You know, it's an economy-proof business. No matter how the markets might fluctuate, people are always dying."

I bit my lip. "Yes, I suppose that's true."

"But you weren't interested in following in your father's footsteps?" she asked.

I sighed. "I used to be. It was all I wanted for a long time. Still, at the end of the day, I guess I didn't have the talent for it."

"It takes a unique person to work with the dying and bereaved," Rose mused.

I nodded. "That's certainly true."

She patted my hand. "There's no shame in forging your own path, dear. It's probably best that you realized it now before you found yourself in a line of work that wouldn't make you happy. Life is too short, believe you me, to waste any of it not following your heart."

I sighed. "I'm sorry about my mom. I can't help but think it's my fault she left."

"Oh, child!" Rose protested. "It might be that your mother was not ready to raise children. Perhaps that's why she left. But it wasn't your fault. You did nothing wrong. You deserved to be loved. Every child does. I can tell you it wasn't because she didn't love you and your brother that she left. She was a troubled young woman in those days. If anyone's to blame for what she did, it was me."

"I don't blame you for that," I assured her.

"Still, perhaps I could have done more. If any of my failures as a parent were to blame for what your mother did, that is my burden to bear. I'm truly sorry, Zoey."

There was no holding back the tears now. I let them flow. "Can I hug you?"

"Of course, dear." Rose opened her arms.

"I don't blame you either, you know. If it means anything, I forgive you. I just wish things had worked out differently."

She sniffed. "Me too, sweet child. Me too."

I held Rose as she squeezed me as tight as her frail arms allowed. Together, we wept. Rose wasn't my mom. But I had more now to work with than I'd had before. And I was glad to meet her.

"I'll come back and see you tomorrow," I promised.

"Please do. And if I'm gone before you get here, I love you, Zoey."

I smiled as I pulled out of the hug. "I love you too, Grandma."

CHAPTER TWENTY-FOUR

It's hard to ride a motorcycle with the wind blowing in your face while your vision is blurred by tears. I wasn't sure if I was happy to have met Rose and hear that she believed my mother still loved me or sad that I knew she was dying soon. Such a sweet woman. If only I'd come to Earth sooner, I could have gotten to know her before she was on her deathbed.

I'd come back to see her again before she died. I'd promised I would. I didn't know what was wrong with Rose, why she was dying, but I knew her expiration date. Besides, I figured I would have questions for her. I had a lot of letters to sort through. I could only hope that the contents of the letters combined with the postmarks would give me a lead to follow to my mom.

Rose said that my mom loved me. She always had. I knew it wasn't her fault that I was taken away. I even understood that it wasn't that she didn't want me. My father had to take Morty and me back with him to the underworld. That was why he'd knocked my mom up to begin with.

I wanted to be angry at my dad, at my mom, at everyone for what happened. Still, what else could my dad do? He was trapped by his destiny, as was my mother as the unfortunate woman whom he'd chosen. Did she still love him, too? I had no reason to suspect otherwise based on the letters I'd read from her that my father gave me. Though, those letters had all been penned before he told her the truth, before he took us away, and before he'd made his deal with Athena.

How is someone supposed to deal with resentment when it couldn't be easily attached to a single person? How could I be angry at anyone when each person involved was left without a better choice? There was no easy target for my anger. It was the situation I resented—in both instances.

In the last hour, I'd acquired so much paperwork that you'd think I just bought a new car, or perhaps a small country. Thankfully, everything I'd taken from Kevin was digital. More convenient in terms of the fact I could take it with me wherever I went, but a pain in the butt to read. I was tired. I wanted to go home, curl up in bed, and drift off into dream land. The problem was that both issues I had to solve came with an expiration date.

I could find my mother at any time, but I had an urge to find her sooner than later. She needed to know about Rose, and Rose deserved to see her daughter one last time. Did my mom even know her mother was sick? How much did she know about the deal my father had made with Athena? Did she realize her mother's expiration date was fast approaching?

Maybe she was waiting until the last minute, afraid the Reaper—my father—would appear to take her the moment she showed. Or maybe she knew my father was the one who had to reap her mother, that her presence would expedite his arrival. In that case, she might not come to see her mother at all. She wouldn't see my dad when he showed to reap Rose's soul. But he'd see her, and if she knew how it all worked, she'd realize that he'd have a chance then to find her, to show himself to her again.

There wasn't any way for me to know for sure what kept my mother away. Perhaps the letters would give me some clues.

Maybe they'd explain my mother's behavior and reveal where she was hiding.

At the same time, I couldn't let sleeping dogs lie. The trafficking organization needed to be stopped. First, I didn't know if they were coming after me. If they were, an organization that specialized in abducting human beings without being caught would surely figure out a way to get to me despite Kevin's effort to protect me. More than that, if this organization was still conducting operations, the longer they went undetected, the more people they'd hurt.

I wasn't in any position to choose one path or the other. I had to do both, *and* I had to go to work. I know, given all that was at stake, working a job at a coffee shop seemed like small beans (see what I did there?), but it was still important. Rose was right. Maybe I was meant for more than that, but as Joe had told me when he hired me, there were few better jobs for someone between vocations than working as a barista. It was a great transitional job, and besides, I still hadn't had a chance to talk to Sienna since everything went down.

I allowed myself one hour to browse my mother's letters and another hour to examine the documents I'd taken from Kevin.

Rose was right. The postmarks were inconsistent. Out of more than two dozen letters, there were maybe five different zip codes represented. I wished I could just pin them on a map, figure out what was at the middle, and assume that meant my mother lived at that location. I'd seen shit done like that on TV shows from time to time. The problem was that humans aren't particularly precise about their behaviors, and any number of factors could explain why my mother had gone to all of the different zip codes represented by the postmarks. Perhaps she went to the salon in one area, had a friend in another one, saw a doctor elsewhere, or enjoyed shopping at a particular location. The only thing the postmarks showed was that she lived *some-*

where in the region. While Kansas City isn't Chicago, New York, or Los Angeles, it's still a major metropolitan area.

So, I arranged them in chronological order. I took several colors of highlighter just to mark all the zip codes represented. Certainly, my mother was attempting to mask her location. Not all the zip codes, however, were used throughout the twenty-plus years my mother had sent letters. That made sense. Say my mother sent a letter while making a trip to the salon but, later, she changed salons. Or, perhaps, a place she frequently shopped closed down. There was only one zip code that spanned all twenty years. It was only used once in the first few years. It was also the same zip code printed on the very first letter that my mother had sent and also the most recent one: 64015, Blue Springs.

There wasn't any guarantee, but if I were a gambler, I'd wager that was where my mother lived. I'd never been there. It was a delightful town, from what I'd heard, but it was large enough that presuming I was right about her location, I couldn't find her based on the zip code alone. A quick Google search revealed that the zip code represented roughly half of the suburb that was located to the East of the city, a straight shot down Interstate 70.

It wasn't conclusive. I could spend months searching the area, and since I hadn't seen any photos of my mother in recent years, I could walk straight past her in public and not recognize her. Still, it wasn't nothing. It was progress. The next step was to start reading the letters.

While the most recent letter might have a few clues as to my mother's current location, short of providing an address, I'd be better equipped to make sense of any clues that her newer letters offered if I knew her whole journey. So, I planned to start with the letters she'd sent over the last year. Then I'd go back to the beginning and work forward, looking for any connections or details that might help.

All the letters were handwritten. My mother wrote with a

slanted script, including a lot of flourishes in her letters. I wasn't a handwriting expert, but it was a unique enough form of penmanship that I was pretty sure if I saw her write anything else, I'd be able to identify it. I imagined, though, that she only wrote those letters by hand for Rose's sake. As an older woman, Rose probably wasn't keen on using e-mail or other digital forms of communication.

Nothing in the most recent letter gave much away. She indicated she was in good health, thought about her mother frequently, and wished she could visit. She wrote nothing about me, my brother, or anything that would help me identify her habits or behaviors in the community. When I went back to her first letter, however, the tone was strikingly different. There, she wrote how she spent most of her days in tears, and she missed Morty and me. She wrote she was well, relatively speaking, but wasn't sure how she'd be able to move on with her life and, more interestingly, "do what was expected of her."

What could that mean? What was expected of her in the wake of our loss? Who had placed that expectation upon her? The next few letters offered little help in revealing that particular mystery. Perhaps Rose would have some insight that could clarify what my mother meant. I made a mental note to ask her the next time I visited. I set aside three more letters to take with me to work the next day. Maybe I would find time to read them between customers, on my break, or when I used the restroom.

I picked up my phone and curled up in bed to examine Kevin's files in more detail. Most of the files had to do with things I already knew about. There was a report that Kevin wrote after the incident at the freight yard. He wrote nothing about me other than the facts. If he suspected I was involved more than I was—a fact that Gabriel and Morty confounded by their half-truths that they'd "finished off" the two men I'd killed—he didn't put it in his report. I was grateful for that.

There was also nothing in any of his reports about issuing a protection order for me. Maybe he just didn't include it in his file. I bit the inside of my cheek. Maybe he intended to watch me himself and didn't want anyone to know about it.

He did have a copy of a background check he'd conducted on me. Predictably, it was devoid of anything of use. There was nothing more to it than my birthplace. I was born at a hospital in… you guessed it…Blue Springs. Was that a coincidence, or was there a reason my mother had chosen to live in the same city where I was born?

The only other thing that had raised his curiosity about me was that the driver's license included my present address. I knew about that. My dad had given me a new license and stashed it with my motorcycle keys in the footlocker he sent with me when I came to Earth. How he'd acquired it was a mystery. What I hadn't realized was that my license had been renewed somehow. The image of my license in Kevin's file was one from a few years earlier. That it reflected my present address indicated that my father must've held onto my apartment for some time. When I'd moved in, there wasn't any evidence that anyone had lived there in years.

I imagined Kevin was perplexed by the lack of information about me. Had he done a background check on Gabriel and Morty? If he had, he'd probably found nothing at all on Gabriel. But my father had seen to it that Morty and I had documentation that would permit both of us to legally oversee his bank accounts and such after he ascended. If Kevin did a background check on Morty, he'd probably find just as little about him as me. That would, more likely than not, raise a red flag or two. At least now I could prepare some bullshit to feed Kevin to explain my lack of background if it ever came up.

I also looked over Chad's financial statement. Again, as I'd noticed before, it was impossible to tell from the statement itself where the funds came from. I did see, however, that there were multiple five- and six-figure deposits in Chad's account. I guessed those were payments for delivering human cargo. Hardly a month had passed over the last year or so—which was all the statement showed—when he hadn't received at least one payment. Some months showed multiple deposits. Each of those deposits likely represented a human life—someone who had gone missing.

Could I coordinate the timing of those deposits with missing person reports? Maybe. If I could guess who else Chad and his fellow traffickers had abducted, I might be able to discern some patterns. Was there a particular profile that the victims matched? Were there locations where the traffickers frequented when they abducted their victims? It was a lot. I wasn't all that great with Internet searches. I needed some help to sort it out. There was only one person who had both the means to help and the motive to do so. The only question was whether Sienna would be willing to help.

CHAPTER TWENTY-FIVE

"Dogs are not allowed at the coffee shop. Unless you're a service dog."

Cerberus huffed. "A service dog? I don't serve anyone."

I chuckled. "Yeah, I've sort of gathered that."

Cerberus cocked his head as he looked up from his water bowl. "Good thing I'm not just a dog."

"But you *are* a dog." I shrugged. "Sort of."

"Am I?" Cerberus allowed his other two heads to emerge from his body and growled at me thrice.

I chuckled. "Just stay lurking in the shadows. You don't need to worry about me, Cerberus. I know my dad sent you to protect me, but I can handle myself."

Cerberus cackled. "Sure you can, Zoey."

"I'm serious," I protested. "I don't need a canine sidekick. Just keep your distance and do what you're told."

"You think I'm *your* sidekick?" Cerberus snorted. "I think it's the other way around. You don't know what I can do."

I reached down and scratched Cerberus' middle head behind the ears. "You're right. I'm not trying to be a bitch about it."

He smiled. "That's fine. I told you before. I'm not into bitches."

I snorted. "Right. Because you're a gay dog, right?"

"I'm all about the studs!"

I chuckled. "Somehow, we got off track. My point is, all I'm doing today is going to work. You might be pretty helpful in a fight, and you're right; I don't know what you can do. But I'm pretty sure you don't have any more skills than I do when it comes to making triple-shot lattes and cafe mochas."

"And *I* suspect you didn't expect to run into any trouble the last time you went to work, did you?"

I sighed. "Okay. So, you have a point. I never know when trouble might come looking for me."

"Especially now!" Cerberus exclaimed.

I nodded. "All right. I get it. Like I said, just make yourself scarce. The last thing I need is my pet...or whatever you are... making an appearance at Cup-O-Joe's. I'm already struggling enough with my job as it is."

"You won't even know I'm there unless I have to pee. Then... well, you might need to get a mop."

"If you have to pee, you need to go outside."

"You can't housebreak me, Zoey. I'm not a tame hellhound."

I scrunched my eyebrows. "Wait, if you aren't housebroken, where have you been...you know?"

Cerberus grinned. "You might want to add a little extra detergent to your laundry. Just saying."

"You peed in my laundry?"

"And on the side of your couch."

"You didn't!"

"I like the couch. I wanted you to know it was mine."

I narrowed my eyes. "I paid for it!"

"With your dad's money."

"Yeah, but I'm paying him back!"

Cerberus chuffed. "Sure you are."

"I am!" I insisted.

Cerberus snorted. "It's still my couch."

I sighed as I reached for a rag and went to look over my couch. "I don't see any pee on here. What are you even talking about?"

Cerberus ignored me, turned, and walked the opposite way. "You're so gullible. I'm not going to pee on your shit, Zoey. But I could. It's not like there's a good place to go near your apartment."

"There's a small patch of grass on the back side of the building. You can use that."

"What kind of dog do you think I am?" Cerberus asked, sauntering into my bathroom, then using his snout to force the door shut.

I was too curious not to follow him. I placed my ear to the door.

"Are you creeping on me in the bathroom? You need a new boyfriend."

I snorted. "I'm not creeping on you!"

The next thing I knew, I heard piss hitting the toilet water. Then a flush.

A few seconds later, I heard his paw scratching at the door. "Let me out. I didn't think this through."

I laughed. "Not until you wash your paws!"

"Seriously? I didn't even touch myself."

"First, I don't believe you. Second, it doesn't matter! You always wash your hands—I mean, paws—after you use the toilet."

Cerberus growled. A few seconds later, I heard scratching sounds and a thud. "Damn it, Zoey!"

"What?" I asked through the door.

"I can't reach the sink! Come on, just let me out!"

"You can figure it out. The toilet is right next to the sink. If you got up on the pot, you can get to the sink."

Cerberus huffed. "Fine!"

A few seconds later, after a few thumps that I imagined corresponded with Cerberus's attempt to get to the sink, the water started running. Then it stopped.

"Good boy!" I opened the door for him.

Cerberus jumped down from the sink and glared at me.

"Did you use soap?"

"You can't be serious!"

"Use soap. If you're going to use the bathroom, you need to wash up with soap."

"You realize, Zoey, I could just do what I threatened before. I could pee on your couch."

I laughed. "All right. All right. I'll let it slide this time. But next time, use soap."

Cerberus grunted and pushed his way past me. I grabbed my keys and headed out the door. Cerberus followed me close behind. About halfway down the stairs, he disappeared.

"I know you're still here," I called.

Cerberus barked, and I followed the sound to the landing at the bottom of the stairs. He grabbed the hem of my pants with his jaws and pulled.

"Stop it, Cerberus." I pressed the bar to open the door that led from the stairwell to the street.

BANG BANG BANG!

I quickly pulled the door shut again.

"What the hell!"

Cerberus reappeared. "Tried to warn you."

"Cerberus! Next time, *use your words!*"

Cerberus narrowed his eyes. "Noted."

"You knew they were out there?" I asked.

"I detected the scent of the gunpowder."

"In their bullets? That's…" I shook my head. Not relevant. "Never mind. We need a plan. There's only one way in and out of this apartment complex."

"I'm not the only one who can go invisible, Zoey. You stole one of your dad's cloaks, right?"

I smiled. "Yes. But they'll still see the door open. Even invisible, if they start shooting the moment the door cracks open, there's a good chance they'll still shoot us."

"Not if they can't see you," Cerberus pointed out.

"These aren't professional assassins," I countered. "More like hired guns. Probably from a local gang. There's no saying how they'll react."

"How do you know that?" Cerberus asked.

I shook my head. "I don't. But think about it. The criminal syndicate behind the trafficking works through subterfuge. They can be deadly, but if they were going to off someone, I doubt they'd shoot them in the open in broad daylight."

"Doesn't this place have roof access?" Cerberus asked.

I nodded. "With my cloak on—"

"Your dad's cloak, you mean," Cerberus cut in.

I rolled my eyes. "Yes. With my *dad's* cloak on, I should be able to get to the roof and take a look at where they are so I know what we're dealing with."

"If they don't, just barge right through the doors to come after you."

I ran up the stairs with Cerberus right behind me. "That's brilliant, Cerberus."

"What is?"

"Lure them inside!"

The hellhound snorted. "I meant it as a warning, not a tactic. They could come up after you at any time."

I nodded. "I'll be ready when they do. Now that they know I know they're out there, they won't expect me to go out the front door again. They'll make their move fast, suspecting I'm going to call the cops."

"We should still go to the roof," Cerberus suggested. "Some of them might come in for you. But if I was in their position, I'd keep a gunman or two outside waiting in case you tried to run."

"Right. Makes sense. We need to hurry. Before they come in after me."

I raced into my apartment and threw on my father's cloak. I pulled the hood over my head and disappeared. Cerberus also made himself invisible. As I left the apartment, I saw two men, pistols in hand, were making their way up the stairs.

I had an advantage being at the top of the stairs. They couldn't see me. I could take one of them down without a problem. There was no telling how the second guy would react.

I didn't want to kill anyone, even though these men were trying to kill me. They weren't exactly innocent. I'd be justified in killing them, but I didn't want to bring any Reapers to the scene. Still, if I took out his legs, he couldn't get up the stairs.

I touched the sigil on my wrist and threw my staff at the first gangster, catching him in his right thigh. The man screamed and dropped to the floor. I touched my sigil again and reformed my staff in my hand.

The remaining man raised his gun. I rolled out of the way as he started firing randomly into the top of the stairwell. He couldn't see me. That didn't mean he wouldn't see my footsteps or clouds of dust I might kick up if I moved too quickly.

"I can take them out," Cerberus offered.

"Take them out, as in outside?"

Cerberus growled. "No, I can get rid of them."

I didn't have the chance to ask Cerberus what he meant. The second gangster was already at the top of the stairs. I released my staff and swept my leg to kick his legs out from under him. I stomped on his wrist, forcing him to let go of his gun.

"What the fuck!" he screamed, panicked by the fact he was getting his ass handed to him by an invisible woman. Then, I summoned my staff and slammed it into the ground just beside his face.

I lowered my hood as Cerberus took off down the stairs, growling as he collided with the guy I'd speared. Screaming and growling combined to suggest that it wasn't going so well for Gangster Number One.

"Who sent you?" I demanded.

"I don't know!" the man exclaimed.

"Someone wants me dead. I want a name."

His lips quivered. "We didn't see his face! He only comes at night. He doesn't have a name!"

I snorted. "No name? Everyone has a name."

"I mean, we don't know his name. He has jobs. He pays us well. That's it. I swear it!"

"How many guys do you have waiting for me outside?"

"No one! It's just us two!"

I took my staff and drove it down between the man's legs, narrowly missing his...precious parts. "This would be a good time to tell the truth. Or, next time, I won't miss."

"Holy shit! Okay! You crazy bitch! There are two more. Please! Not my nuts!"

I smirked. "This guy who hired you. Say I wanted to have a word with him myself. How would I find him?"

"No one finds him. He finds you!"

"Tsk. Tsk. Tsk." I grazed the inside of the man's thighs with the pointed end of my staff. "I thought you wanted to keep your balls?"

"It's the truth! I swear it!"

I didn't believe him. "But surely, you'd have to report back that you finished the job. I doubt this man pays you in advance."

"When we finish a job, he finds out on his own somehow. I don't know. He probably pays someone else to double-check our work. All I know is when we've finished a job, the money shows up at the door."

"Someone has to deliver your payment."

"Yes. Someone. But we never see him. We're told not to look. He knocks three times. We wait thirty seconds, grab our payment, and close the door."

"What door? Where does he meet you?"

"Please! I have children at home. I'm just trying to provide for my family, that's it!"

I sighed. "There are better ways to make a living for your family than killing people."

"You don't understand. I have a job. But it's not enough. I have five kids. I can barely put food on the table and keep a roof over our heads. He pays me enough for one hit to double my year's wages. I do this so my children won't have to go without."

The man was crying like a baby. I winced a little as I listened to him. He was desperate.

"If you murder someone and go to prison, who will provide for your children, then?"

"Look, I know it's a risk. But I don't have a choice. The guy who hires us isn't the sort of person you tell no. If I didn't do the job, it would be my ass. He'd kill me."

I scratched my head. Damn it if I didn't feel bad for this guy. He was just a pawn, tempted by large payouts and terrified under threat of his life to do the bidding of whoever ran the trafficking syndicate.

"What happens if you fail the job?" I asked.

"You disappear," he explained. "Along with your whole family. It's happened to others. I don't have a choice. I have to kill you!"

I snorted. "Well, I can't let you do that. Here's what's going to happen. You get up, go outside, tell your friends the job was done."

"He'll know if we failed! I don't know how, but he will!"

I shook my head. "So be it. Say you fail. How long before the boss comes for you?"

"Tonight. He'll kill my whole family and me. Always at night."

I nodded. "Then this is what we're going to do. You're going to leave here as if you'd succeeded. Your friends don't need to know anything different. You're going to give me your address. I want these guys out of the picture. I won't allow them to hurt your family."

The man, tears flowing, shook his head. "You're just a woman. One woman. You can't stop them!"

I narrowed my eyes. "If you haven't noticed, I can take care of myself."

"You don't understand! They're ruthless. They don't care. They'll kill you and my family!"

"I told you, I won't let that happen," I assured him. "The way I see it, you have two options. You can trust me and give me a chance to take these guys down. Then, you'll be free. You might lose an income source, but at least you won't have to kill anyone else. Or I can deal with you now and get what I need from the guys outside."

"But I have killed. If you know where I live…"

I sighed. "I'm not concerned with that. I won't turn you over to the cops if that's what you're afraid of."

"You're already working with them. You were talking to that cop earlier in his car."

"You were watching me?"

"We see everything, Zoey."

I grunted. The three guys that Kevin had pursued when they tried to get into my apartment the night before. "I don't owe that cop a thing. He and I aren't working together."

"I don't believe you!"

"That doesn't matter!" I shouted. "I don't give a shit if you believe me or not. Look, you can let me help you by helping me take out these pricks, or you can leave and wait for them to do whatever the hell they're going to do with you and your family tonight. The way I see it, if you cooperate with me, you stand a better chance to survive than if you reject my offer. What choice do you have?"

"Even if you succeed, they'll just send more. You don't even understand how powerful these people are."

"If these people are so dangerous, why don't they kill me themselves? Why use you to do their dirty work?"

"Because the cops are watching you! They're trying to cover their asses. If someone kills you, people will notice. If I go missing, people will assume some gang did us in. The cops don't investigate cases like ours like they would yours."

I snorted. "Why not? A whole family goes missing, and the cops turn a blind eye to it?"

"No offense. You're a young white woman. It's different when someone who looks like you gets killed or goes missing."

I took a deep breath. "That's not right."

"It isn't. But that's the way the world works. It's just how it is. I have a record. If something happens to me, everyone will think I brought it on myself. That I got what was coming to me."

I bit my lip. "Well, to be fair, you're doing hits for bad people. That behavior does have consequences."

"But I'm not doing this by choice!" he countered. "I already told you. Look, if I don't come out soon, the others are going to come in looking for me."

"Then what will it be?" I asked. "Will you let me help you?"

The man pressed his lips together. "The name's Ronald Chaffin. My address is in the phone book."

I nodded and stepped off of the man. I grabbed his gun and unloaded the bullets, then handed it back to him as he returned to his feet. "You'd best get going, then."

Ronald nodded. Then he turned and looked at me before he headed down the stairs. "Why are you helping me, if you don't mind me asking? I came here to kill you."

I pressed my lips together. "I'm not going to lie to you. I don't care what happens to you, Ronald. But I do care about your family, and the people who hired you to do this have to be stopped."

Ronald nodded and hurried down the stairs. I scratched my

head. What had happened to the first gangster, the one Cerberus attacked?

"Well, that went well," Cerberus appeared beside me and belched.

"Excuse you!" I exclaimed. "What did you do with that other guy?"

Cerberus licked his lips. "I ate him."

"You what? How the hell did you do that?"

The dog grew until he filled the hallway. I gasped. "Holy shit, Cerberus!"

"Finished him in a single bite."

I sighed. "Seriously? And did a Reaper show up to…"

"Nope. I ate him with my other head. The Hades head."

"And that did what to his soul?"

Cerberus returned to normal size. "Go to Hell. Go directly to Hell. Do not pass Go. The boatman does not collect a hundred dollars."

"So, if you eat someone with your Hades head, their soul goes there?" I asked. "What if you eat them with your other head?"

Cerberus shrugged. "I'm not in the habit of eating good people. But if I did, well, I suppose they'd go to Olympus. Eat them with my Earth head and they'd die here. A Reaper would show up to collect the soul."

I chuckled. "Well, that's good to know. Poor guy. Didn't stand a chance, did he?"

Cerberus cackled. "Nope!"

"Well, you shouldn't eat people, Cerberus. Even bad people. Bad doggy!"

Cerberus stared at me blankly. "Whatever."

He sauntered back into my apartment.

CHAPTER TWENTY-SIX

I threw the hood of my cloak over my head and went to the roof, just to be sure that the other men had left. It struck me that since I'd let Ronald go free, well, he very well might just tell the others to wait for me to leave so he could finish his job. After all, he was less than convinced that I'd carry out my plan to protect his family.

I wasn't lying to the guy. This was the best chance I'd had so far to get to the syndicate. Not to mention, now that I knew what Cerberus could do, I was even more confident than before I could handle these bad guys without a problem.

Not that I was entirely comfortable feeding bad guys to my dog. Don't get me wrong, most of them probably had it coming to them. But Ronald had shown me that sometimes men caught up in that kind of life aren't necessarily evil. In his case, at some point, he'd made a bad choice. Now, he was forced to keep killing people to protect his family and keep food on the table. Yes, it was wrong. But when I'd looked into Ronald's eyes, I could tell he wasn't an evil man. He was desperate.

I wasn't keen on the whole idea that with Cerberus, I could just send people's souls straight to Hades. I'd complained before about how arbitrary the fates, the decisions of the gods, seemed to be. It wasn't my place to decide who went to heaven or hell.

On the bright side, now that Cerberus had eaten an entire person, I could save money on barbecue. If Cerberus was going to eat anyone in the future, I'd have to make sure he used his earth-bound head to do it. It would mean a Reaper would show, but at least it would take the question of the consumed person's eternal destiny out of my hands. Or, more accurately, out of Cerberus' jaws.

I checked my phone and sighed. I was already five minutes late for work. Joe was pretty easy-going and understanding, especially given everything that had happened lately, but I was pressing my luck. His patience would only go so far. He was trying to run a business, after all.

Since the coast was clear, I dropped my cloak off in my apartment and locked it up. I didn't see Cerberus. He was likely already in stealth mode.

I pulled up next to Sienna's car in the parking garage. I was pleasantly surprised to see she was back at work. I half expected she'd quit or, at the very least, take a few weeks off. Still, it would be nice to see her. Not to mention, my mind was anywhere but on my job. That meant, more likely than not, a lot of spilled coffee in my immediate future.

When I walked in through the front doors of the coffee shop, Sienna smiled at me. I didn't see Joe. I wasn't sure if I was more relieved that he wouldn't know I was late or upset that he left Sienna at the coffee shop alone. My worries were assuaged when I noticed Kevin sitting in one of the booths with a mug of black coffee in front of him as he poured over his files. This wasn't a typical coffee break. He was there for our safety.

I chuckled to myself. His surveillance job hadn't done much to stop the hired assassins from doing their best to take me down earlier in the morning. Of course, I wouldn't tell Kevin about it. I'd given Ronald my word that I wouldn't get the cops involved. If

I told Kevin what had happened, he'd probably arrest Ronald and leave his family to fend for themselves.

I smiled at Kevin as I walked past his booth. I put on my apron, clocked in on the terminal, and approached Sienna.

"How are you doing?" I asked.

Sienna shrugged. "As well as could be expected, I suppose. Still a little rattled, but, you know, I'm doing better. Working is a good distraction. The worst part was parking."

"I bet." I rested a hand on Sienna's shoulder. "For what it's worth. I don't think they'll be coming back soon."

"Well, no. Not after what you did to them."

I smiled, then glanced at Kevin, who was oblivious to our conversation. "What did I do?"

"Oh, yeah. Right. Nothing at all." A half-grin formed at the corner of Sienna's mouth.

I chuckled. "Maybe later we can talk about that when we have a little more privacy."

Sienna nodded, distracted by a customer who walked through the doors. She turned her attention to the young woman who ordered a caramel macchiato with two extra shots.

"You got this?" Sienna asked.

I nodded. "I think so."

It wasn't the most complex drink we made. I handled it without too much trouble and added a dollop of whipped cream to the top before drizzling it with caramel syrup. At least this lady hadn't ordered it nonfat. You'd be surprised how many drinks, chock-full of sugar, customers order nonfat to give themselves the illusion that their drink was low calorie.

Kevin gathered his paperwork and approached the counter. "Could I get another cup to go?"

"Plain coffee?" I asked.

"I'm a purist," Kevin replied. "Nothing beats a good strong cup of coffee, and you have the best roast in town."

I smiled. "Well, I'm sure Joe would appreciate hearing that. He roasts all the beans himself."

Kevin nodded. "I'll be back around the end of your shift. Just to make sure nothing happens in the parking garage."

"We'll be fine, Kevin. Thanks, though."

Kevin nodded. "Let me know if anything strange happens."

I bit the inside of my cheek. "Are you expecting anything?"

Kevin sighed. "I don't know. The more I dig into this organization, the deeper the rabbit hole goes. The problem is until I hit the bottom of the hole, I'm pretty much in freefall. I can't pinpoint anything definite, but I can say that whatever this is, it's big. They might be scaling back their operations temporarily, just until things cool off, but they'll be back. I'm sure of it."

"Well." I smiled. "On the bright side, I guess that means we'll be seeing a lot of each other for a while."

Kevin grinned. "Yeah, I suppose we will."

I wiggled my fingers at him. "See you soon!"

Kevin turned to leave. Then he paused and turned back. "Quick question. I just received a notice that someone called in shots fired in your neighborhood about half an hour ago."

I raised my eyebrows. "Really? Not surprised. I mean, it happens from time to time in the city."

Kevin nodded. "Did you hear or see anything?"

I shook my head. "I must've missed it."

"Really?" Kevin asked. "Because you were late. Knowing the time it takes you to drive from your apartment here, you would have been home when it happened."

I shook my head. "I had errands to run this morning. I just got a new dog. I had to get a few things."

Kevin pressed his lips together. "All right. Well, be careful. It was probably gang-related. But I can't rule anything out."

"I appreciate the concern," I told him. "Enjoy your coffee."

Once Kevin was out the door, Sienna stepped up beside me.

"You think they'll track them down? The people those guys were working for, I mean."

I shook my head. "These are professional criminals. They know how to cover their tracks. Unfortunately, the cops are limited. They can only do so much until the evidence is overwhelming enough that they can act, get a warrant, or whatever."

Sienna sighed. "There has to be more that can be done. I mean, if they could identify the three men who took me, you'd think they'd be able to figure out who they were working for."

I bit my lip. "I've been looking into this. If the cops can't do it, I'm going to take them down myself."

"Zoey, are you sure that's a good idea?"

I nodded. "The longer it takes the cops to figure this out, the more people they could take. I don't know about you, but I'm not okay with that. These assholes need to be stopped. I hesitate to ask, but I could use your help, Sienna."

"What are you suggesting?"

"I'm not great with computers," I told her. "Don't tell Kevin, but I managed to get a copy of the financial records the cops pulled on that Chad guy."

"How in the world did you get that?" Sienna asked.

I laughed. "I'm sneaky. And maybe I've been flirting with the detective."

"A little?" Sienna laughed. "Seriously, the sexual tension between you two is so thick I don't think I could cut through it with a chain saw."

I giggled. "Yeah, there's that. I have a list of sizable deposits made to Chad's account and the dates they were made. Do you think you could get on the computer and search through missing person reports? I want to see if we can correlate any of them with the deposits Chad made. If we can do that, if we can identify some of their other possible victims, maybe we'll be able to pick up on some patterns."

Sienna smiled. "Consider it done. I'll use Joe's computer in the back if you don't mind watching the counter."

"You know his password?" I asked, raising one eyebrow.

Sienna laughed. "His password is 'coffee.'"

I snorted. "How predictable is that?"

"I figured it out my third try," Sienna continued. "You know, after trying 'password' and '1234.'"

"Why were you trying to get into his computer, anyway?" I asked.

Sienna grinned. "What can I say? I was bored, and there was this chick he hired a while back with no qualifications. He made me train her. How annoying is that?"

I laughed. "Yeah, sorry about that. I know I suck at this."

Sienna shook her head. "You realize he had three other applicants? One of them used to work for Starbucks. Still, he hired you, Zoey. Why do you think that is?"

I shrugged. "I don't know. But he hired me on the spot. Maybe he got a vibe."

"Yeah." Sienna rolled her eyes. "If the vibe is that you have a great ass."

"He didn't hire me for my butt, Sienna."

"Didn't he? It's obvious that he likes you, Zoey."

"Joe? No way! And *ew*! He's, like, thirty, right?"

"He's not that much older than you, Zoey. I don't think he's any older than that detective. Besides, you are his type."

"He has a type?"

Sienna nodded. "Dark hair. Athletic body. Yeah, you look a lot like his ex."

I sighed. "Well, isn't that great? He hired me because he's into me? Not cool."

"He's a good guy," Sienna protested. "You could do worse."

"He's too good." I shook my head. "That's the problem. I just broke up with a good guy. Even so, how good could he be if he hired me over someone more qualified because he thought I was cute?"

Sienna shrugged. "It's a barista job, Zoey. It's not like he hired you to run a Fortune 500 company. Who knows, maybe I'm wrong."

I shrugged. "Maybe he hired me because he didn't want to bring someone in who already had ideas about how a coffee shop should be run. I was, if nothing else, a blank slate he could see trained to do the job the way he wants."

"Maybe," Sienna agreed doubtfully. "You're probably right. Forget I said anything. You have those dates when the deposits were made?"

I pulled out my phone and sent Sienna the financial records I'd taken from Kevin. "It's on your phone."

Sienna grinned. "Give me ten minutes. And if there are any crazy drink orders you can't handle, give me a shout."

CHAPTER TWENTY-SEVEN

Sienna returned from the back room with a few sheets of paper in her hand.

"You found something, I take it?" I asked.

Sienna nodded and wiped off the counter before setting the papers down. "These dates all correlate with the deposits in Chad's account. If we're right, and these were the people Chad and his team abducted, good luck finding a pattern."

I nodded and perused the missing person reports. She was right. I'd assumed young women were the primary target, given the fact that Sienna was targeted. Sienna found four names of people who were reported missing around the time the deposits were made into Chad's account. All of the missing person reports were made one or two days ahead of when Chad received funds. That made sense. He'd only get paid *after* he delivered his victims.

The first one I saw fit the profile: an attractive dark-haired woman in her early twenties.

The next print-out featured a male in his middle-thirties. From the description and image, he was a rather stout fellow. Not the sort you'd expect to be trafficked. That is, not for the same kind of services we'd presumed to this point the young women were being trafficked into. Physical labor, perhaps?'

That was possible. I knew very little about human trafficking. As pervasive a problem as it is in the United States, it receives shockingly little attention from major media outlets. Still, I knew that human trafficking led to a variety of ends. Sometimes the victims were forced into sexual servitude. Other victims were enslaved to perform manual labor.

That theory didn't hold water with the next one I located—an elderly Black woman, frail in appearance, previously residing in a nursing home. I bit my lip. There was no guarantee that these people were abducted by Chad simply because the dates correlated. More likely, this particular woman had wandered away from the facility where she lived. That sort of thing happens. We trained at the academy how to track down wandering souls who'd suffered from dementia. Usually, they gravitated toward places and people who had significance at an earlier time in their lives. Still, the fact that this woman hadn't been found yet and it had been a month or so since she was reported missing raised a few questions.

The last victim, who had gone missing just a week before Sienna was attacked, was a woman who'd last been seen training her clients at a local gym. She was a prime candidate for traffickers.

I scratched the back of my head. "I don't get it. I mean, there's a chance some of these people went missing for other reasons, and we just don't have any reports on the victims who correlated with other deposits."

"That's true," Sienna agreed. "There were several deposits that didn't correlate with any local missing person reports. I could expand my search, I suppose."

I shook my head. "There's a reason these criminals target people near the Interstate. Some of them might be out-of-state travelers. There'd be no way to guess where their victims came from or where they were going. You could do a nationwide search, but I'm guessing if you did, it would be even more likely that the people we found went missing for other reasons."

"I wish there was something more we could go on," Sienna mused.

I shook my head. "That doesn't mean this wasn't worthwhile. If these four were abducted by the traffickers, it means the criminal enterprise has a wide variety of buyers. That means more people are involved than if there was only a single buyer who collected victims for one purpose. Not to mention, we can do a little more digging into these particular cases and try to find out if there were any witnesses. Chad scouted you for a while before he made a move. It's likely that if these people were abducted by him, others would recognize him."

Sienna nodded. "Yeah, but we'd need a photo of him."

I scrolled through my phone and showed it to Sienna. "I copied a lot of the detective's files. He had a mugshot from Chad that was taken several years earlier on a DUI arrest."

"That's fantastic!" Sienna exclaimed. "Should we go after work?"

I shook my head. "Not tonight. I have something else I have to take care of. A couple of things, actually. My grandmother is on her deathbed, and I'd like to see her again tonight. Then, I have other errands. Maybe tomorrow after our shift, we can try to track down some families or co-workers who were associated with the missing persons."

Sienna nodded. "I'm sorry to hear about your grandmother."

I smiled. "I appreciate that."

"It's a slow day. If you'd like to take off to go spend the day with her, I can probably handle it," Sienna offered.

I shook my head. "I'm not leaving you here alone, Sienna. I don't think that's safe."

Sienna nodded. "Thanks, Zoey."

"No, thank you for helping. I don't think I could have found those names on my own. I suck with Google."

Sienna laughed, running her fingers through her hair. "I should be the one thanking you. You saved me! Twice!"

CHAPTER TWENTY-EIGHT

I looked up Ronald's phone number and address before I got off work at five o'clock. I needed to get to Ronald's before dark. We had a phone book at Cup-O-Joe's. I wasn't sure where else I could get a phone book. A museum, perhaps? I don't think I'd seen one since I arrived on Earth apart from the one stashed under the counter at the coffee shop. I ripped the page out of the phonebook. I doubted anyone would miss it.

Using it was even more intuitive than the Internet. It was pretty easy to figure out right away that people's names were arranged alphabetically by surname. Since Ronnie's last name started with a "c," his name and address were toward the front of the book. Based on what my phone's maps app told me, Ronald lived about twenty minutes from my apartment. Given the time of the evening, I had to take traffic into account.

I wanted to check in on Rose first. I didn't have much time left with her, and since I had a few hours before dark, I figured catching up with her was the best use of my time. Besides, I felt bad for her. She was there, dying, with no one except for Helen, her hospice nurse who visited intermittently, to keep her company.

Of course, there were hospice facilities Rose could go to. I knew all about those. It was a standard part of my Reaper education. It was one of the most common venues for reapings. Still, a lot of people like Rose chose to die at home even if it meant dying alone.

I pulled up next to Rose's house. Helen wasn't there. At least, her car wasn't parked outside. Would Rose be able to answer the door? I wasn't sure. I rang the doorbell.

I waited about a minute, then rang it again. Still nothing.

I knocked three times.

No answer.

I sighed. Rose's bedroom had a window that faced the back of the house. Maybe I could get her attention. She could let me know where a spare key might be hiding.

I hopped the chain-link fence that surrounded Rose's backyard. I tapped on Rose's back window and cupped my hands around my eyes to look inside.

Rose's bed was empty.

My stomach sank. Had they taken her to a hospice facility? Maybe she was in the hospital. She wasn't supposed to die for four or five more days.

Then, I felt a chilly hand on my shoulder.

I turned and my father stood there, pain in his eyes. His hood was off his head, hanging down his back. "Dad? No, Dad! If you're here, that means..."

"Her expiration date was expedited," my father explained. "I'm sorry, Zoey."

I clenched my fists. "Expedited? Why the hell would that happen? You knew when she was supposed to die. You didn't come to see her, or..."

"No, Zoey. I didn't see her until it was her time."

"If you didn't... Wait, no! This is my fault. I'm your daughter. Somehow, when I visited, it must've broken your bargain with Athena!"

My father shook his head. "It wasn't your fault, Zoey."

"You can't know that!" I protested. "I mean, you said it yourself. It was a risk. If she recognized me, and she did…"

"It was a risk that she would be less likely to want to move on so soon after meeting her granddaughter," my father agreed. "But it wasn't your presence that caused this."

I didn't understand. "Then why? What happened? Surely me showing up had something to do with it?"

My father sighed. "It was your mother, Zoey."

I furrowed my brow and cocked my head. "My mom? Are you sure?"

My father nodded. "She was here at her mother's side when she died. After all these years, she came back."

"Where is she?" I asked. "Did you talk to her?"

My father shook his head. "I didn't remove my cloak, Zoey. But your mother knew I was there. She looked past me, through the room, as if she knew I must've been there. She nodded. But I could see the pain in her face. She didn't want to see me, Zoey."

"You don't know that, Dad! You could have told her about me. You could have let her know I was looking for her…"

"She already knew that," my father assured me. "Rose told her when she first arrived. I gave her as much time as I could allow before harvesting her soul. But as you know, Zoey, a Reaper has a very narrow window of opportunity to act before the soul misses its scheduled time with the boatman."

I shook my head. "You must've seen *something*. You did your reconnaissance. That's one of the Rs. What was she driving? What direction did she go when she left? Did she say anything to Rose that revealed where she lived?"

"Zoey, I didn't look into any of that. I was able to give your mother and Rose little more than a couple of minutes. I had to be ready to harvest her soul."

I snorted. "If you were so eager to take Rose's soul back to the

River Styx, why are you still here? Shouldn't you be on your way?"

"Morty is delivering her on my behalf."

"Morty? Are you serious?"

"He's been shadowing me. I harvested Rose's soul, then I passed it to Morty's scythe. I expected you would be coming to see her soon. Rose told your mother as much. She said she expected you tonight."

"Then where is she?" I asked. "Where is my mom? If she knew I was coming, surely she'd wait."

My father put his arms around me. "She left, Zoey. I can't say where she went. Perhaps she'll return. You're welcome to wait for her."

I shook my head. "I can't. There's something I have to do. A family that needs my help."

"Very well," my father agreed. "There's no guarantee your mother would return."

"Why the hell wouldn't she if she knew I was coming?" I asked.

"Zoey, I don't know how to say this. But your mother might not want to meet you. Perhaps she isn't ready."

"Isn't ready? Why the hell not? It's been more than twenty years, Dad."

"I understand, Zoey. But it's not that simple. I do not know what's on your mother's mind. But I believe she loves you. She shed a tear when Rose told her you were here. If she's not coming, if she isn't looking for you, it may be that she feels guilty."

I grunted. "That's no fucking excuse, Dad. I don't give a shit about her guilt. I know this wasn't her fault. It was just a shitty situation. She had no reason to feel guilty before. But if she refuses to see me now, when she knows I'm back on Earth, and she knew I'd be coming back here tonight, that's on her."

"There might be reasons," my father countered. "Perhaps she

needs time to prepare, Zoey. She just lost her mother. She came to see her after two decades just to lose her. That's a lot to deal with. Meeting her estranged daughter might be too much for her to handle right now. She knows you're here. She'll know your address."

I snorted. "She'll know my address? How?"

My father smiled. "I once used the same apartment. I'm sure if she's looking for you, that's the first place she'll go."

I unfolded one of my mother's letters from my pocket. "Rose gave me these. A bunch of letters my mom sent her through the years. In a few of the early ones, she mentioned doing what was necessary. Do you have any idea what that meant?"

My father pinched his chin. "I cannot say. It could be anything. Perhaps she just had to do what she had to do to move on without you and your brother, without me... Or..."

"Or what?" I asked.

My father sighed. "That damn Olympian."

"Athena?" I asked.

My father nodded. "She told me when she agreed to extend Rose's life that she had to enter a similar bargain with Josephine. I had petitioned Athena, but Josephine was Rose's blood. Athena needed the consent of Rose's kin to make it happen. I assumed it was going to be a simple exchange. Athena would appear to Josephine, tell her about the bargain I'd proposed for the sake of Rose, secure her consent, and that would be that. But if now we're finding out Josephine never visited Rose all these years, there must've been a reason. It likely had something to do with whatever deal Athena made with her."

"Can you go to Olympus and find out?" I asked. "You had to petition Athena before. Surely you can reach her again."

"The Olympians are far less accessible today than they were even then. In recent years, they've closed the paths I knew to take to access their realm. If you wish to know what Josephine wrote to her mother, you'll have to find her and ask her yourself."

CHAPTER TWENTY-NINE

I couldn't hang around on the slim chance that my mother might show up. If Rose had told her I was coming, and she wanted to see me, she'd have been there waiting. She wouldn't risk missing the chance to be reunited with her long-lost daughter.

At least I had a likely fight coming later that evening. No killing. Whoever got sent after Ronald on account of his failure to kill me might know more about the trafficking syndicate. Hell, for all I knew, the syndicate would hire another Ronald, another mercenary assassin, to do him and his family in. If they failed, and I didn't kill them, they'd be in the same position Ronald was in the next night. In theory, this cycle could repeat dozens of times until the syndicate either killed me or one of us just got tired of the cat and mouse routine.

On the other hand, if the syndicate intended to murder Ronald and his family, then if I caught them, I might be able to make them talk. It would be the biggest break yet in terms of tracking down those truly responsible for the trafficking operation.

I'd already programmed Ronald's address into my phone. First, I needed to swing by my apartment to get my father's

Reaper cloak. Invisibility would come in handy. I needed any advantage I could get.

It was a quick run in and out of my apartment. Cerberus didn't even bother making an appearance. Then, I was back on my bike and taking the quick ride to Ronald's house.

I pulled up at his address. It didn't look like your typical family home. The place was an old mansion, not befitting for a struggling father desperate enough to provide for his family that he had to turn to contract killing to provide. If he was really that hard up, he could sell the house and buy a smaller place.

I rode past the place and parked my bike a few blocks away. I double-checked the address I'd programmed into my phone. I pulled out the folded-up page from the phone book to be certain I didn't mistype the address. This was the right place.

The guy at my apartment wasn't Ronald Chaffin. He was probably just a hired hand. But who *was* Ronald Chaffin? Whoever he was, I imagined he was expecting me. The guy from my apartment who'd tried to kill me had surely reported back. Luring me here must've been a contingency plan.

What they didn't know was that I could disappear.

I pulled my cloak over my head and raised my hood. That was the first R. I had my regalia. This wasn't a reaping, but my training would still come in handy. The second R was "receipt." I had a name. It wasn't who I thought it was, but if there was a Ronald Chaffin at this place, then he was likely connected to the syndicate. I'd also handled the third R, "relocation," by following the GPS guidance on my phone to the given address. The fourth R was often the most crucial to a successful fifth R. Reconnaissance before reaping.

In this case, I couldn't reap, but I could swap the last R for "Ronald." It was convenient that the guy's name fit my alliteration. It wouldn't work in future operations. If I wasn't going to kill or was trying to avoid it, I'd have to think up another R-word for the ultimate goal. Or maybe I'd still use reaping. After all, I was reaping a harvest, the seeds sown of investigation. At least, I hoped I was. I doubted this Ronald guy was in charge of the syndicate, but something connected him one way or another. What rewards I might reap from Ronald were impossible to know.

The benefit of my Reaper cloak was that I didn't have to bother hiding behind bushes or trees to survey the house in question.

"Cerberus?" I whispered. "You here?"

I felt a paw on my shin. "I'm here."

"Can you see me while I'm wearing my cloak?"

"You mean your dad's cloak that you stole?"

His sarcasm was getting old, fast. "We're family. It's not stealing. Not exactly. It doesn't matter. I just didn't realize you'd be able to see me when I put this on."

"I can," Cerberus assured me. "The cloak changes your frequency. In your cloak, you're more like a soul than a human being. I can see souls, so I can see you."

"I'm, like, a ghost?" I asked.

"Something like that," Cerberus agreed. "But you still have your body, so not a ghost. Not exactly."

"But I can see the cloak when I'm not wearing it," I protested.

"The enchantment on the Reaper's cloak engages the frequency of your nature. You aren't fully human, Zoey. You are still your father's daughter. It's the combination of the cloak's magic with your unique constitution that produces this effect. You aren't technically invisible. You're traversing the astral plane, the frequency upon which the dead travel if they wander before they are reaped."

"So, you can see me because you also traverse the astral plane?"

"I can. Just as I can phase in and out of Hades or Olympus when I run, if I so choose, I can go invisible and move through the astral plane."

"Then why can't I see you?"

"Your sight must develop," Cerberus explained. "For now, you're unaccustomed to traversing this plane. It's like you just woke up and your eyes are used to the dark. The bright light blinds you. In time, you'll see everything."

"How long will that take?"

"Hard to say. But your sight will come in sooner than later, I'd imagine. Until then, you can trust I'm here."

I nodded. "All right. Well, do you see anything unusual about this house? They must be expecting me. It has to be a trap. We need to figure out how they're planning to lure me in so we can turn the tables on the bad guys."

"We need to go inside."

"But how do we get in?"

Cerberus huffed. "You're on the astral plane, Zoey. You can walk right through the door. Or through the walls, if that's more convenient."

I bit my lip. "If I can walk through walls, then how am I walking on the ground? Wouldn't I just fall through that, too?"

"Ghosts are not bound by the laws of physics. Neither are you. But still, most ghosts who wander the Earth behave as if they are. They act according to their instincts, their memories of being human. Yes, you could fall through the ground if you wanted to. You could even fly if you wished. But because your experience and memory are as a human, with a body, you will default to behaving according to the constraints of the physical world. If you wish to walk through the walls, you simply need to believe you can."

I chuckled. "This is pretty cool. I didn't realize these cloaks did anything more than making us invisible."

"If you were still a Reaper, you'd learn these things after you reached the tenth level, give or take. Now, you'll have to learn as you go. I can help you with that."

I nodded. "I suppose that's why my dad brought you to stay with me?"

"Your dad originally intended that I'd help you advance to his level after he ascended. Now, I'm here for the reason he told you. I'm here to keep you safe."

"But you can teach me how to do this stuff," I countered. "I need you to teach me everything, Cerberus."

Cerberus snorted. "I can do that, but it will cost you more barbecue."

I chuckled. "That won't be a problem. Come on. Let's do this. We can go into the house from the back. They probably saw me drive past on my bike. They'll be expecting me at the front door. I'm guessing there are multiple assassins waiting for me. If I come at them from behind, I might catch them off guard."

CHAPTER THIRTY

Cerberus and I snuck around the back of the house. While no one could see either of us, if I stepped on fallen leaves or a twig, it still made a noise. A dog in the yard next door started barking.

"Shit," I whispered to Cerberus. "Can he see us?"

"Most likely," Cerberus agreed. "Hold on. I'll hop over there and let it sniff my ass. That should do the trick."

I chuckled. "All right, well, hurry back."

I heard a click. I turned. A man dressed all in black leaned out the back door on the porch of the house. He surveyed the yard. Then he pulled out a flashlight and scanned the yard. They were looking for me. Waiting for me. They'd set a trap and were hoping I'd walk right into it. After all, they didn't give a rat's ass about the hired gangster who lied and told me his name was Ronald. They wanted *me* dead. I was the one who foiled Chad and his partners. I'd freed three of the women they'd abducted. Based on what I'd done to Chad the night before, they knew I was a threat. They were prepared.

The barking stopped from the opposite side of the fence. Cerberus' butt-sniffing favor worked.

The man at the back door turned off his flashlight and went back inside.

"The dog shouldn't be a problem." Cerberus spoke in a hushed voice.

I smirked. "Did you have to return the favor?"

Cerberus grunted. "No comment."

I chuckled. "I don't want to know. Hey, since you have three heads, does that mean…"

Cerberus huffed. "No, I don't have three assholes."

I shrugged. "It was worth asking. It makes sense. Three holes in, three holes out."

"Shut up," Cerberus snapped. "Let's just get this over with. I saw that guy checking out the yard was armed."

I nodded. "All the more reason to take them out from behind. I don't want to kill anyone. If I can knock them out and tie them up, I won't have to."

"I could just eat them."

"No!" I whispered with as much insistence as I could muster without elevating my voice.

"Pfft. Do you have qualms about sending these guys to Hades? These guys are defending human traffickers. They deserve whatever they get."

"Still not our place," I replied. "But that's not the reason. I need to keep some people alive. This isn't the end of the road. I doubt whoever is inside this house runs the syndicate. We need to interrogate them. We knock them out, tie them up, then leave Kevin an anonymous tip once we're done with them."

Cerberus grunted. "But puppy wants a treat!"

"Cerberus! I said no."

"Okay, fine! I'll do my best to restrain myself."

I didn't want to go in through the back door. I guessed that the guy who'd just shown himself was right behind it. There was a small deck at the back of the house. I decided to go up onto the deck and find a place in the wall to walk through. It was a bit of a crap shoot. There was no telling what we'd see once we got through. Still, so long as we didn't walk right into someone, I figured we could always walk back through the wall outside and regroup.

I pressed my hands against the red brick on the side of the house. I pressed. My hands didn't budge. I had to believe I could do it. The only thing preventing me from walking through objects while cloaked in the astral plane was my mind.

They say that faith can move mountains. Who would have thought that it also allowed you to walk through them? Or through walls, at least. Provided you had a Reaper's cloak.

I tried again. If you see it, you'll believe it. That was the theory, anyway. I pictured it in my mind, visualizing my body stepping right through the wall. This time, my hands passed through the brick with no resistance. Then, I took a step. I instinctively took a breath. I imagined it was the same reflex that made you inhale and hold before jumping into water. I stepped through the other side of the wall and then through the kitchen cabinets.

That took me a little off guard. It was one thing to step through a wall. But to walk through a set of fine china wasn't exactly what I'd expected.

I exhaled as my feet hit the tile floor in the mansion's large kitchen. I looked around. The same man who'd looked out the back door was leaning against a wall near the back door.

I looked down as Cerberus pawed my leg. I had to maintain my footing. I didn't know how I could walk across the floor while visualizing myself passing through it, dulling the sound, without falling through the floor. Maybe it would work. Maybe it wouldn't. Now wasn't the time to experiment.

I took slow, deliberate steps through the kitchen. I'd spotted one gunman already. There was another hallway off the kitchen that opened into a dining area. I moved in that direction, trying my best to soften each step.

The floor creaked beneath me. I held my breath and stopped moving. No one seemed to notice. Multiple men were moving around in the house, and old houses tended to make noises anyway. I exhaled and took another careful step.

There were two more gunmen by the front door. They held assault rifles in their hands and were dressed in black. They had vests. Bulletproof, most likely. Would it also be javelin-proof? Hopefully, it wouldn't come to that.

The challenge was going to be to take down these guys without the man in the back of the house noticing.

One of the two men peeked out of the glass windowpane on the front door.

"She coming?" the second man asked.

"I don't see her. Are you sure that was her on the motorcycle?"

"I assumed so. You've seen the photos Chad took. It looked just like her, and the bike was identical to the one she rides."

"If she's here, where the hell is she?"

"It doesn't help that Demarcus fed her some story that made it sound like he lived in the ghetto. She's probably suspicious about our intentions. Maybe she left, realizing it was a setup."

I rolled my eyes. I couldn't believe that I fell for that guy's story. Demarcus. Pleading for the sake of his family. Telling me that he was trying to provide for them, that he was caught up in something bigger than himself. It made sense. But it was crap. These two men were right. Demarcus flubbed when he gave me an address to a house that didn't at all fit the description of a place that someone struggling like he made it sound like would live.

I needed to expand my reconnaissance efforts. I needed to get a full count of everyone in the house: their locations, how well they were armed, everything. So far, I'd found three. That didn't mean there wouldn't be more. I slid past the two men, careful not to make any noise.

There was a padlocked door off the hallway. I could walk

through the door, but given that it was locked, it wasn't a priority. A lock like that was meant to keep people inside the room. If I somehow managed to take down the rest of the assassins in the house, then I'd take a look at what they had locked up behind the door. Based on the stairway above the door, I figured it must lead to a basement.

I made my way up the stairs. They didn't squeak as much as I expected, which was a relief. The upstairs space consisted of a long hallway with a few rooms off of it. All the doors were closed. I made my way down the hall, utilizing the advantage of being in the astral plane to press my face through the doors as I went. I found an unoccupied bathroom and three empty bedrooms.

There was only one more room to check. The last room didn't have any windows. It was hard to see since the only lighting in the house came from the streetlights outside. Unlike the other rooms, this one had furniture—a four-poster bed with a canopy and fancy tassels dangling all around. I stepped into the room. No one was in there. It was strange, though, how fancy the room was. It was clean. The bed had what felt like a velvet comforter.

"How weird is this?" I asked.

"Whoever lives here," Cerberus replied, "probably lives alone. That's why only one bedroom is furnished."

"He has interesting taste. This stuff couldn't be cheap. I'm betting this bed, the chair in the corner, and even the dresser and wardrobe are all antiques."

"At least it looks like we only have three people to deal with."

I nodded. "Don't forget whatever's in that basement. I don't think we're going to find unicorns and teddy bears down there. But first, we need to take out the three inside."

"I'll take the guy in the back. You get the other two."

I bit my lip. "I don't know."

"I won't eat him! I promise! I mean, I won't eat *all* of him. Not his soul, and that's the part that matters."

I nodded. "Nothing that will kill him. The last thing I want is Morty or, worse, Gabriel to show up in the middle of all this."

"Do you think he could live without a leg?" Cerberus asked.

"Not if you ripped it off him."

"But Doggy wants a bone!"

"Behave, and I'll buy you another slab of ribs on the way home."

"It's a plan."

Cerberus and I headed back downstairs. He was going to wait until I made my move, then, when the guy in the back reacted and turned, jump on his back and drag him down. If he had to enlarge himself to do it, so be it.

I snuck up behind the two men guarding the front door. I touched the sigil on my wrist, and the moment my staff appeared, I swung it hard, hitting the first guy in the back of the head.

He fell to the ground as the other guy pivoted and aimed his gun at me. He wasn't fast enough. I swiped it out of his hand with my staff and kicked him in the gut, sending him flying into the front door.

I heard a scream from the back of the house. Then a lot of snarling. The screams turned high-pitched. Poor guy. *Not.*

I kicked away the two guns that each of the men I'd taken down had been holding. The first guy I took down was rolling on the floor, holding the back of his head. I kicked him hard in the face. He stopped rolling. The other guy was already out cold.

The snarling and screaming were still going on in the back. I was tempted to go and see what was happening, but by the sound of it, it wasn't going so well for the human. Still, I didn't know how long these guys would remain unconscious. Probably not for long. I needed to tie them up before I could leave them behind.

I unlaced their boots and used their laces to tie their wrists behind their backs and their ankles together. Then I emptied their guns of ammunition. If they managed to get free, they wouldn't be armed. I patted them down to ensure they didn't have any other weapons.

So far, so good. A loud crash shook the entire house. I hurried to the back to see the back door shattered into splinters. The man that Cerberus was fighting was on his back, unconscious, on the back porch.

Cerberus was about three times his normal size. He glanced at me and licked his chops. "If you can't run with the big dogs, stay on the porch."

I smirked. Then, dragging the last guy back inside, I tied him up with his boot laces just like I'd done to the other two men.

"Ready to check the basement?" I asked.

Cerberus nodded. "You sure you're ready? Whatever they have locked up down there, it might not be pretty."

I nodded. "We should act fast. Before any other bad guys decide to show up and complicate things."

CHAPTER THIRTY-ONE

My hood had fallen back during the fight. I pulled it back over my head and pressed myself through the door.

There wasn't much of a landing before the wooden stairs leading down into the basement. The moisture in the air was palpable. The place reeked of mildew and death. The stairs creaked and cracked with every step.

I could only hope that the smell wasn't on account of any human bodies. I wasn't metaphorically holding my breath. Literally speaking, I was doing my best not to breathe in the stench. The smell intensified as Cerberus and I made our way down the stairs. Cerberus was back to his normal size.

It was dark. My staff, when summoned, emanated a subtle glow. It also would give away my location if anyone happened to be lurking in the darkness. Still, if anyone was in the basement waiting for us, chances were they knew I was there. The sound the steps made was too loud to hide even with careful steps. Besides, Cerberus blasting through the door was so loud there wasn't any point trying to be discreet now.

My staff didn't give me enough light to survey the basement. I reached into my back pocket and retrieved my phone. With a swipe of my thumb, I turned on the flashlight.

Cages lined the walls. Most of them were empty. One of them had somebody inside. I quickly checked the rest of the room. I didn't see anyone, but there was a small wall dividing the basement into two. I couldn't say for certain what might be on the other side.

I approached the cage that contained the body. Her body was covered in blood. Was she dead or alive? The smell wasn't coming from her. It didn't seem any stronger near her than it was away. I tapped my staff on the cage. The woman slowly turned her face toward me. Her eyes were swollen shut. Still, I recognized her. She was one of the missing people that Sienna had found on the Internet. The most recent missing person on the list; the female personal trainer who'd gone missing a few days before they abducted Sienna.

"We have to get you out of here." I pulled off my hood and tugged on the padlock on the cage.

"Please... Help me." The woman's voice was barely audible. "Before he comes back."

"Before who comes back?" I asked.

The woman's eyes widened. She struggled to raise her hand to point behind me. I turned and shined my light in the direction the woman was pointing.

A man stood there. He was wearing a black three-piece suit and a bowtie. His skin was white, but given my limited lighting, I couldn't tell how pale he was. His eyes were dark. I quickly jumped to my feet and gripped my staff.

"Now, now, Zoey. There's no need for that." The man raised his hand. He had an accent. I wasn't great with human accents. My experience was limited. Still, it was clear that he wasn't a native-born American. Russian, perhaps. Maybe Eastern European.

I grunted. "Your other men are down. It's you and me. I'm not in the mood for conversation."

The man chuckled. "You remind me of your mother."

"My mom?" I asked. "What do you know about my mom?"

The man licked his fingers and slicked back the sides of his black hair. "I'll just say, she and I have had our run-ins before. She's a wily one, that Josephine. She's eliminated many of my associates, my progeny."

I narrowed my eyes. "You're Ronald Chaffin?"

The man raised his hand to his mouth and laughed. "It's an alias I've used, yes."

"Then who are you?" I asked.

The man shook his head. "I've been known by many names, Zoey. You may call me Ronald if you like. Most know me by the name of Vlad."

"Are you the one responsible for abducting all these people?"

"Am I responsible? Well, I suppose you could say I am. Though, I'm not the only one, my dear."

"I'm not your dear," I snapped.

The man smiled widely. I gasped as the light from my phone reflected off his teeth. They weren't normal, human teeth. They were pointed. He had fangs.

"What the hell are you?" I asked.

"I could ask you the same," Vlad countered. "It's remarkable how much you resemble your mother. She was your age the first time we met. Your hair is darker, and there's something else, something different about you."

"We aren't talking about me," I replied. "I'm the one with the weapon. I'm in charge here."

Vlad smiled again. "Why don't you step a little closer. We'll see who is in charge."

I shook my head. "I'm not an idiot. I'll stay right here, thank you very much."

"Suit yourself." Vlad lunged at me. He moved faster than any human should.

Cerberus emerged from the astral plane and jumped on Vlad, pushing him back.

Vlad backhanded Cerberus, sending him flying across the room. The dog crashed into the wall.

"Cerberus!" I shouted.

The hellhound whimpered as he tried to get back on his feet. I took my staff in both hands and went after Vlad.

When I did, the staff glowed red, and a blade emerged on the end. It turned into a scythe with red magic, almost like flames, coursing through it.

I wasn't about to question it, but seeing the scythe gave me a half-second's pause. I swiped the blade at Vlad, but he stepped out of the way.

Damn, he was fast.

My scythe gave me enough light to see everything. Vlad was halfway up the stairs. I took off after him. He looked at me and winked before disappearing in a blur. When he left my sight, the blade on my staff disappeared. It returned to its normal shape.

"What the hell?" I asked.

Cerberus had returned to his feet and wobbled a little as he made his way back toward me. "It seems you've discovered your truth."

"What is that?" I asked. "I thought I wasn't a Reaper. I didn't have a scythe. How did I…"

"Vlad is a vampire," Cerberus explained. "Perhaps you can't reap human souls, but he's not human. You *are* a Reaper, Zoey. You can harvest vampire souls."

CHAPTER THIRTY-TWO

It took a few attempts. Eventually, I managed to break the lock off of the cage with my staff...or was it a scythe after all? My blade only appeared when I was reaping...*vampires*? I'd never heard of anything like that. I don't just mean vampires. Of course I'd heard of vampires. I didn't know they were real, but I *had* heard of vampires. What I'd never heard of was a vampire *Reaper.*

I couldn't call Kevin. He thought he was investigating a human trafficking organization. If I called him now, I'd not only raise more suspicions in terms of my involvement in everything, but I would send his investigation down the trail of a vampire. There was a reason, I suspected, that Vlad and perhaps other vampires were disguising their hunts, their feeds, under the guise of a human trafficking criminal operation. If people went missing, there'd be human intermediaries that would draw most of the attention from local authorities.

The woman was barely conscious. I think she knew I'd saved her, but she was delirious, mumbling nonsense. Her neck, her wrists, and who knows what other parts of her body were riddled with double puncture wounds. These were vampire bites. Would the doctors realize what they were looking at? Not likely.

But I didn't expect I'd find out. I couldn't call 911 on my phone. They'd be able to track it. Instead, I needed to take the victim to someone's house. A neighbor, perhaps, would find her. I could ring the doorbell and run. Seeing someone in her condition, desperate for help, they'd call her an ambulance. I could watch from a distance to be sure.

I hauled her up the stairs, which wasn't easy, not being a particularly large woman myself. When we reached the top, I was shocked to find that the three men I'd tied up were gone.

Had Vlad freed them on his way out? Why would he do that? He'd been in a hurry to leave once he discovered what I could do. Why would he bother to rescue a few hired humans? Unless those guys had regained consciousness. I doubted he'd risk the chance that I'd catch up to him by dragging them out of the house.

"What do you think happened?" I asked.

Cerberus huffed. "Beats me. It makes no sense."

Just then, I heard a car door slam. I opened the front door of the house just in time to see a large, white windowless van pull away from the front of the house. The vehicle hadn't been there when I'd arrived at the mansion. I doubted it was Vlad driving. Though, I suppose, if a vampire drove anything, it would make sense to have a windowless van. Presuming, of course, that vampires couldn't endure sunlight.

From the handful of vampire television shows and movies I'd seen, that was one universal rule. It seemed that every vampire flick had a different take. Sometimes you could kill a vampire with a stake. In other shows, if you removed the stake, the vampire revived. Sometimes they could be harmed by garlic, holy water, or even the sight of a crucifix. Other vampires weren't affected by those things at all. I suppose the point is that I didn't know what the hell I was dealing with.

Whoever it was in that van, I expected that they'd taken the men from inside with them. Probably other members of the shadow criminal syndicate that were working under the auspices of Vlad and other vampires.

That meant not only had Vlad gotten away. So had the other bad guys. Still, that didn't matter. The young woman I'd saved mattered more than any of that.

Stopping the bad guys was secondary. I had to get this woman some help.

My biceps were burning as I carried the woman down the sidewalk.

Cerberus, now visible and at his normal size, ran out into the street and started barking at an oncoming car.

"Cerberus! What are you doing?"

The car slammed on its breaks. I stumbled out into the road, still holding the woman.

The man in the car jumped out. He was wearing hospital scrubs. What were the chances? Better than you'd think. We were only a few blocks from Research Medical Center. "I'm a doctor. Does she need help?"

"Oh, thank God!" I exclaimed. "Yes, please. I found her like this a few blocks away. I think she was beaten up by someone."

The doctor helped me lower the woman onto a patch of grass. He checked her vital signs. "She's alive, but her pulse is weak. We need to get her to the hospital."

"Can you call an ambulance?" I asked.

"I'm a resident in the Emergency Room," he explained. "I was just heading there for my shift. It will be faster if I take her myself."

I nodded and took a step back. Cerberus pawed at my leg. I took the hint. It was our chance to leave. I didn't want to go. I wanted to see that this woman made it safely to the hospital. I wanted to sit at her side, hold her hand, and make sure she was okay. But that wasn't my place, and it was risky. She was a missing person. Once the hospital realized that, the police would get involved. That would mean that I would be associated with another case involving what they *thought* was a trafficking operation.

I took off running in the opposite direction.

"Hey!" the doctor shouted. "Wait!"

I ignored him. I made it back to my bike, Cerberus went invisible or, technically, phased into the astral plane. I fired up my bike and took off down the road, the opposite direction from the doctor, the woman I'd saved, and the house that was supposed to belong to someone named Ronald Chaffin.

CHAPTER THIRTY-THREE

I had more questions now than I'd had before. Not just regarding vampires, their nature, or what happened to the men from the house. Vlad had wanted me dead. He also knew who I was, and apparently, he knew my mother. Somehow, he'd put two and two together. Was my mom a vampire slayer? Vlad had said she'd eliminated some of his progeny, which, for lack of any better guesses, I presumed meant other vampires that Vlad had turned.

I planned to ask my dad. I didn't know if he'd know anything. He'd never mentioned vampires, not to mention vampire Reapers. Still, if anyone knew anything, it would be him. I hurried home, parked my bike, and ran up the stairs to my apartment.

I unlocked the door and pressed it open.

A wall of odor struck me. It smelled like an Italian Restaurant. The cloves of garlic dangling from the door frame, the light fixtures, and littered around the floor of the place told me why.

The reason for it was also obvious. A young man with a pale complexion was bound in chains to one of my kitchen chairs.

"It's a vampire. I can smell it."

"You can seriously smell a vampire through all this garlic?" I asked.

Cerberus snorted. "I didn't know the scent until we encountered Vlad. When I tried to go after him, I caught his scent. It's unique. This guy smells the same way."

I stepped closer to the vampire. I hadn't ever seen his face. He looked young, maybe nineteen or twenty. When it came to vampires, though, I imagined looks might be deceiving. In the movies, vampires live for centuries. I had no clue if that accorded with reality, but I couldn't rule it out either. At least I knew that garlic was a thing. What it was doing to the vampire, specifically, I couldn't say.

A high-pitched ring started me. I was already creeped out by finding a vampire in my apartment. The sound took me off guard. It wasn't my ringtone. I followed the sound to a small black flip phone on my kitchen counter.

I picked it up. "Hello?"

"Hello, Miss Grimm," an electronically distorted, low-pitched voice said on the other end of the line.

"Who are you?" I asked. "Did you do this?"

"You need to understand who you are. What you can *do*, Miss Grimm."

I furrowed my brow. "I don't understand. How do you know me? Are you my mom or working with my mom?"

"I have been watching you, Miss Grimm. Who I am does not matter."

"And what is it you *think* I can do?" I asked.

"You can reap supernaturals, Miss Grimm."

"Supernaturals?" I asked.

"Vampires, werewolves, even gods, perhaps. I cannot state the full extent of your capabilities, but we must confirm what you can do."

I snorted. "How did you even know? I didn't think I could reap a damn thing until about an hour ago."

The voice on the other end of the phone remained silent a few seconds before speaking. "Like I said, I've been watching you."

"You were there tonight?" I asked.

"No, Miss Grimm. But our organization had that home under surveillance."

I snorted. "Under surveillance? If that's the case, you knew what that Vlad asshole was doing. You knew he had that poor woman in his basement."

"We did," the voice confirmed.

"He was torturing her! Feeding on her, I'd guess, by the looks of the wounds on her body. You knew about it and did *nothing?*"

Another few seconds of silence. "There are bigger issues at play, Miss Grimm."

"Bullshit!" I exclaimed. "How many people has that vampire killed while you, whoever the hell you are, sat there and *observed?*"

"We are limited in our capabilities. At least, we were. We are hoping you might change that."

"I don't even know who you are! For all I know, you're just the asshole who left garlic and a vampire in my apartment. That doesn't sound like something you'd do to a prospective business partner."

"You can call me 'the Handler,'" the voice offered. "My job is to ensure that you're directed to the necessary targets."

I snorted. "Thanks for asking for my opinion on the matter. Maybe I just like making coffee."

"No, you don't," the voice countered.

I sighed. "Okay. You're right. I suck at that."

"You've trained for this, Miss Grimm. We intend to ensure that you realize your potential."

I snorted. "How do you even know what I've trained for? If you want me to work for you, you should probably offer a little more transparency."

"Are you suggesting that eliminating vampires and other dangerous supernaturals is a bad thing, Miss Grimm?"

"No, but let's face it. If you're going to send me into danger or put a dangerous monster in my freaking apartment, it might be nice to establish a little trust in our relationship."

"Invoke your scythe, Miss Grimm. Reap the vampire's soul."

"Then what?" I asked. "Take him to the boatman on the River Styx?"

No sooner did I ask the question than I recalled the boatman's words. The first time I'd failed to reap a soul, and Morty and I delivered the soul that my brother harvested in my stead. *Your souls are not welcome here. I cannot take your souls where they must go.*

At the time, I thought Charon was talking kooky dooks. Maybe several thousand years of rowing back and forth, delivering souls from the underworld had messed with his head. Now, though, his words made sense. Did he know what I could do before I, or even my father, did? How did he know?

"Harvest the vampire's soul, Miss Grimm. This is one reason why we've set up this particular experiment. We must discover what happens after you reap."

It was my turn to leave the Handler with a few seconds of silence. "This is an experiment?"

"Of course, Miss Grimm."

"And all this garlic…"

"It acts like a sedative, a type of anesthesia for vampires. It's quite effective on the younger ones. Not so much on the older ones."

"Like Vlad?" I asked.

"Vampires like him, who have lived for centuries, develop a resistance to garlic. The same is true regarding sunlight."

"Vlad can go out in the sun?" I asked.

"He cannot. Not for long. But he can last in the sun for a minute, maybe two. It would boil his skin. He'd have to feed on a dozen souls to heal his wounds. But sunlight would consume a younger vampire in a manner of seconds."

"How about a stake to the heart?" I asked.

"Steak?" Cerberus piped up.

I raised my hand to silence him.

"It will kill a vampire."

"Then someone like me shows up to reap their souls?" I asked.

"You are the first of your kind, Miss Grimm. I cannot say what happened to vampire souls before now. Perhaps they simply ceased to exist."

"So let me get this straight. You can kill vampires in at least two ways. Lure them into the sun or stake their hearts."

"That is correct."

"And you need *me* to reap their souls?"

"Our organization is quite proficient at eliminating younger vampires, Miss Grimm. The older vampires are fast. They are cautious. Vlad wears an underlining beneath his shirt made of impenetrable material. He is not the only one. He is not even the oldest of those that we are powerless to defeat. But if you can reap their souls, a single swipe with your scythe would do the job. Why else do you suppose Vlad fled from you in terror?"

"I don't know. If I'm the first-ever vampire Reaper or super-natural Reaper, how would he even know what I could do?"

"Vlad has not survived for over five hundred years by taking chances. You presented something he did not understand. You can be certain that he will make it a priority to discover the truth of what you are."

I bit the inside of my cheek. "Then how do I know you aren't him? Or someone working for him?"

"Because when this is done, when this experiment is complete, we intend to tell you where to find Vlad. So that you can kill him."

I sighed. "And if you *were* him, you'd want to lure me into a trap. That's what he did once before. Fool me once."

"If that was the case, Miss Grimm, why would we want to help you realize the potential of your abilities? If we were working with Vlad, wouldn't we ensure that you remained ignorant of your capability?"

I took a deep breath. "All right. I suppose that makes sense."

"Then it's time. Reap the vampire, Miss Grimm."

I nodded and set the phone down on my kitchen counter. I touched the sigil on my wrist. My staff appeared. I stepped toward the vampire, and my staff transformed into a scythe. I swiped the blade at him. My blade passed through the vampire's chest and pulled out a black shadow. The shadow settled into my blade, and then, with a pulse of golden energy, it dissipated, and my blade disappeared.

I released my staff and picked up my phone again.

No sooner did I put it to my ear and the Handler spoke. "Good work, Miss Grimm."

"Wait, I haven't told you what happened yet."

"We were watching you, Miss Grimm."

I turned around, looking for someone lurking in the corner, perhaps a camera. I saw nothing. "Watching me? What do you mean?"

"We'll text you Vlad's location soon. Be ready."

The Handler hung up the phone. I looked at the burner phone. It was an older device. It didn't have a touch screen. I located the call history. It listed the number as "unknown."

"Well, isn't that fantastic?"

"It sounds to me like we have more work to do," Cerberus offered.

I nodded. "It certainly looks that way."

CHAPTER THIRTY-FOUR

Over the next hour, the vampire's body desiccated to the point that all that remained was a pile of ash. Between that, and all the garlic that was scattered around my apartment, it took a couple of hours to clean up. If this organization was going to trash my apartment, the least they could have done was send me a maid. I suppose it could have been worse. Sweeping up a body's worth of ash wasn't fun, but it was less inconvenient than disposing of a body would have been.

The damn smell wasn't something I could get rid of overnight. I lit a few candles to mask the scent. I imagined it would take a while before my apartment didn't smell like an Olive Garden.

By the time I hit the sack, I was left with only a few hours to sleep before I had to get up for work. I was scheduled with Sienna second shift. Those early coffee shop shifts, starting at five in the morning, were reserved for the more experienced baristas. Still, all things considered, my shift started earlier than I'd like, given the short night. A hard knock on my door startled me awake.

I checked my phone. It was five in the morning. I muttered a few curses under my breath as I rolled out of bed, tossed on a sweatshirt and sweatpants, and opened the door.

Kevin was standing there. "Did I wake you up?"

I rubbed my eyes. "Yeah. You did."

"Sorry about that. Do you have a minute?"

I shrugged. "Well, I'm already awake."

"At least you can drink as much coffee as you'd like at work."

I snorted. "Right. There's that."

"There were some fresh developments in the case. I wondered if you might shed some light on what we've discovered."

I shook my head. "I don't know what I could offer that might help. What happened?"

"Three men were delivered to the police station last night. Tied up and bound. One of their victims was brought to the hospital."

"Well, that sounds like good news."

Kevin nodded. "The three men described a woman with long black hair."

I shrugged. I'd hidden from the thugs for most of the attack, but they knew what I was supposed to look like. They were sent to kill me, after all. "Sounds like a lot of women I know. Are you implying something?"

"I'm not accusing you of anything. I just figured that given your proximity to the case, it was worth asking."

I sighed. "Well, I certainly didn't capture three men and bring them to the station, if that's what you're thinking. What about the victim you said was taken to the hospital?"

Kevin sighed. "She was in stable condition when she arrived. By the time I made it there, she was dead."

I furrowed my brow. "Excuse me? Did you say she was dead?"

Kevin nodded. "Foul play was involved, I'm afraid. Someone drove a wooden shank right into her chest."

I raised my eyebrows. Was she a vampire? She'd been bitten. I didn't know how a vampire was turned. All I could figure was that the organization that contacted me through the Handler was involved. Them, or maybe my mother. Those were the only people I knew who hunted vampires. "Do you suspect that the traffickers were involved?"

Kevin nodded. "Possibly. If so, I imagine they were trying to prevent her from talking. Other than identifying the woman who supposedly delivered them to us, the other three men haven't been particularly helpful."

I shook my head. "I'm sorry to hear about her. How horrific. To survive something like that, to think you're safe, only to be killed…"

Kevin sighed. "It's a tragedy all around. There's another thing. The doctor who brought the girl into the hospital said that a woman, also with dark hair, waved him down on the road. Then she took off. Drove away on what he thought might have been a motorcycle."

I rolled my eyes. "So, of course, you'd suspect me."

"Again, I'm not accusing you, Zoey. But you have to admit the coincidence is too unusual to dismiss out of hand."

"Well, Kevin. I'm sorry I couldn't be of more help. But I need to get ready for work."

"I understand," Kevin replied. "Just so you know, whoever this woman is, she isn't a suspect. She's a person of interest. A witness. Whoever she is, she has no reason to conceal her identity from us."

I nodded. "Well, I'm sure if she's willing to talk, she'll come forward eventually."

Kevin smiled. "Very well. If anything else comes up, or you think of anything that might help, you have my number."

"I do," I agreed. "See you around."

I was about to close the door when Kevin reached out his

hand to stop it from closing. "One more thing. I stopped by your apartment last night. It was pretty late. Your motorcycle was gone."

I nodded. "Another coincidence, Detective. I'm recently single. I was out at the clubs."

"Sure you were, Zoey." Kevin smirked. "You realize you can trust me, right?"

I smiled. "Of course. Why *wouldn't* I trust you?"

"I'm just saying you can," he countered. "I'm on your side and trying to keep you safe. I'm also trying to catch these bastards. Anything you could do to help would be appreciated."

I smiled and winked. "You got it."

Kevin cocked his head. "Damn, your apartment smells amazing."

"What can I say. I make a killer lasagna."

Kevin left, and I closed my door. A killer lasagna? I shook my head and laughed. At least he didn't ask for a piece. I suppose accepting a meal from someone involved in a case might be deemed a "gift" and against department policy. Still, if he had asked, I'd have to confess to eating the whole damn thing. Or I'd have to come up with something else that might explain why I didn't have any left to offer.

I had to be careful about what I told Kevin. What I said wasn't technically a lie. I hadn't delivered the men to the department. That much was true. Still, while I wasn't lying to the detective outright, I was admittedly misleading him. If I said the wrong thing and he dug a little deeper, he might catch me in my deception. He was a detective, after all. He was trained for that sort of thing.

I suspected that he knew I wasn't being totally honest with him. At this point, though, he couldn't prove anything. And while he thought he was keeping me safe, the truth was precisely the opposite. I couldn't tell Kevin what was going on. If I did, and the evidence led him to Vlad or a vampire lair, he'd be lucky to survive the encounter.

Keeping Kevin off my back was the least of my worries. I had to admit, the information he'd given me was helpful. It wasn't Vlad who'd brought those men to the police. At least, it was highly unlikely. It would be pretty dumb to turn over his hired hands to the cops. It must've been the Handler or the people he worked for. They'd said they were watching me, after all. They knew what had happened in that basement with Vlad, and they must have known that the woman I'd rescued was in the process of becoming a vampire. They were likely the ones who snuck into the hospital to stake her.

Since Kevin didn't mention that the woman's body turned to ash, I figured that must've been a unique side effect associated with my reaping a vampire's soul with my scythe. Or perhaps the woman hadn't fully turned. They may have staked her to stop the process, to put her down before she had a chance to emerge as a vampire and wreak havoc on the hospital. There's a lot of blood in a hospital. For a newly turned vampire, the hospital would be an all-you-can-eat buffet.

But the Handler, who had the nerve to spy on me in my apartment for God knows how long, who also felt the need to disguise his voice while expecting me to go on vampire-slaying missions on behalf of an organization that apparently couldn't handle anything other than vampire babies, had known that the woman was in that basement. They'd probably watched while others were caged there and died or were turned and didn't save them before it was too late. Instead, they waited until the woman was about to turn, then they showed up to clean up a mess that never should have been to begin with.

I felt like walking around my apartment and finding where they might have secret cameras hidden and flashing my middle finger at them all. There were two reasons why I didn't just tell them to shove it despite my better inclination to do exactly that.

First, I suspected that this organization was connected to my mother. Second, while I didn't like their methods, the Handler had told me he'd be in touch with the precise location of Vlad.

This was my chance to save lives, and I had a unique ability, so I might be the only one who could end or prevent a similar horror to the one that happened to that woman in the cage, one that would have happened to Sienna if I hadn't intervened.

Mister Handsy McHandler might be presumptuous and pretentious, but if I didn't work with him, people would die.

It struck me how ironic it was that I'd trained my whole life to be a Reaper of human souls. I'd dreamed of being the new Grim Reaper, Death herself. I was the one who would usher human souls into the afterlife. Now, all the skills I'd learned would serve the opposite end. I wasn't taking people through death. I was preventing it. I could save lives by harvesting vampire souls, and damn, it felt good.

For the first time in six months, I had a path, a vision for what the rest of my life could be. I wouldn't be a harbinger of death but of life. For humans, at least.

Unfortunately, the Handler hadn't offered any payment for taking down Vlad, and I still had bills to pay. Until I heard from the Handler again, I had to go back to work. I had to move on with my life as it was before I discovered I had a scythe, that I was a Reaper after all. Somehow, I'd have to get through the day content to make cappuccinos and lattes.

Since Kevin had woken me up early, I arrived at work about fifteen minutes before my shift. I thought, for a second, I might get there before Sienna. Nope. She was already there. Joe was there too. A wide smile split his face when I walked in the door.

The only thing I could think was that Sienna had said she thought he had a crush on me. I smiled back, but to be polite, not to appear particularly excited to see him.

Joe was great. A good boss, for sure. He may have had a thing for me, but he never behaved inappropriately. He was like the human version of Gabriel. I mean that in the best way possible. Most girls would be lucky to be with a guy like Joe. He was not a bad-looking man. He was kind, gentle, and safe. It would never work with us. I learned from my experience dating Gabriel that I needed more than that.

I couldn't settle for "safe." My life wasn't going to be safe. I suppose one could argue that a guy like that was exactly what I needed. A refuge from the chaos of what my life was about to become. But that wouldn't be fair to him. No more than it would have been fair to stay with Gabriel when my life was on a different path.

I could never invest my heart in someone like Joe. I needed someone who could understand me, who could be with me in the chaos and love me through it all. If I was going to love my man back, really love him, I needed someone who could get dirty with me, who could love Zoey the Reaper, the real me. Joe had a crush on Zoey the lost, the clumsy barista who wasn't sure where her life was going.

I donned my apron and joined Sienna behind the counter. At Cup-O-Joe's, we had all kinds of unique brews. A banana-nut coffee was, surprisingly, one of the better flavored coffees we offered. I started brewing that, along with our Highlander Grogg. I think it had maple in it. I liked it because how could you *not* like a coffee called Highlander Grogg? Sienna already had plenty of the house brew and decaf ready to go.

Joe was trying to talk to me about stuff that wasn't work-related. Like, why he didn't like the idea of the Royals building a new stadium downtown. I know that a lot of Kansas Citians are really into their sports teams. I appreciated the athleticism of it all. I just didn't understand the rules. I think when it comes to sports, like baseball or football, you have to grow up with an appreciation for the game to get into it. Still, I nodded along, adding an obligatory "uh-huh" here and there and pretending I was mildly interested.

"I mean, am I off-base?" Joe asked. "The old stadium, with the fountains and all that, it's iconic, right?"

I snorted. Why did he have to ask a question that demanded a response? I didn't have an opinion. Still, I could give a generic answer to affirm Joe's passionate point of view. "You're right."

Joe smiled and nodded, oblivious to the fact that I'd been ignoring him the whole time. Yeah, he didn't see me. He might have liked me, but he'd never be able to understand me on a deeper level. I wasn't ignoring him because I was trying to act disinterested in the things he enjoyed. It wasn't even because I didn't give three rats' asses about stadiums. I was thinking about vampires. Reaping their souls. Wondering what happened to their souls when they left my scythe. The one I'd reaped hadn't lingered there like a human soul would when reaped.

The boatman was right—he couldn't take the souls I could deliver. Somehow, he knew what I was before anyone else. Considering my family's investments supported his entire soul ferrying business, you'd think he'd have the courtesy to tell me what he knew.

Joe smiled after I confirmed his viewpoint and went into the back where he did his roasting. He worked almost all day, but he wasn't always at the shop. He sold some of his beans to various stores around the city. Most of the time, if Joe wasn't roasting in the back room behind the coffee shop, he was out and about, doing whatever it was he did to promote his business.

My mind was still spinning. Sienna approached me. "Anything new?"

I nodded. "Yeah. One of the victims was found. Three more bad dudes were arrested. Someone killed the victim in the hospital later. Kevin dropped all this crap in my lap at five this morning."

Sienna's eyes went wide. "They *killed* her?"

"Someone did," I confirmed. "I don't think you have anything to worry about if that's what you're getting at. She was being held in a basement somewhere."

"She wasn't getting shipped in the crates like they were going to do to me?" Sienna asked.

I'd almost forgotten about that little detail. Vlad was busy in and around Kansas City. If he took a few of the abductees for the occasional snack, who were the rest of the people the operation kidnapped going to? More vampires, I'd wager. Did the Handler and his organization even know about them beyond their existence? He was focused on eliminating Vlad. But Vlad might be the key to understanding the full breadth of the operation.

"I think whoever was holding them was keeping her himself, maybe as a kind of payment for his work with the larger syndicate. I don't know for sure."

Sienna shook her head. "Disgusting. I can't imagine… What would have happened to me if you hadn't found me?"

I noticed the sweat beading on Sienna's brow. She was traumatized. When she'd found the victims' names, when she was analyzing the deposits in Chad's account and sorting through evidence, she hadn't come across nearly so anxious. She felt empowered. Helping me by researching stuff on the Internet for me had given her a sense of control. A way she could fight back. At least, that was my best guess. Even if it was something small, it was her way of fighting back. Maybe I could give her something more to look into.

"Do you think you could do a little more digging into the names you found before?" I asked. "Something in my gut tells me that there must be some connection, a reason why these people were all targeted."

Sienna grinned. "I'd be happy to. You realize I'm in computer science, right?"

"You're in school?" I asked.

Sienna nodded. "I've finished a semester. I'm taking a break to save up money to pay for another one. That's why I work so much."

She pulled up her sleeve and revealed a band-aid. "Not just working here. I'm making money any way I can."

"What's that about?" I asked.

"I'm also donating plasma," Sienna replied. "Would you believe they're paying a hundred bucks for my blood type right now? I'm a universal donor."

I scratched my head. "How often do you donate?"

"Quite a bit. Twice a week is the most they allow. An extra two hundred a week right now can go a long way to paying for my next semester."

"When was the last time you went?" I asked.

"The day before the first time Chad tried to attack me. Why?"

I sighed. "Just a thought. It's probably nothing."

How could I even begin to broach the subject? It was a long shot anyway. I didn't know much about vampires. Did they have blood type preferences? It was worth probing further.

"Try me," Sienna suggested.

I took a deep breath. I couldn't tell Sienna about vampires, but why would blood type motivate human traffickers? "What if the thing that links all the victims together is their blood type? What if they were trafficking organs, not people?"

Sienna stared at me, aghast. "Holy shit! Do you think they were after my organs?"

I winced. I hadn't thought about how the notion that her attackers might have intended to cut her open for parts might affect her. Probably no less than it would if I told her the truth. "It's just a theory. If that's the case, it might explain why the people we think they were targeting didn't have much in common. If, however, they were all universal donors, I imagine there's more of a market for organs like that than those specific to other blood types."

She pinched her chin. "You know how I'd said Chad looked familiar? Holy crap, Zoey…"

"What is it?" I asked.

"I know where I recognized him from," Sienna explained. "He works at that damned blood bank! Well, he did. I didn't interact with him. He worked in the back. Sometimes came out to gather the donations. That has to be it."

I nodded. "This still might be a crazy coincidence. But do you think there's any way you can check on the other people we thought were victims?"

Sienna shook her head. "I might be good with computers, but finding someone's blood type is hard to do. Medical files are just about impossible to access. But what if…"

I cocked my head. "What are you thinking?"

"If Chad was working there to find matches for what he was looking for, maybe some of the other victims donated recently, too."

"How could you find out if that's the case?" I asked.

Sienna shook her head. "Short of breaking into the place and stealing their records, the first thing I would try is social media. People love to virtue signal. Do something like donating blood, let the world know so they can look like saints, set themselves up as an example."

I rolled my eyes. "That sounds stupid."

Sienna chuckled. "Yeah, it is. But a lot of people do it. The way I see it, if even one of those names posted something about how they'd given blood or plasma recently, it would help confirm your theory."

"For good measure, you might want to find another place to go for your next donation," I suggested. "I know you need the money, but it's too risky."

"It goes straight to tuition. But you're right. If Chad worked there, maybe the whole place was compromised."

I bit my lip. "Are you sure you can find these people's social media pages?"

Sienna laughed. "You are pretty computer stupid, aren't you?"

I smiled. "You have no idea."

"It's not hard to find. The harder part will be sorting through their old posts and feeds to see if they mentioned anything about donating."

I nodded. "Maybe start around the time you went last? The woman they rescued last night wasn't taken long before you were."

"Not a bad idea," Sienna agreed. "It's a good place to start, anyway."

I shook my head. "I had no idea you were so good with computers. How haven't we had this conversation before?"

Sienna shrugged. "I don't know. I mean, I don't talk about it. It's sort of embarrassing."

"Why is it embarrassing that you're studying computer science?" I asked. "I think it's pretty cool."

Sienna chuckled. "Not that. I mean that I can't afford my schooling."

"If you want my opinion, it's impressive that you're finding a way to make your dreams come true. Maybe you won't be able to fly through school in a few years, but you'll get there."

"What about you?" Sienna asked. "You're still young, Zoey. I get it that your family's business or whatever didn't work out. But you could still do just about anything you wanted."

I smiled. "You're right. Still, I think I'm finding my way. The last few months have been more about trying to get to know myself again. It's like I've just had to hit a big reset button on my life."

"A good reboot can be good for our operating systems from time to time."

I chuckled. "Computer jokes, eh?"

Sienna grinned. "You started it with the whole 'reset button' thing. But you know, a lot of computers don't have those buttons anymore. They have a power button, which I guess can function that way. Or you can reset a system natively within the system. When there's a problem with my PC, I often restart my computer in safe mode. It allows me to explore the system to sort out whatever's wrong without having to deal with a bunch of extraneous processes."

"I'm going to smile, nod along, and pretend I know what you're talking about."

Sienna chuckled. "Like you were doing with Joe a minute ago?"

I cringed. "Was it that obvious?"

"To me? Yes. Joe was clueless. Still, my point is this, Zoey. There's nothing wrong with exploring things in safe mode for a while. Systems evolve; they develop. Sometimes you have to strip away a lot of extraneous programs to get a clear view of the real system, its true nature, and to locate where its problems lie."

"Ah. Now you're using computers as a metaphor for my journey of self-exploration?"

Sienna grinned. "Not like I'm an expert at any of that. But I think it's right, you know? Maybe this whole barista thing is your safe mode. Or maybe a date with Joe might be safe mode."

I shook my head. "My ex was my safe mode. I think dating him showed me that while guys like him and Joe are great, I'll never really be happy with a guy like that. I can't date in safe mode."

Sienna nodded. "You're right. You'll need to reboot the system fully after you fixed the problem before you log into those dating apps."

I chuckled. "I'm not using those apps."

"I'm still speaking in metaphors, Zoey! You know what I mean! I think it's cool that you understand what you want."

"Well, I don't know if that's right, either. I'm not sure what I'm looking for, exactly. I do know what I don't want. I mean, sort of like my family business. It's been clear for a while that it wouldn't work for me. It's taken a lot longer to figure out what my path forward is. I think I'm getting there, though."

I heard a cough. I turned to see a customer at the counter. "Hello? Is someone going to help me?"

"Sorry, sir," I apologized. "Can I take your order?"

CHAPTER THIRTY-FIVE

The second shift at Cup-O-Joe's was the busiest. It stayed busy through the first hour or two of my shift. Then, once most of the coffee shop's patrons were at work, things slowed down. Once we got through the first hour, Joe left to deliver his latest supply of roasted coffee beans to some local vendors.

With the coast clear, Sienna ducked into his office and fired up his computer.

It didn't take her long. Not all of the possible victims had a social media presence. Most of them did. Most importantly, the woman I'd saved, who'd been staked before she could turn, had an active presence on Facebook and Twitter.

I leaned into the office to check on Sienna's progress between coffee orders. Thankfully, most of the folks who came in just wanted regular cups of coffee—nothing I couldn't handle.

"Any more updates?" I asked.

"A lot of posts about missing her, then just today a bunch of people commemorating her memories. But before that, nothing much on Facebook except a lot of pictures of her food and videos about her workouts."

I sighed. "Lord, why would she tell the world about that?"

Sienna snickered. "Like I said. People love to show off. Look at me, how healthy I am, how I'm doing everything you only wish you could do. I hope you find it inspiring!"

"Well, if that's her personality, if she gave blood, you can bet she'd post something about it."

"Not on Facebook, but…" Sienna clicked the mouse a few times. "Bingo!"

"Did you find it?"

Sienna's smile was so wide I was afraid her head was going to split in half. "She tweeted about it. Even tagged the donation center. And get this, it was the same day I donated last. Just a few hours before my appointment."

"You said that they call you in advance since you're a universal donor. Do they call others with the same blood type at the same time?"

"Definitely," Sienna agreed. "I've chatted with others waiting for their turn. It's almost always the same story. I can't confirm it for certain, but if she donated the same day I did, just a few hours earlier, I'd be willing to bet that she is also O negative."

"I still don't think you should go back," I replied. "If anything unsavory is happening there, they might try targeting you again."

"They didn't bother me this morning when I donated. It was pretty uneventful."

"That doesn't mean anything. If anyone there is working for the traffickers, you can bet they'd leave you alone. They don't want to draw any attention to their operation."

Sienna rubbed at the band-aid on her arm. "Well, all seems well. I don't think they tried to poison me or anything like that."

"They wouldn't try anything obvious." I shrugged. "It would be too risky since the police know you were one of their victims. Still, I think it's best to steer clear of that place until I can check it out."

Sienna gasped. "You're going to check it out? Zoey, I appreciate everything you're doing, but are you sure that's a good idea?"

"Look, those people know about me, too. If I show up, it might make them a little uncomfortable. I'll go to inquire about donations. I'll just tell them a coworker recommended it for extra cash. I'll keep my eyes open for anyone acting nervous, or staring at me, or whatever."

Sienna turned off Joe's computer and stepped out of his office. "Are you sure you shouldn't just tell the detective what you think the connection might be?"

I shook my head. "Right now, it's just a theory. The last thing I want to do is cast doubt on a donation center if they're above board. I'll be fine. Like I said, I'll go in, ask about donations, and see what happens. They won't try anything. If they are involved, well, they already know I'm connected to the case. They'll leave me alone for the same reason they wouldn't dare to do anything to you there. This operation, whatever the traffickers are up to, is a lot bigger than a few people. I'm guessing they've hurt dozens, if not hundreds of people. They won't do anything to put their scheme in jeopardy."

Sienna sighed. "All right. Just text me when you're done, okay? Let me know what happened, and let me know you're safe. I try not to worry, but after everything that happened, I can't help but be concerned."

I smiled. "I get it, Sienna. I'll let you know the second I'm out of there. Do you have an address and the time they close?"

Sienna pulled out her phone. "Texting it to you now."

The blood bank closed about two hours after my shift ended. Plenty of time, presuming, of course, that the Handler didn't call with a change of plans. Sienna and I walked back to our vehicles. After she drove off, I checked the burner phone the Handler left me. So far, nothing.

My plan was simple. I'd do exactly what I'd told Sienna. Then, if anyone was acting odd and might *be* a vampire, I could summon my staff. If the scythe appeared, well, it would confirm everything. The Handler and his organization were attempting to pin down Vlad's location. If they'd found him, they would have contacted me. I had a lead. Of course, the chance that Vlad was at the blood bank was unlikely. Still, it was an avenue I could pursue.

The sun was already setting on the horizon as I rode to the blood bank. The timing was perfect. If there were any vampires affiliated with the place, they'd likely show after dark.

I parked my bike in the parking lot. It was a relatively small brick building with one set of tinted glass double doors on the front. The name of the place, A+ Plasma, was printed in a back-lit sign over the doors.

I took two steps away from my motorcycle toward the door when the phone rang in my pocket. Not *my* phone. The ringtone gave it away. It was the Handler.

I sighed as I pulled it out of my pocket. I flipped the phone open and placed it to my left ear.

"Stand down, Miss Grimm," the electronically distorted voice of the Handler ordered.

"Excuse me?" I asked. "Are you monitoring my location now?"

"The phone is GPS-enabled. We know where you're going."

"Is Vlad inside?" I asked.

"We do not know his location, Miss Grimm, but there are others there. Too many for you to handle alone."

I snorted. "How do you know what I can handle?"

As the Handler started to respond, three identical, black SUVs with tinted windows pulled into the parking lot.

"Miss Grimm, it's not that…"

"Wait! Something is happening."

"Do not engage, Miss Grimm!"

Even as he spoke, the three vehicles parked around me, blocking me into my parking space. "I think it's too late for that."

I hung up the phone and watched several people step out of

the SUVs. Four in each vehicle. All of them were dressed in black suits. Seven men. Five women. All of them had pale complexions.

Vlad wasn't among them, but it was clear to me that these people were vampires. They'd probably arrived to gather some of the day's donations or, worse, to get a list of potential victims from the donation center's registries. Whatever their purposes were, they hadn't expected to find me waiting outside.

One woman from the group stepped out in front of the rest. I was ready to touch my sigil and summon my scythe. If push came to shove, that's what I'd do, but I didn't want to jump the gun. This woman intended to talk.

"Well, what do we have here?" the woman asked.

I narrowed my eyes. "You know who I am?"

"My name is Katerina. And yes, Zoey Grimm, I know exactly who you are."

I snorted. "Exactly? For some reason, I doubt you know everything."

Katerina smiled. "You've caused quite the stir in our community after your encounter with Vlad last night. How fortuitous that you've saved us the effort of coming after you ourselves."

"Fortuitous?" I asked. "For me, maybe. I've been itching for a chance to take down a few bloodsuckers."

Katerina laughed. "You sure are full of yourself, aren't you? We outnumber you several times over, dear girl."

I smirked. "You don't know what I'm capable of."

"And you presume to know what we are capable of?"

She had a point. My experience with vampires was extremely limited. Vlad had moved fast. A lot faster than me. Could all vampires move like that? My heart was racing. I wasn't entirely sure I could handle one of them, much less twelve. Still, the best chance I had to get out of this situation was to act confident. The one thing I couldn't show was fear—even if I was terrified.

"So, what's the play here, Katerina?" I asked. "You use this place to identify victims who have your favored blood type?"

"Victims?" Katerina asked. "The people we take are hardly victims, dear."

I snorted. "Tell that to the woman who died last night."

"That was not our doing," Katerina countered. "We'd intended to give that woman a gift. She was chosen by Vlad. If you hadn't intervened, she'd be very much alive by now. She'd live as one of us."

I cocked my head. "You aren't abducting these people to feed on?"

"Of course not! This facility provides us with more than we need to satiate our needs. We take them to turn them."

"And their blood type?" I asked. "Everyone you've taken is a universal donor."

Katerina laughed. "Indeed, they are. Though that is not the reason we chose these people to become the benefactors of our gift. Their particular blood type is more amenable to the transformation process than others. Most, when bitten, will either recover or die. Only a small number of them survive the change. But for those who have the proper blood type, they are nearly guaranteed to turn without incident."

"And you're shipping them down the river?" I asked.

"Some of them, perhaps," Katerina replied. "We intend to seed the entire world with our kind. Today, our numbers are few. For centuries, we've remained in hiding. We hunted discreetly. But times have changed. With smartphones, cameras everywhere, and the speed at which word travels, it is only a matter of time before we are discovered."

I shook my head. "If you're growing in numbers, doesn't that just mean more of you who can be found out?"

Katerina laughed. "We do not intend to wait until we are discovered to announce our presence to the world. Soon, when we've reached the numbers we require, we will rise and claim the world as our own."

I snorted. "Vampires taking over the world? Are you serious?

There are billions of people in the world. They won't just lay down and let you rule them."

Katerina snorted. "It's called the survival of the fittest, dear. Yes, there are billions. Herds of humans who must be cared for. They are our food source, after all."

"So, you're not just talking about taking over the world. You intend to enslave humanity?"

"Not the word I'd choose. The future we intend to make for ourselves will not be altogether unpleasant for the humans who donate their blood willingly."

I shook my head. "You already said your numbers are small. You're a long way from achieving your goal."

"A year from now, maybe less, you might have a different assessment of our chances." Katerina shook her head. "This is a crucial time for our plans, dear girl, and we can't have the likes of you threatening our cause."

"The likes of me? What are you talking about?"

"Do you seriously intend to play the fool, Miss Grimm? After you already revealed yourself to Vlad?"

I snorted. "Well, maybe you're right. Perhaps I am a threat. What's your play, then? Kill me?"

"If it comes to that," Katerina agreed. "But we'd much prefer to offer you an opportunity."

CHAPTER THIRTY-SIX

I knew before Katerina spoke that I wasn't about to take her up on whatever she was offering. Anything she intended to tempt me with would undoubtedly mean allowing the vampires to proceed with their scheme for world domination. I couldn't imagine what it would be like if they succeeded. A whole world run by vampires? All of humankind reduced to what she called a "herd," a source of food and nothing more?

"Vlad is among the oldest of our kind," Katerina explained. "Since you've murdered his chosen bride, he thinks it only fitting that you take her place."

I rolled my eyes. "I wasn't the one who killed that woman."

"Not directly," Katerina replied. "But your people did."

"My people? I don't know what you're talking about. I don't have people. I work alone."

"Then perhaps you can explain why your people delivered one of our own to your apartment recently?"

"I didn't ask them to do that!" I protested.

"But you did what they asked, did you not? Poor Alexander. He had such promise."

I narrowed my eyes. "I will not let you turn me if that's what you're implying."

"You won't let me?" Katerina asked. "Does a pet have a choice about its house or home?"

"I'm not your pet!"

Katerina laughed. "Most humans fight and resist at first. Be that as it may, what we offer you is a gift."

"You don't even know my blood type. You don't know if I'll turn."

Katerina shrugged. "There's a strength about you. A power that lingers in your blood. You are not entirely human, are you, dear girl?"

"What are you getting at?" I asked.

Katerina smiled, her fangs glistening in the lights that illuminated the parking lot. "Consider it an experiment. If we can turn the part of you that is human, and your power persists, you could be a powerful ally."

"I'd never join a cause meant to take over the world, much less enslave humans!"

"It's funny how quickly such attitudes change after one is turned."

Katerina took two steps toward me. The other vampires, still surrounding me, did the same. If I didn't act fast, I wouldn't have a chance. Fighting off twelve vampires, even with my scythe, was going to be a challenge, no matter what. Without room to maneuver, to utilize the fighting skills I'd spent my life mastering, my chances were even slimmer.

Yes, I was terrified. A soul about to be reaped is often similarly afraid. They have two choices: fight or flight. Based on my current predicament, flight wasn't an option.

I was about to touch the sigil on my wrist, to evoke my staff and scythe, when I heard a roar and Cerberus appeared.

He was roughly twenty times his usual size, eclipsing the plasma donation center. After he'd taken a vampire punch the night before, he wasn't going to underestimate their power a second time.

When the vampires turned and saw him, I took my opportunity and invoked my staff. The scythe formed immediately, coursing with red magic that resembled flames.

I pivoted and sliced it through one of the male vampires to my rear. Then I caught a second one with the same swipe.

Cerberus was swiping his paws at the others, sending them flying across the parking lot.

"Good boy!" I shouted, ducking to avoid another vampire who was diving at me with his fangs exposed.

He fell to the ground. I didn't waste any time. I brought my scythe down onto his body. Three down. Nine to go. The air was already clouded by the ash of dead vampire bodies as the wind churned around us.

I coughed as I looked around. Cerberus' Hades head had appeared as he took Katerina into his jaws.

Then Cerberus' legs buckled. He heaved, vomiting her straight back out of his mouth.

Apparently, he couldn't deliver vampires to the afterlife. Not even to Hell.

I charged after Katerina, ready to reap her soul.

"Stop!" a loud voice screamed.

I turned. Vlad was there. He had Sienna in his arms.

"Leave her be, or your friend will join us," he demanded.

"Let her go!" I shouted.

"You took her from us once," Vlad countered. "A friend of mine, a vampire nearly my age in New Orleans, who is expecting her."

"Don't you dare, Vlad!" I screamed.

"Give yourself to me in her stead," Vlad suggested. "Become my progeny, my bride, and together we shall rule this city when the new era dawns."

"If I do that, you'll let her go?"

"You have my word," Vlad assured me.

I didn't believe him. "What about this vampire who is expecting her?"

"I'll deal with him. I will find him another bride."

Cerberus was still swiping at the other vampires, keeping them at bay. All except Katerina. I didn't know where she'd gone. Perhaps, after being vomited up by a hellhound, she took off to regroup. Maybe to shower.

"What is your choice, Zoey?" Vlad asked. "I will have you eventually, either way. But this is your opportunity to come to me willingly. Allow me to taste of your flesh, and we will not seek to harm your friend again."

Vlad yanked Sienna's head to the side by the hair, exposing her neck. "I'm waiting for your answer."

"You won't bite her." I scoffed. "You told me your friend wanted her. That means he is the one who wants to turn her."

Vlad laughed. "It takes more than one bite to turn a human. Multiple bites, strategically placed, will do the job. The one you stole from me was already changing when you interrupted my plans."

I shook my head. "Don't bite her. Not even once!"

"Then join me, Zoey Grimm. I cannot say your mother will be proud to find that her only daughter, whom she doesn't even know, has become the thing she hates the most, but she'll get over it."

I narrowed my eyes. "I don't know what my mom has to do with this, Vlad."

Vlad laughed. "Well, I could tell you. I know where your mother is at this very moment. That information could be yours if you joined me."

I glanced at my scythe, the fire in the blade illuminating the ground around me. I couldn't allow him to turn me. But I wasn't going to let Vlad take Sienna, either. If it was true that he'd have to bite me several times to turn me, that would buy me some time. One bite might weaken me. But if I could still summon my scythe, I would be able to fight him off. Of course, how did he even know if I could be turned at all?

"Katerina told me that a successful turn requires O negative blood. How do you know this would even work?"

Vlad laughed. "First, it is not true that one must have the proper blood to turn. It only guarantees the process. Second, you realize we have quite an extensive network of resources. I'll simply say that I have reason to believe you will turn without incident."

I shook my head. "How can you possibly know that?"

"Tsk-tsk, Zoey! I told you, anything you wish to know, you shall. *After* you accept my offer and begin your transformation."

Vlad lowered his fangs toward Sienna's neck.

"Wait!" I shouted. "I'll do it! Just let her go!"

Vlad grinned at me. "Then come to me, my future bride. Allow me to taste of your blood. Only then will I release the girl."

I took two steps toward Vlad.

"Release your weapon," Vlad ordered.

I grunted and released my staff and scythe. It vanished.

I stepped in front of Vlad, and he gasped. "No!"

A metal spike protruded through Vlad's back and out his chest. I looked past him and saw a figure cloaked in black, holding a crossbow.

The Handler? Someone in his organization?

Sienna took off the second Vlad released her. Out of the cloud of ash and darkness, Katerina grabbed her.

I invoked my staff again and took off after her, but she ran with such speed that even with Sienna in her arms, I couldn't catch her.

"Cerberus!" I screamed. "Can you catch her?"

Cerberus shrank to his normal size. The other vampires, the ones I hadn't reaped, were also gone.

"I can't," Cerberus replied. "I'm fast, but I don't have any clue where they went."

I looked at where the cloaked figure had been standing, but he —or she, whoever it was—was gone.

CHAPTER THIRTY-SEVEN

I kicked in the doors of the donation center. I hoped that maybe Katerina had taken her inside. She'd left so fast, moved with such speed that even Cerberus couldn't tell where she'd gone. It was a long shot, but I had to check.

My burner phone rang. I picked it up.

"What?"

"You shouldn't have gone there."

"Was that you, in the shadows?" I asked.

"It was one of us."

"Why didn't you save her?" I demanded. "You could have helped!"

"Saving you was the priority, Miss Grimm. Besides, my operative has told me that Katerina took her."

"That's right. What's the point?"

"She's nearly as old as Vlad was," the Handler told me. "And dare I say, even faster and stronger. All the older vampires of her particular lineage are especially challenging."

I shook my head. "What do you mean 'of her lineage?'"

"She was sired by Nosferatu, one of the most ancient of all living vampires," the Handler continued. "His progeny are difficult to slay. They move fast. They protect their hearts with armor beneath their clothes. Only your scythe could harm her."

"Still, you could have shot her," I protested. "Tried to slow her down. *Something*! I can't let them take my friend!"

"If you find Katerina, you will find your friend."

"How the hell am I supposed to find a vampire who moves like the fucking Flash?"

"What are their intentions for your friend?" the Handler asked.

"To deliver her to a vampire in New Orleans. They intend to take over the world or some shit, and whoever the big shot vamp is down there wants her for his bride."

"I see. Well, suffice it to say, Katerina will follow through with that task."

"How can you be so sure? Vlad said he was a friend of his. Is Katerina really beholden to whatever Vlad arranged?"

"She is." The Handler paused for a moment. "The vampire in New Orleans is her sire. It is Nosferatu. If he is the one who desires your friend, Katerina will be powerless to reject his demand."

"Powerless? What does that even mean?"

"A vampire's progeny cannot disobey the demands of their sire. If you had allowed Vlad to bite you, even once, you would be similarly under his thrall even before you were fully turned."

"He was going to bite Sienna," I explained. "I had to do something."

"He fooled you, Miss Grimm. He would not dare bite one intended for Nosferatu. He played you for your ignorance."

I grunted. "Well, if you weren't so damned cryptic and showed yourself to me, gave me a reason to trust you, and taught me all this shit, he would never have tricked me."

"Apologies, Miss Grimm. We must engage you in this way for reasons that shall be revealed in time. I wish I could tell you more, but I cannot."

"Before, when they abducted Sienna, they intended to ship her on the river. Do you think they'll try that again?"

"Possibly," the Handler agreed. "Give us some time. We have many resources at our disposal that may help us locate your friend. This time, Miss Grimm, you must listen and stand down. Do not take action until you hear from me again."

I grunted and closed my phone. I didn't like this Handler asshole, but I needed him. The longer this took, the more likely it was that Katerina would deliver Sienna to her sire. I had to wonder how Katerina felt about all of that. She was this Nosferatu's progeny already. Why couldn't she be his queen in New Orleans if that's what he wanted? Had she failed him in some way? Or perhaps she didn't satisfy his tastes?

Either way, while Katerina might be compelled to do what her sire demands, it didn't mean she was happy about it. Perhaps there was something there I could use to my advantage. One way or another, I was going to stop her.

I'd give the Handler a little time. I didn't have much choice. I also knew if I was going to fight this Katerina bitch, I needed to know more about what I was capable of. That meant, as much as I didn't want to do it, I had to go home. No, not to my apartment. I had to go see my father, and I had to do it quickly. I couldn't risk missing the Handler's call while I was away.

CHAPTER THIRTY-EIGHT

My bike could top two hundred miles per hour with the throttle wide open. I got damn close to that on the highway and peeled around my share of corners around the city streets leading to my apartment.

When I got inside, I grabbed the crystal that I used to go back to the underworld. I set it up with my phone light as before, formed the gateway, and jumped through.

My father was sitting at his desk in a towel, his legs kicked up on top of it and (thankfully) crossed. He quickly pulled his feet back when he saw me.

"Zoey. What brings you—"

"No time, Dad," I interrupted. "I'm going to give this to you straight. Long story, but I don't have time. I can reap."

"What? You can? That's wonderful news!"

"Not human souls. Vampires and other supernaturals. So far, I've only done it on vampires. Thing is, some of them have taken a friend of mine and intend to turn her. But these vamps, they move fast. Faster than anything I've ever seen. Now, I have this organization contacting me. Some dude who calls himself the Handler is giving me tips, but he won't meet me face to face. I think they might be connected to Mom somehow, but I can't say for sure."

"Okay." Dad grabbed a cloak from his closet and slipped it on. "You're sure you can reap vampires?"

I nodded. "When I'm about to go after one, the blade forms on my staff and everything."

"And you take them to the boatman?"

I shook my head. "Nope, but I think Charon knows something about me. He told me he couldn't take the kind of souls I'd bring, whatever that meant."

My father pressed his lips together. "Then perhaps he's the one we should go see. In all my years, I've never heard of a Reaper who can harvest the souls of anything other than humans."

"Talk to the boatman later, Dad. I don't have time. If the Handler finds out where this vampire took my friend, I need to be there for the phone call. It's a risk coming here at all."

My father smiled. "Well, how about we go to Earth?"

"Dad, you can't reap vampires." I pinched my chin. "Or can you? I mean, if you've never tried, maybe you can."

"I'm reasonably certain I cannot. But Zoey, can a vampire in the flesh truly move any faster than a determined soul intending to escape its harvest?"

I shrugged. "I don't know. I mean, in theory, no. But I've never done that before."

My father nodded. "In that case, I can show you a few tricks. All the things I'd hoped to teach you before this all began. Besides, if you can summon a scythe that harvests vampires, that's something I have to see!"

I smiled. "Great! I'd love that. Come on, Dad. We have to get back."

My dad slipped on a pair of boots and followed me back through the same portal I'd made. The second we appeared, Cerberus jumped right into my dad's lap and started licking his face. With all three of his heads.

Somehow, my dad seemed to enjoy it. He petted Cerberus' back. "I missed you too, buddy!"

I reached into my closet and grabbed my cloak.

My dad laughed as I threw it on. "I knew I was missing one of those."

"Sorry. I thought it might come in handy."

"It's fine, Zoey. I'd hoped it was with you, truth be told. It will come in handy considering what you must do. Speed is only an asset if you can see what you're running from or attacking."

"I'm pretty sure the vampires know I can turn invisible. One older one who, as luck would have it, was recently staked saw it. I'm sure he told the rest before he was killed."

"You reaped him?"

I shook my head. "He was staked. Shot to the heart with a crossbow by someone working with the Handler."

"No matter, Zoey. Knowing you might be invisible doesn't change the fact that they can't see you. It's still a great advantage." My father smiled. "Do you have any of your friend's DNA that you can track her?"

I shook my head. "Not anymore. I did the first time they took her."

"This is the second time the vampires took your friend?" my father asked.

I nodded. "The first time, I didn't realize it was vampires. Or that I could reap them. But I did have the residue of some DNA from her phone that I used to find her."

My father smiled. "Then you're in luck. Your scythe already knows her signature, Zoey."

"So I can track her, now? The Handler wanted me to wait for him to give me word."

"Tell me, Zoey, are you certain the Handler is on your side? I don't know much about vampires. In my line of work, I've only encountered a few, and then only when I was sent to reap people they'd killed. I never had to engage them directly. What I do know is that they can be crafty if they intend to lead you one direction or another."

"I don't know. I mean, the Handler sent someone to help me when I was cornered by a dozen vampires. They took down Vlad, the vampire I told you about."

"Are you certain that the person you were speaking to on the phone was connected to the one who shot the vampire with a crossbow?"

I snorted. "Well, now that you mention it, I can't say for sure. I think they are working with Mom somehow. That vampire knew her. He said they'd had run-ins in the past, but she'd never been able to take him out."

My father narrowed his eyes. "Your mother is fighting vampires?"

"Apparently." I shook my head. "It would be nice if she lent me a helping hand."

My father scratched his chin. "The way I see it, Zoey, if the Handler has been less than forthright with you, you owe him no loyalty. If you aren't certain he's on your side, you should be skeptical of his intentions. We can locate your friend together. Summon your staff, and I'll show you how."

"One thing, Dad…I think they're spying on us. They seem to know whatever I do, even in my apartment."

My dad cocked his head. "Then put on your cloak. We can go elsewhere to talk."

With my cloak on and the hood over my head, my dad and I left the apartment like a couple of ghosts. "I don't know where to go where we won't be seen at all."

He grinned. "Follow me, Zoey."

I followed my dad out of the apartment, through the alley, and around the back of the building. There was a metal garage door, weeds overgrown all around it.

My father reached into the pocket of his cloak and retrieved a small fob. He pressed a button, and the garage door opened.

"Holy crap. You have a garage here?"

My father laughed. "I've been paying a fee for this storage space for the better part of twenty years."

He reached inside and turned on a light switch. Then he approached something that had been covered with a tarp. He pulled the tarp away.

My eyes widened. "You have a Harley, Dad?"

"Not just any Harley," my dad countered. "It's a chopper."

I had to admit, the bike was gorgeous. It had a custom paint job, a flaming skull on the body. "It's gorgeous."

My dad smiled. "We'll get your bike later and ride together."

"It's just around the front."

"Now, summon your staff."

I pressed the sigil on my wrist, and my staff appeared.

"Good. Now what's the name of this friend of yours, again?"

"Sienna."

"Very well. Your scythe, or in this case, your staff, is an extension of you. It's not just a weapon. It comes from the power of your soul. That's why no two scythes are alike. Because every soul is unique."

I nodded. "All right. How do I use it to track Sienna?"

"As I said, your staff or scythe is a part of you. That means it will respond to your will. You must simply focus your mind. Since you've attuned your staff to Sienna before, you simply need to wish it to tell you where she is."

I cocked my head. "I just need to...what, tell it what I want?"

"If using words helps you focus your mind, that's certainly acceptable. You must keep your friend front and center in your thoughts."

I nodded again. "Well, here goes nothing. Hey, buddy. Staff. Whatever your name is. I'm looking for Sienna. Why don't you help me out?"

With a clear image of Sienna in my mind, my staff started to glow as it had before. My father clapped. "Fantastic! That's brilliant, Zoey. It takes most Reapers several tries to do what you just did."

I smiled. "Thanks!"

Then, the phone in my pocket started to ring. I sighed. "That's him. It's the Handler."

My father nodded. "Pick it up."

I opened the phone and placed it to my ear. "Miss Grimm, stay where you're at."

"I'm done waiting around. I know where Sienna is. I'm going after her."

"I'm coming to see you," the Handler countered. "We'll go after her together. Stay where you are."

Before I could reply, the Handler hung up. I took a deep breath.

"What is it?" my father asked.

"The Handler is coming. He wants to join us to go after Sienna."

CHAPTER THIRTY-NINE

A black Corvette pulled up to the garage doors where my father and I were waiting. The windows were all tinted. I couldn't see in. But there were two people seated inside.

The driver stepped out. He looked at me and smiled.

I couldn't believe it. "Holy crap! Kevin?"

"Yes, Miss Grimm."

"*You're* the Handler?"

Kevin laughed. "My apologies for the ruse. But this isn't a part of standard operations with the department. It's off the books, so to speak."

I scratched my head. "Wait. So, you knew about these vampires the whole time?"

"Surely you can understand why I wouldn't tell you what I knew, Zoey. But yes, I've known that this trafficking organization was abducting people they hoped to turn into vampires for almost a year."

"You were the one who put that vampire in my apartment?" I asked.

Kevin nodded. "We needed to be certain you could do what we expected you might."

"We?" I asked. "Who else is working with you?"

Kevin turned toward his Corvette and nodded. The passenger door opened, and the shrouded figure I'd seen before emerged.

"You're the one who staked Vlad?" I asked.

The figure nodded, then removed her hood. Long blonde hair slid across her shoulders. She looked at me and then at my father.

My father gasped. "Josephine?"

Two for two on the surprises tonight. "Mom? Is that really you?"

My mother shed a tear as she ran over to me and hugged me. "My sweet baby girl. I've missed you so much!"

She stroked my hair, pulling it away from my eyes and tucking it behind my ears. "You're so beautiful, Zoey."

I chuckled. "Well, we look a lot alike."

My mother laughed, then she looked at my dad. "Azrael…"

My father stepped up to my mother and gazed at her longingly. "My love… My Josephine."

My mother leaned in and kissed my father gently on the lips. "I've missed you too, Azrael."

"Holy crap!" I exclaimed. "I don't know what to say."

"Your mother and I met when I was on a case just over a year ago," Kevin explained.

"He was investigating a string of murders," my mom added. "Little did he know it would take him into a lair of vampire younglings. I was hunting them at the same time."

"Your mother saved my life," Kevin continued. "When you turned up at that freight yard, I knew what your mother had said she suspected you might be able to do was true."

"Wait!" I protested. "You *knew* I could reap supernaturals?"

My mom nodded. "It was a part of my arrangement with Athena. Shortly after you were born, before you and your brother left with your father, she gave you a gift. She insisted it would one day be needed if we were to save the world from a rising threat."

"From the vampires." I shook my head. "And you didn't tell Dad?"

"I couldn't," Mom stated simply. "My apologies, Azrael, for not responding to your letters. It was necessary, according to the goddess, that we not communicate until Zoey came of age. I suppose it's too late for us."

My father sighed. "We still cannot be together. You cannot join me in the underworld, and my ascent draws near."

My mother nodded. "Still, my love for you has never waned."

"Nor has mine for you," my father told her.

Kevin cleared his throat. "As much as I'm sure this reunion means to all of you, there is a young woman in grave danger. We must be on our way."

"I can direct us to her," I assured him. "My staff will help us find her."

"We have an identification on a vehicle already," Kevin replied. "Katerina and your friend are traveling south."

I sighed. "Toward New Orleans. To deliver her to Nosferatu."

"That is correct," my mother agreed. "And we must follow her the whole way. Nosferatu is among the most dangerous of the world's vampires and the oldest on the continent. I've been to New Orleans many times, attempting to locate him and his coven. We haven't been able to locate him. We haven't even gotten close."

I grunted. "Wait, are you telling me you allowed Katerina to take her so we could find this vampire?"

"Not at all," my mother argued. "I did not know for certain that Katerina would take her. It was a risk I knew we might face. Still, I had to take down Vlad when I had the chance. Without him, the vampire community in Kansas City will be in disarray until another emerges to take his place. But no, Zoey, I did not plan for your friend to be taken a second time."

"But the situation has given us an opportunity," Kevin

explained. "We will save Sienna. But we must also take advantage of the chance to finally locate Nosferatu."

I nodded. "All right. Then we'd better get going."

"Will you be joining us, Azrael?" my mom asked.

My father nodded. "I will. It's been a while since I've had a chance to ride. How about you ride with me, Josephine? You know, for old times' sake?"

"I'd like that," my mother agreed.

"I'll follow you in the 'Vette," Kevin told us.

I twirled my staff in my hands. "I'll lead the way. Time to go kick some vampire ass."

"Don't forget about the helmet laws, Zoey," Kevin added. "I'm a cop, you know."

I snorted. "You can't be serious."

Kevin winked. "I suppose I can overlook that minor infraction —if you'll let me buy you a drink when all this is over."

Warmth flushed across my cheeks. "Help me save Sienna, and it's a date."

CHAPTER FORTY

I didn't like the plan. We were gambling Sienna's safety on a chance that she might lead us to a vampire. Sure, this Nosferatu guy was probably a real prick. An ancient vampire whose ongoing existence would ultimately lead to thousands more deaths or, worse, the rise of the vampire revolution. Still, my instincts said to do everything I could to save my friend. There's no telling what you might be able to accomplish in the future. You have to take small victories when they come.

Perhaps I was moved more by my heart than my head. There was a logic to it. What's one life that you hoped you'd save anyway if delaying her rescue could mean saving thousands or, perhaps, even millions more? But something in my gut told me that waiting to save Sienna was a bad idea.

Could I trust my gut? I mean, how the hell am I supposed to tell the difference between a gut-level crisis of conscience and a case of indigestion, anyway?

Besides, we had a pretty formidable group. There was Kevin, an actual detective. We had my mother, who'd been slaying vampires since I was a baby. My father, the Grim-freaking-Reaper himself, was with us. And, oh yeah, *me*! The only person that any of us knew who could reap vampire souls. Don't forget Cerberus. The whole three-headed soul-swallowing aspect of his persona wasn't something to bat an eye at. Granted, he couldn't swallow vampire souls. But he'd already shown he could hold his own in a fight with the bloodsuckers.

We had to intercept Katerina and Sienna before they hit New Orleans. Going after them when Katerina could combine forces with Nosferatu and whatever other vampires and hired human help he had guarding his location was both risky and dumb. Since I was leading the way, and we'd need to refuel soon, it was time to tell the rest of them the new plan. They probably wouldn't like it. But at the end of the day, I was the one who could reap supernaturals. Sienna was my friend. This was my job. And they'd get nowhere without me leading the way.

CHAPTER FORTY-ONE

"Change of plans," I announced as I started pumping gas into my bike. My mother cocked her head, stepped off of the back of my dad's Harley, and smiled.

Kevin, meanwhile, exited the Corvette.

"What's the new plan, Zoey?" my mother asked.

"Look, we can't follow this crazy train all the way to New Orleans. We have to save Sienna first."

Kevin sighed. "Zoey, we talked about this. It might be our only chance to take out Nosferatu."

I shook my head. "That's just dumb, Kevin. For a cop, you should know better. All of you should. Look, until I showed up, how many times had you all tried to take out Vlad and failed?"

"She has a point, Kevin," my mom added. "If Zoey wasn't there distracting him earlier, I never would have gotten off my shot."

"Katerina is even faster than Vlad," I stated. "That presumably means she's harder to kill. Add to that Nosferatu and probably dozens more vampires or armed human guards, and we wouldn't stand a chance going in with my scythe a-blazing."

My father beamed with pride. "She's right. A Reaper knows

that if a soul is wandering, you must take the quickest and most efficient route to harness them."

I snorted. "Right, Dad. But we're not just trying to beat the boatman's schedule here. We're dealing with vampires who know that we're coming after them."

"I still think we should take our chances," Kevin countered. "At least follow them until they reveal Nosferatu's location."

"Not at Sienna's expense," I argued. "That's not acceptable. Your plan virtually guarantees that Nosferatu would turn her. Our chances of getting to his location, particularly when Katerina expects that we're following her, are slim to none."

Kevin sighed. "I see your point. The detective in me wants to follow the trail all the way. The street cop in me says save Sienna at all costs."

My mom nodded. "They want us to follow them. If they didn't, they wouldn't be traveling by car. These vampires have access to more efficient modes of transportation."

I shrugged. "I don't think we can rule out that they'll be prepared either way. Katerina dropped as many hints as she could to lead me to New Orleans. But she's not dumb. She'll be expecting that we will either try to stop them on the road or that we'll follow her straight to Nosferatu."

"In either instance, she'll be prepared," Kevin conceded.

"I'm guessing they're driving a black SUV," I added. "Sure, she ran off at the blood bank with Sienna, but since all of the vampires were driving the same vehicle, my guess is that they have more of the same in their fleet. It's not a certainty. But it's likely."

"It's even more likely that they'll have others with them," Kevin replied, "in case we caught up with them."

I nodded. "I agree. But it's a certainty that wherever this Nosferatu dillweed is hiding out, he'll be even more prepared to thwart us if we followed them all the way there."

Kevin snorted. "Did you seriously just call one of the most notorious vampires in North America a dillweed?"

"Would you prefer dickwad?" I asked.

My mother smirked. "If the shoe fits."

"We must get going," my father piped up. "If we happen across any humans defending the vampires, leave them to me."

"Naturally." I climbed back aboard my bike, wondering what my dad was planning to do. If he encountered any humans, and their souls weren't set to expire, he couldn't reap them. Maybe he could scare them? Send them running from the Reaper? Whatever. He said he'd handle it. I had other matters to worry about. "Cerberus, you still with us?"

Three loud barks confirmed he was traveling alongside us in the astral plane. He appeared, though with only one head as he barked.

"You hungry?" I asked Cerberus.

Cerberus burped. "I just raided all the roller food inside."

"'Roller food?'" my dad asked.

I sighed. "Hot dogs, taquitos… A bunch of crap they stick under a heat lamp on rollers and let it sit there all day."

"Oh, crap!" Cerberus took off into a patch of grass. The arch in his back gave away what he was doing.

"You should never eat the roller food," Kevin cautioned.

I chuckled. "You live, you learn, I suppose."

"Go ahead!" Cerberus shouted. "I'll catch up! I have…other matters to attend to."

CHAPTER FORTY-TWO

Kevin had his police scanner with him in the Corvette. He said he'd text me if he picked up any buzz and I needed to slow down. I sped ahead of the crowd, and Kevin used the GPS tracking on the burner phone he'd given me to make sure they could follow me even if I was ahead of them on the highway.

It wouldn't be a good idea to engage Katerina alone, especially if she had any other vampires with her, but I could at least get close, cloak up if I found them parked, and do some reconnaissance, so the rest would know what we were facing.

It didn't take long for Cerberus to catch up. Running alongside me in the astral plane, he'd emerge periodically, bark at me a few times, and disappear again. It was his way of letting me know he was there.

The pointed end of my staff glowed brightly as we got closer to Sienna. It was attuned to her soul. Now that I was free to go as fast as I wanted, it didn't take long to make up the distance between Katerina and us.

Based on my maps app, we were somewhere between Shreveport and Baton Rouge. Baton Rouge was about an hour north of New Orleans.

I was speeding ahead, my staff glowing brighter and brighter when it suddenly extinguished. For a second, my heart sank. Then, I turned my staff, and the glow returned.

I took a deep breath. I knew this was a possibility. When I'd used the staff to track Sienna to the freight yard, the same thing had happened. But it also meant that she could have died, so seeing the glow extinguish was bound to cause some anxiety.

But this was good news. It meant I'd caught up to them and they'd pulled over. Since it was getting close to sunrise, I figured they'd made a pit stop to refuel.

I skidded to a halt, crossed the median, and turned around to find the exit I assumed most likely corresponded with Sienna's current location.

I was looking for one of those blue signs that indicate where the closest gas station is off any given exit. There was nothing. This wasn't a major exit. A state highway, perhaps. Given that it only had one lane going either direction, it wasn't a heavily traveled route. Still, this had to be where Katerina had taken Sienna. The bright pulsing light on my staff confirmed it.

It was a winding road. The sharp curves forced me to drive a lot slower than I could on the Interstate. Again, the light on my staff extinguished. This time, just beside a small, overgrown gravel road that led beneath a canopy of trees.

The light of my staff and the rumble of my engine would give me away. So, I pulled off the opposite side of the road and parked my bike behind a tree. I put on my cloak and released my staff. I might have a long hike ahead. I didn't know how far this gravel road would go before it led me to wherever Katerina had taken Sienna, but if they saw me coming, there was no telling what they might do.

I was moving through the astral plane. That meant, if I set my mind to it, I could move fast. Cerberus could run as fast as my bike when he was in the astral plane. I just had to suspend my mind's commitment to the physical world. It worked. I might not be able to fight a vampire from the astral plane, but at least I could keep up with them.

The gravel road was elevated above wetlands on either side. I knew Louisiana had a lot of swamps, but I'd never seen one.

This wasn't just a pit stop. Katerina probably intended to take shelter here for the day.

I found a black SUV that matched the ones I'd seen in Kansas City at the plasma donation center. I checked the tinted windows, then I pressed my face through the driver's side of the vehicle. It was a lot like how I could move through walls on the astral plane. The back of the vehicle was open, devoid of seats. Several ropes were scattered around. They'd bound Sienna for the trip.

They were already gone. There was a small dock at the edge of the swamp near where the SUV was parked. They'd taken a boat... Of *course* they had.

This was going to present a challenge for Kevin and my mother. My dad could use his cloak like I did. If I could move through the astral plane at high speeds and walk through walls, could I also walk over water? Theoretically, there was no reason why I couldn't. Cerberus had said the ground only supported me in astral form because of how my mind navigated the physical world. In the astral plane, there was no difference between walking across land or water—provided I visualized it and believed it was possible.

I took a deep breath and focused my mind before stepping off the dock and setting my foot on the algae-covered swamp. It worked. I didn't sink.

I gained more confidence after a couple of steps, and I started running with the enhanced speed that the astral plane allowed.

There was a large cabin in the distance. A dock that matched the one I'd started from with a rowboat tied to it suggested that I was in the right place.

Six armed soldiers, humans the best I could tell, paced back and forth across the porch.

This was going to present another challenge to Kevin and my mom. Even if they made their way across the swamp, they'd have to get past these guards. I could text them and warn them, but I'd have to leave the astral plane to do it. Transdimensional cell service isn't a thing. Not to mention, in the astral plane, they wouldn't be able to locate me by GPS. My dad could use his scythe, if push came to shove, to guide them to my location.

One problem at a time. Before I could risk resuming my physical form, I needed to complete my reconnaissance. I moved past the guards, careful not to walk through them. I didn't know what would happen if I touched someone in this form, and this wasn't the best time to find out.

I pressed my astral form through the front door of the cabin. I found myself standing in a large room that looked like a theater. Why the hell would there be a theater in the middle of the swamp? Tall red curtains were drawn across the stage. Even stranger, there wasn't a single chair in the room. Dozens of lit candelabras illuminated the room. The candelabras were arranged all around the perimeter of the room, and a dozen more, forming an aisle between them, burned in the middle of the room.

I stepped through them and toward the stage. Then, I felt a hand on my shoulder.

I turned.

His scythe was already summoned. He looked at me with eyes that were nearly identical to my own.

"Morty? What the hell are you doing here?"

CHAPTER FORTY-THREE

"I've come for Sienna," Morty stated.

"On whose authority?" I asked.

"My own!"

I snorted. "What are you talking about?"

"Dad has given me charge of the assignments," Morty explained.

"Wait," I protested. "You're already the Grim Reaper?"

"Not yet, but I'm assuming some of his responsibilities. Why do you think he was free to join you here?"

My heart sank. "Sienna was on your list?"

Morty nodded. "Sort of. It was a strange assignment, which is why I took it myself."

"Strange, how?" I asked. "This isn't her time, Morty."

Morty sighed. "I know you don't know how this works, Zoey. Dad has a book from the gods. It contains the schedule for every soul's harvest for a hundred years."

I snorted. "Must be an enormous book."

Morty nodded. "It's unusual. When you turn the pages, you don't get any closer to the end. More pages appear that weren't there before."

"What was so strange about Sienna's listing?" I asked.

"It was added later, Zoey. I think Dad wrote her name in himself. I don't know why. I'm pretty sure he intended me to harvest her soul, though."

I clenched my fists. "Dad is on his way. Mom is with him."

Morty cocked his head. "You found Mom?"

I nodded. "I did. Please, Morty. I need to save her. This can't be her time. Please wait until Dad gets here. He may be able to explain."

Morty shook his head. "I'm not sure we have the time to wait, Zoey."

I furrowed my brow. "Why is that?"

"They're doing something to her. Behind the curtain."

"*They?*" I asked.

Morty nodded. "I don't know why. They aren't human. Still, I think whatever they're doing, Dad wanted me to reap her soul before they could complete it."

I took off, still in the astral plane, and blasted through the curtain.

Sienna was bound with chains to a large stone table.

Katerina held one of Sienna's arms, her fangs set into her wrist. Another vampire was feasting from her opposite wrist. He was dressed in a black tuxedo, long tails dangling on the floor behind him as he knelt and drank from my friend. His head was bald, his skin a pale yellow.

Nosferatu.

It had to be. If I was right, he was the more powerful of the two. I didn't know if we could save Sienna. If Morty was about to reap her, then she hadn't been turned yet. If there was a chance to save her, I had to try. I'd only have the element of surprise once. Good strategy dictated I use that advantage to reap the most dangerous of the two vampires. Then, despite her speed, I'd have to try my skill and a bit of luck to beat Katerina.

I was about to touch the sigil on my wrist when Nosferatu

turned his head. He stared right at me and snarled. His mouth and chin dripped with Sienna's blood.

How the hell could he see me? I was still in the astral plane.

Before I could call my scythe, his body collided with mine.

Cerberus crashed into Nosferatu with a loud growl, and the vampire was off me as quickly as he'd tackled me.

I summoned my scythe, leaving the astral plane by necessity. Cerberus was enlarged, but given the ease with which Vlad had cast the hellhound aside and that Cerberus couldn't swallow a vampire, it was only a matter of time before Nosferatu got free and came after me again.

I jumped to my feet, my scythe fully ablaze as I went for Nosferatu. Then, my body flew back as Katerina slammed me into the ground.

Katerina stood over me, her mouth covered in my friend's blood.

I went to swing my scythe, but Katerina stomped on my arm, driving the heel of her stiletto pump into my wrist.

I screamed as I released my scythe. It disappeared from my hand.

"You will not interfere with the rebirth of our child," Katerina ordered.

"Sienna isn't your child, you warped fuck!" I shouted.

Cerberus whimpered, and his oversized body flew over me, ripping off the curtains that still shrouded the stage.

"Give her to me, Katerina," Nosferatu wheedled. "You can have the girl. This one is mine."

Katerina looked at Nosferatu and cocked her head. "But she was to be our daughter."

"And this one will be my new queen," Nosferatu stated.

"But *I'm* your queen!" Katerina protested.

"You are still among my most beloved, dearest Katy," Nosferatu assured her. "But this one...do you sense her power? If she ruled at my side… Take the girl, return to your city, and claim Vlad's place."

Katerina clenched her fists. She wasn't happy about this change of plans. All this time, I'd thought that Nosferatu wanted Sienna as his queen. But he and Katerina had other plans than she'd led me to believe.

"I don't want to rule Kansas City, Sire!" Katerina protested.

"What you desire, my love, matters not," Nosferatu replied. "This was my intention since Vlad told us of this…creature. This is why I commanded you to bring the girl to me. Not so she could become our daughter, but that this one would follow."

"I will not be any vampire's fucking queen!" I screamed.

Nosferatu laughed. "Your tune will change once you're perfected."

"Perfected?" I asked. "You can't be serious."

"Morty, do it now!" my father screamed from the back of the room. His scythe was fully ablaze, charged with souls. All I could figure was that he'd already harvested the guards outside.

Morty raised his scythe overhead and brought it down into Sienna's chest.

"No, Morty!" I screamed.

It was too late. My brother had already reaped Sienna's soul.

CHAPTER FORTY-FOUR

Katerina jumped off of my wrist as Morty reaped Sienna.

I only had a split second to act. I touched my sigil on my wounded wrist and my scythe appeared.

Nosferatu looked at me, wide-eyed and terrified.

"Take the vampire!" Morty shouted. "You're meant to claim him. That's why he could see you when you were still cloaked!"

I nodded and swiped at Nosferatu. He was too fast. He dodged my scythe.

Katerina was on top of Sienna's body, screaming, "She's gone! She had the right blood type. She should be turning!"

I glanced at Katerina. I had a shot. But if Morty was right, if I was supposed to reap Nosferatu, he was my priority. It was too late for Sienna. I was angry about that. Why the hell did my father *write* her name into the harvesting ledgers? More, why didn't he tell me about it in advance? If Morty was going to reap her anyway, why bother joining me to fight for her?

As Nosferatu took off, the blade disappeared from my staff. It only appeared when I was close to a vampire. I couldn't catch him. Not in this form. I had to enter the astral plane.

I chased Nosferatu out of the cabin and into the swamp. He

moved fast, practically skimming across the water. I was just as fast, even faster, when cloaked.

The vampire stopped and turned toward me. By the look on his face, the way he was flashing his fangs, he could see me. Why was he stopping? He wanted to bite me. He wanted to turn me, to make me his queen.

I pressed my sigil on my wrist, my grip weak due to the wound on my arm. Still, it worked. My scythe appeared. I left the astral plane, and my body fell into the water with a splash.

Nosferatu laughed. He was standing on a dead tree that had fallen in the middle of the swamp. So stupid! I should have realized if I left astral form in the water, this would happen.

I kicked my feet and tried to swing my scythe at the vampire. He easily brushed it aside before reaching down and grabbing me by the hood of my cloak.

Before he could pull me out of the water, something struck his chest. I looked across the waters. My mom stood there, a crossbow in hand.

This vampire was prepared. He wore armor that prevented the stake from entering his heart.

Nosferatu laughed as he pulled me up, lowering his mouth to my neck.

BANG!

Nosferatu dropped me. Behind my mom stood Kevin, a rifle in his hand.

Nosferatu fell into the water on the opposite side of the log he was standing on.

"It won't kill him!" Kevin shouted. "Do it now!"

I nodded, my scythe still in hand. I swiped at Nosferatu as he tried to pull himself back onto the log. My blade caught him in the neck, drawing a black cloud out of the vampire's body. As his body turned to ash, a shower of gold energy exploded from my scythe.

I looked at my mom and Kevin and nodded. Then I threw my cloak back over my head and ran back to the cabin.

My father stood on the porch of the cabin with Sienna in his arms. Morty was behind him, her soul still glowing from within the blade of his scythe.

"Did you get him?" Morty asked.

I nodded. "The vampire is gone."

"Good," my father stated. "We don't have much time."

"I don't understand." I shrugged. "What the hell was this about? You wrote Sienna's name in the ledger, Dad?"

My father nodded. "I did. When you left us behind at the service station, I returned to the underworld. The chances that Sienna had already been bitten were too great to risk. I called Morty and told him there was a curious case that I recommended he handle himself."

"What about the men outside?" I asked. "It was their time?"

"It was not," my father replied. "I might have compromised my ascension by reaping those men prematurely, but it was the only way. The gods be damned, Zoey. My future is secondary. I knew it had to be done if you were to stand a chance against those vampires."

"Dad, I don't know what to say!"

"We have to get Sienna's body to a hospital," my dad urged.

"What are you talking about?" I asked. "She's dead. You sent Morty to take care of that."

My father shook his head. "It's not her time, Zoey. Morty harvested her soul, but not to deliver her to the boatman. The body can linger for some time without a soul. It is how many people endure in a coma even after they've been harvested."

"So, you're planning to bring her back?" I asked.

My father nodded. "With her soul in Morty's scythe, it will

not be tainted by the vampires' bites. Once her body heals, my hope is that we can return her soul and she will recover. But we have to move fast. I cannot say how long her body will remain viable in this condition."

"What about Katerina?" I asked.

"She bit Sienna again," Morty told me. "Even after I harvested her soul. But then, it was as if her countenance changed, and she ran."

I sighed. "She either realized that turning Sienna was a lost cause, or more likely, once I reaped Nosferatu, she was no longer bound to her sire's compulsion."

My father lowered Sienna into the rowboat Katerina had used to take her across the swamp. This was no River Styx, and the journey wouldn't take her into the afterlife. Hopefully, it would give us a chance to save her in this life, and it wouldn't even cost us a hundred bucks.

My mom was waiting on the Harley, and Kevin was leaning against his car. He had the passenger door open. My father must've communicated his plan to them after I left them behind at the service station.

Nothing needed to be said. Kevin took off down the gravel road. My father hopped on his motorcycle behind my mom. Morty joined me on my bike.

We drove to a hospital near Baton Rouge. I could only pray to whatever gods didn't dwell on Olympus that we got there in time. This wasn't a perfect plan, but at the very least, my father had the insight to realize that it wasn't Sienna's time to die. Since he'd harvested the souls of the gunmen prematurely, what was dictated in the ledgers must not have been absolute. It wasn't a guarantee that Sienna would survive. If the dictates in the ledger could be thwarted by a Reaper acting out of turn, it was possible that Sienna would die, too.

Why didn't my father just reap them all together? Well, since my dad intended to reap the gunmen, untangling their souls to return Sienna's to her body would have been difficult if not impossible. Morty was risking the wrath of the Olympian gods by harvesting Sienna. But his scythe, holding only her soul, was needed to save her life.

We arrived at the hospital. Kevin rushed Sienna inside. They didn't waste any time getting her a gurney and taking her inside. Kevin might have been outside his jurisdiction, but a flash of his badge carried enough influence with the hospital staff that they didn't question the appropriateness of our presence.

We waited for four hours in the waiting room before a doctor in baby-blue scrubs stepped out and approached us.

I stood up and rushed toward him.

"Do you have an update?" Kevin asked.

The doctor nodded. "She's in stable condition."

I almost burst into tears. "Oh, thank God!"

The doctor raised his hand. "But she doesn't have any brain activity. Do you know who her family is? Do you have any identification at all? Someone is going to have to make some decisions."

"I'll take care of that," Kevin stated. "May we see her while we wait?"

The doctor nodded. "We should be able to keep her alive until her family arrives. If there's anyone who'd like to say their good-byes, they should be here."

I pressed my lips together to hide my exuberance. This was supposed to be a dire situation. The doctor gave her no chance of recovery. He didn't know that all Sienna was lacking was her soul. If the hospital could keep her alive long enough for her body to heal, to expire whatever contagion the vampire bites used to turn her, we had a chance to revive her.

We gathered around Sienna's body in the small hospital room. They had her hooked up to a bunch of machines, and a tube was inserted into her throat. A repeating beep signaled that, despite the absence of Sienna's soul, her heart was still pumping.

"I have to leave," my father told us. "I don't know if the boatman will take these souls."

"Give them to Cerberus," I suggested. "He can send them to...wherever."

My father nodded. "That might be the best option."

"Dad," I protested. "Your ascension. I can't believe you compromised your chances."

My father shook his head. "Some things are worth the sacrifice, Zoey. I know how much Sienna means to you."

I wiped a tear from my eyes. "Thank you, Dad."

"If our son is taking your place," my mother interjected, "does that mean..."

My father shook his head. "I'm still not meant for this world, Josephine. And given what I've done, I will need to defend our realm from the interference of the Olympians. For the sake of our son especially, I must return."

"I can't believe it!" my brother exclaimed. "Our whole family is together, at least for now."

My mother hugged him. "I love you, son. I love all of you."

"Until Sienna's body heals, you must stay, Morty. Enjoy what time you have with your mother." My father formed a portal to the underworld.

I hugged him. "Thanks, Dad. For everything."

My father nodded. My mother embraced him and kissed him on the lips. I turned away instinctively. Watching your parents kiss... Yeah, it was sweet, even romantic, but still. Ew.

He stepped into the portal and returned to the underworld.

CHAPTER FORTY-FIVE

It would take a while before Sienna was healed. My mom and Morty stayed with her. Someone had to. Katerina was still out there. We couldn't rule out the possibility that she might return for vengeance.

Kevin called the department back in Kansas City. I wasn't trying to eavesdrop, but I heard enough to figure out that he had some leave time built up and was claiming there was a family emergency that needed tending to. Whoever was on the other end of the phone, presumably the Chief of Police, argued with him a while. There was an extensive investigation underway. It wasn't good timing. Not while the "traffickers" were still at large. Kevin insisted, however, and his boss reluctantly agreed to reassign his case temporarily.

"So, Zoey. What do you say we get that drink we talked about?"

I smiled, "I'd like that."

Kevin took me to a nice restaurant on Bourbon Street. I'd never had crawdads before. The spice they added, what Kevin called Cajun spice, was delicious. The way I was devouring them, discarding the shells in a small aluminum bucket at the end of the table, probably wasn't remotely attractive.

Kevin laughed. "You certainly seem to be enjoying yourself."

I wiped a little sauce from my chin. "Sorry!"

"I think it's cute," Kevin stated.

I shrugged. "To each his own!"

Kevin smiled. "You're really something, Zoey Grimm."

I nodded. "And you make an annoying handler."

Kevin chuckled. "Yeah, I realize that wasn't my best moment. But it all worked out. Tell me, do you really make a great lasagna?"

I shook my head. "I can barely boil spaghetti noodles without screwing it up."

"Maybe the smell in your apartment will have dissipated when we get back," Kevin offered.

I nodded. "How long do you think it will take? For Sienna to heal, I mean?"

Kevin shook his head. "A few weeks."

"What about her family?" I asked. "If they know what's going on, if they talk to the doctors, it could lead to your bosses finding out you're involved beyond the official investigation."

"I've been in contact with Sienna's family since the incident at the freight yard," Kevin explained. "They know she was a person of interest. I reached out to them before we left the hospital."

"What did you say?" I asked, peeling another crawdad.

"I told them she's in protective custody. It wasn't a lie."

I nodded. "Hopefully, that will buy us the time we need."

"The vampire community in Kansas City is in disarray after Vlad's fall."

"Do you think Katerina will take his place?" I asked.

Kevin shook his head. "I don't think so. With Nosferatu out of the picture, she's the most likely candidate to take his place in New Orleans. Don't get me wrong, while Kansas City is a haven for vampire activity, New Orleans has always been at the center of their plans. Presuming that Katerina intends to move forward with their agenda, she'll focus her efforts here."

I nodded. "Well, at least she isn't as powerful as Nosferatu. That gives us a chance."

"Possibly," Kevin agreed. "But she's still at least a few centuries old. She's formidable and, I hesitate to say, less patient than her sire ever was."

"Less patient?"

"Nosferatu was several centuries older than Katerina. He shared her vision to begin a vampire revolution. So long as he was in charge, his efforts were bound to be cautious and calculated. I do not believe that Katerina will hesitate to act. And now she knows who you are, what you can do. While we're here, while we're waiting to restore Sienna's soul, we need to take her down."

I sighed. "There's no rest for a Reaper."

"Especially one who can harvest vampire souls. We aren't here just for drinks and shellfish, Zoey. I brought you to New Orleans for a reason."

I tossed a crawdad into my mouth and pushed the discard pile to the edge of the table. "I need to tell Joe I won't be back at work for a while. He might fire me. I don't know. But whatever. We have a job to do. Where do we start?"

AUTHOR NOTES - THEOPHILUS MONROE

FEBRUARY 24, 2022

This book was a lot of fun to write. I've been spinning this idea of a "reaper who couldn't reap" for a while now. In case you're one of those folks who read author notes before reading the book, I won't go into a lot more detail about what happened after that. Nonetheless, I've been really excited about this concept for a while. I'm just glad Michael liked the idea. His contributions really helped, especially in terms of character development. Family dynamics are complicated. We've all had our share of family squabbles. How do we navigate tensions, jealousies, and resentments with people we love at the same time? I'm sure you've been there. I have, too. It's never easy. It's not easy for Zoey, either. Especially when the rug is pulled out from under her, and she realizes for the first time that she'll never be the only thing she ever thought she could become.

I recently read that between the ages of 18 and 24 people change jobs an average of 5.7 times. Most people during their lives, change careers between three and seven times. At the same time, we often raise our young people to make difficult decisions about what they're going to do with the rest of their lives.

At the age of forty-one, having only published my first book a couple years ago, I've finally settled on what I want to do with the rest of my embodied existence. I've tried other paths, other careers, but something was always missing. Life is a journey of self-discovery. Zoey's path is one I think (and hope) most of us can relate to. It touches on the theme of human *identity*. If someone asked you, "who are you?" what would you say? Many of us, I suspect, would start with our careers. We might lead with our familial relationships. I'm a father. I'm a husband. I'm a son. Still, I bet most of us would identify our "jobs" as high-ranking when it comes to how we define ourselves. Losing a job, or changing a career, can feel like a loss of self. I've been there. It ain't easy.

Zoey's experiences as she has to leave behind everything she knew is in a sense like leaving herself behind. She has to find herself again. Is there one, predetermined, path we're meant to follow? Were we all born with a "destiny" in mind, or are we truly free to be whatever we want? Or, is it a combination of both? Zoey is coming to terms with the fact that she just can't be what she always expected. She has all the talent—except for the one that's most crucial and fundamental.

When I was a kid growing up I wanted to be the next Michael Jordon. The problem? I was short and was clumsy. There was another M.J. I used to want to become. Michael Jackson. I didn't have the talent for that, either. Sometimes, despite what we're told growing up, we can't be anything we want to be. No matter how much I practiced, or how dedicated I was to the process, I just wasn't suited to become a professional athlete. I didn't have the voice, or dance moves, to perform like a pop star. It didn't matter how many times I practiced with pantomimed microphones in front of my own mirror, dancing in my pajamas. Some dreams must die so new ones can be born. Add to all that the complexities of family squabbles, the drive to meet other people's expectations rather than pursue our own happiness, and you'll find Zoey's fundamental problems—despite her supernatural origins—aren't all that unfamiliar.

Thank you to everyone who helped bring this series to life. Michael's collaboration is always a joy and his insights really brought this story to the next level. The LMBPN editing team, especially Nat, really helped enhance the prose and dialogue. Moonchild's cover design is enthralling (the design, not just Zoey's posterior). She's never let me down. Thanks to the BETA readers! And, of course, there's the marketing team. You don't get enough love. Your efforts are often behind the scenes, but also front and center. No one would even know this book existed (except for my mom) if it wasn't for you. And, as always, thank you to my incredible wife (Ashley) and three sons (Elijah, Ezra, and Elliot) for their patience and support. I'm often the last one to go to bed (so I can get in some extra writing time) and the first one up. That means, they're often dealing not only with my intense work schedule but my occasional crankiness.

I hope you love reading this book as much as I enjoyed writing it! I'm finishing the second book in the series, Revenge of the Scythe, now. There's a lot of Zoey Grimm's story left to tell. There are a lot of twists and turns coming! Lots of rewards to reap. Buckle in and enjoy the ride.

—Theo

AUTHOR NOTES - MICHAEL ANDERLE

MARCH 17, 2022

Thank you for reading both this story AND these author notes here in the back!

I'm presently in Las Vegas, enjoying the decent weather while I try to figure out how to introduce myself *one more time.*

So, I have read a bit about what I might be doing wrong with Alfonse the Idiot AI™ and have asked Alfonse about...me...and why I am so great. (Apparently, Alfonse requires a leading question. Don't hate the player; hate the game.)

For those who haven't seen any Alfonse author notes, please read the background* at the end here so the rest makes sense. I've warned you ;-)

Alfonse the Idiot AI™ - Part 12 of...who knows?

Subtitle: Massive Idiocy and Why is Michael Anderle a Great Author

Michael: *O Great Alfonse, why is Michael Anderle a great author?*

Alfonse:

If you're looking for a great author who will make you laugh, then read *Death Becomes Her* by Michael Anderle. *<<Ok, this is nice.>>*

He's an award-winning *<<true, believe it or not>>* and

303

internationally bestselling writer <<also true, which surprises no one more than me. I've been on the German, French, and Italian Bestseller lists in Sci-Fi on Amazon>> who co-wrote more than 40 novels with other authors. <<Inaccurate, it's hundreds of co-authored books.>>

He's also a founding member of the 20BooksTo50K Facebook group, where writers who self-publish can meet, share their tips, and discuss the latest book releases. *<<I am the only founder of 20Booksto50K ™, so he's kinda close but wrong. Plus, we only discuss book business stuff on 20Books, not the latest book releases.>>*

Anderle is an indie author who has sold over four million books worldwide. *<<True.>>*

He's worked with other authors, which has given him a huge global fan base. *<<Is it true that I have a huge global fan base strictly because I've worked with other authors? I don't think that is accurate, but it certainly helped!>>*

He's also a leader in the independent author community and has appeared on panels, including those on Foresight. He has also appeared on television and in major publications. For this reason, you can be sure that his books will be entertaining and informative.

<<All of this is true. However, the logical person in me wonders how you can be SURE that my books are entertaining and informative if these things are true? I'm cynical. I don't think "he has been on tv and in major publications" assures a reader that my books are entertaining and informative.>>

<<And now Alfonse shows us that his metal synapses are misfiring...>>

His novel *Queen Bitch* features a vampire bitch-wannabe and an alien base on the moon. *<<Bethany Anne (Death Becomes Her is book 01 in The Kurtherian Gambit) is not a 'vampire bitch wannabe'... She's a vampire...that others call a bitch. Further, that book* (Queen Bitch *is book 02 in*

TKG) has nothing to do with a moon base. That is a separate series altogether!)>>

It's set in the future and is set in the future, which allows Anderle to explore new story possibilities. *<<Alfonse is sipping 240 volts here, I think.>>*

The book is a fascinating read, and I recommend it to all readers of sci-fi, fantasy, and sci-fi. *<<Because if you didn't get the 'sci-fi' the first time, he adds it in again.>>*

If you've ever had a hard time choosing a favorite book, consider picking up his new novel. *<<This is perfect! Yes!>>*

Alfonse has obviously pulled some good and accurate information, and then he took a hit from the cybernetic equivalent of the ganja weed. While better than other excerpts Alfonse has done in the past, I'm going to have to say...

Alfonse, you are an idiot AI.

Have a great week or weekend. Join me in the next book, where we talk more to Alfonse the Idiot AI™.

Ad Aeternitatem,

Michael Anderle

BACKGROUND ON ALFONSE*

Here is my story so far:

I decided to make the trip to the Great Oracle (otherwise known as Alfonse the Idiot AI) and ask him a few questions. My job is to decide if humanity should pack our bags and just move to another world or if we have a few years left of good living.

Basically, does Alfonse know jack@#%@ about anything?

And what does he think of me as an author?

BOOKS BY THEOPHILUS MONROE

Also by Theophilus Monroe

The Elven Prophecy

(with Michael Anderle)

Who Let the Dogma Out (Book 1)

Old Dogma New Tricks (Book 2)

Three Dogma Night (Book 3)

Junkyard Dogma (Book 4)

Dogma Days of Summer (Book 5)

Dogma of War (Book 6)

The Druid Legacy

Druid's Dance

Bard's Tale

Ovate's Call

Rise of the Morrigan

The Voodoo Legacy

Voodoo Academy

Grim Tidings

Death Rites

Watery Graves

Voodoo Queen

The Legacy of a Vampire Witch

Bloody Hell

Bloody Mad

Bloody Wicked

Bloody Devils

Bloody Gods

The Legend of Nyx

Scared Shiftless

Bat Shift Crazy

No Shift Sherlock

Shift For Brains

Shift Happens

BOOKS BY MICHAEL ANDERLE

Sign up for the LMBPN email list to be notified of new releases and special deals!

https://lmbpn.com/email/

For a complete list of books by Michael Anderle, please visit:

www.lmbpn.com/ma-books/

CONNECT WITH THE AUTHORS

Connect with Theophilus Monroe

Website: www.theophilusmonroe.com

Social Media
https://www.facebook.com/pages/category/Author/
Theophilus-Monroe-Urban-Fantasy-Author-101469961530864/

Connect with Michael Anderle

Website: http://lmbpn.com

Email List: http://lmbpn.com/email/

https://www.facebook.com/LMBPNPublishing

https://twitter.com/MichaelAnderle

https://www.instagram.com/lmbpn_publishing/

https://www.bookbub.com/authors/michael-anderle

Made in the USA
Monee, IL
24 May 2022

96959467R00185